WE LIVE
HERE
NOW

SARAH PINBOROUGH

WE LIVE HERE NOW

ORION

First published in Great Britain in 2025 by Orion Fiction,
an imprint of The Orion Publishing Group Ltd.
Carmelite House, 50 Victoria Embankment
London EC4Y 0DZ

An Hachette UK Company

The authorised representative in the EEA is Hachette Ireland,
8 Castlecourt Centre, Castleknock Road, Castleknock, Dublin 15,
D15 XTP3, Republic of Ireland (email: info@hbgi.ie)

1 3 5 7 9 10 8 6 4 2

Grateful acknowledgement is made for permission to reproduce from the following:
'Happy House' from Happy House by Stella Maidment and Lorena Roberts.

A CIP catalogue record for this book is
available from the British Library.

ISBN (Hardback) 9781398722606
ISBN (Export Trade Paperback) 9781398722613
ISBN (Audio) 9781398722644
ISBN (eBook) 9781398722637

Typeset by Born Group
Printed in Great Britain by Clays Ltd, Elcograf S.p.A.

MIX
Paper | Supporting
responsible forestry
FSC
www.fsc.org   FSC® C104740

www.orionbooks.co.uk

Sarah Pinborough is an award-winning and *New York Times*, *Sunday Times*, and internationally bestselling author and screenwriter who is published in over 30 territories worldwide. Having published more than 25 novels across various genres, her recent books include *Behind Her Eyes*, now a smash-hit Netflix limited series; *13 Minutes* that she's developing with Carnival/NBC, *The Death House* that she's adapted herself for Compelling Pictures, and her most recent book *Insomnia* which she adapted herself and is now streaming on Paramount+. She lives with her rescue dog, Teddy in the historic town of Stony Stratford.

For Hannah, Oli, and Wilf

It's a house,
It's a happy house,
It's a happy house,
Can you see?
Here's a window.
Here's a door,
Here's a roof,
And here's a floor!
It's a house,
It's a happy house,
It's a happy house,
For you and me!

—'*Happy House,*' *from* Happy House *by Stella Maidment*
and Lorena Roberts

Prologue

The raven watches the stone house on the crossroads through the long year.

Freezing winter turns to gentle spring and then to summer, and his dark feathers heat like the sticky tarmac of the narrow lane that bakes and shimmers below him. He knows his mate is long dead, but he remains, constant, perched on the uneven wall, watching and listening. At night, in the cooler air, he feeds and drinks and calls out, but there is never a reply.

The house does not give up his mate. His mate is dead. He knows that. He should have moved on. Found another to share his solitary life. To nest in the worn rock cavities on the moors. To enjoy the endless skies. Perhaps a better mate. But still he watches.

He does not like the house. He has never liked the house. It stirs something inside him that speaks so loudly of danger that when he heard her cries, he did not follow her in, but now he finds he cannot leave. *Not yet. Not yet,* he croaks, parched, into the sky, as his black eyes stare and wonder if anything will live within those walls again. The house stares back at him, defiant. No, he does not care for the house.

Summer cools to autumn, and as winter stirs once more, a long year of watching over, he is almost ready to take flight, to start again, when suddenly cars arrive and doors open. His mate does not emerge – his mate is dead, he knows this – but his feathers tremble in the wind as he watches, curious now.

Life is coming back to the house.

Me

I.

Emily

The house looks different from how it did in the photos.

Freddie pulls the car up close to the front door and smiles across at me before getting out. I try to reciprocate but my heart is sinking. The pictures were taken in summer when the front garden was full of colour and life. Now, as I push the car door open and swing my bad leg out before gritting my teeth against the pain and hauling myself inelegantly onto my feet, everything is covered in icy grey mist and the ground is hard and dead.

I lean heavily on my stick. My joints are sore from sitting for hours on the drive, and the sharp air is like icing sugar in my lungs, making me want to cough with every breath, the wind coming in from the moor cutting into me despite my thick coat. The quiet of the frozen countryside makes my stinging ears, ring. Everything is awash with shades of grey, but still it makes me squint. There's too much to take in.

'What do you think?' We both rest on the bonnet of the car as I contemplate my answer, looking up at the large house looming over me. *Larkin Lodge* is written in thick black letters above the imposing front door. Larkin Lodge. Our new home.

The house stands alone on a hill, the drive simply a turning off a country lane, marked by old low stone walls. Beyond, all I can see is moorland, wild and untamed, a spattering of snow here and there that has refused to melt. No sheep or cows. Just uneven ground and rough shrubs amid rocky outcrops.

'I feel like I'm in a Brontë novel.' I take his arm, and our feet crunch loud on the gravel as we move toward the front door.

'Does that make me Mr Rochester? Are you my Jane Eyre?'

'Well, you'd better not have another wife locked up in the attic here, otherwise, you're in trouble, my friend.' I don't tell him it's *Wuthering Heights* that had come to mind, and how that one doesn't end so well for the characters in it, the ghost of Cathy pleading at the window to come inside. Freddie only knows *Jane Eyre* because he claimed to like the classics when we met and I'm sure he quickly scanned a couple, when in fact, the years have proven that he's more a-few-Lee-Childs-on-holiday reader than a proper bookworm like me.

'It looks different in the flesh. It's like it's suddenly real.'

'It is real.' He unlocks the door with an old-fashioned key and nods me inside. I step across the threshold, and while the immediate air – *the exhale* – that rushes out to greet me is not exactly cold, neither is it warm, as if Larkin Lodge is perhaps as unsure of me as I am of it.

I do relax a little as the door closes behind us and the warmth from the radiators finally envelops me. There are polished wooden floors and a feature central staircase that is both imposing and austere, but there are also fresh flowers in my vase from Heal's, sitting on the stylish Rose & Grey hallway table Iso bought us for our tenth anniversary. Freddie promised he'd have all the unpacking done by the time the hospital let me out, and he's been true to his word on that.

Further into the house I peer into a bright sitting room, or drawing room, or whatever people who have more than one living room call a second or third downstairs room, and our teal Loaf sofa, wine stain and all, is waiting there for me to collapse on.

'It's bigger than I thought.' I'm trying to be happy but I'm having a massive pang of missing our garden flat in Kentish Town and feel a little sick. *What have we done?* I know I'm being childish. It was my dream, after all, a house in the country, away from the madness of London, with space and air to breathe, and it was me who first saw Larkin Lodge online and made a lot of noise about escaping everything and how it would be perfect.

I didn't, however, expect to wake up from a coma several months later and find Freddie so enthusiastically suggesting we sell and move here that I heard myself agreeing. But then I hadn't been expecting to be in a coma either, and I hadn't expected the gut punch of being let go from work when I'd done so much – so much I didn't want to think about – to get the promotion secured just before my accident.

'Marriage is teamwork,' he'd said as he held up the keys in the rehab center. 'You wanted a life in the country, and I'm on board with that.' The move kept him busy at least. Freddie has never been good with worry, and while I lay between life and death getting all the pieces in place for me to nod a yes to kept him busy.

It would be a lie to say I've had no excitement about the move too. I have. From my hospital bed it felt like exactly what I needed – a fresh start – but as the days ticked round to leaving, the excitement trickled away to something close to regret as the reality of my situation sank in. I wanted the safety of the *known*. The comfort blanket of my familiar nest to lick my wounds in.

Freddie's still looking at me, expectant, and I give him a big grin, shaking away my gloom. A year to recuperate fully, that's what Dr Canning said I needed. The quiet country life will probably be good for me. And it is a beautiful house. I have to get used to it, that's all.

'I guess we live here now,' I say.

'I guess we do,' he answers.

2.

Freddie

Jesus, I can't believe I'm in this mess.

It's getting dark outside, marginally preferable to the endless suffocating grey of the awful winter moors, and even though the heating's on I'm cold again. There's always a draught in this bloody house and it does nothing to improve my mood.

The warmth of the Aga seeps through my jeans as I lean against it, boiling water for pasta. My phone's on silent in my pocket, *just in case*, and I can hear Emily's stick tapping as she explores the house, her walk a slow echo of her usual confident—overconfident—stride. The sound makes me feel worse.

I am not a good person. How could I have done this to her? How can I *still* be doing it to her? After what she's been through. *Everything* she's been through. The guilt—the constant fear of discovery—is a cancer inside me. How have I got myself so trapped?

I turn on the radio, needing distraction, some cheesy nineties local radio station, and whistle along, feigning normality, as I add pasta to the boiling water and dig around in the cupboard for a sauce.

I can sort it. I have to. It's all going to be fine. It is.

As long as Emily never finds out.

3.
Emily

There are so many rooms downstairs I feel almost dizzy. My walking stick *tap taps* on the wooden floor, and I keep one hand on the cool walls as I slowly explore. The wallpaper's thick, lining every room thus far, the different damask patterns in the flock like braille under my fingertips. The rich colours—faded greens, yellows, blues, and reds—remind me of ladies' evening gowns from long ago, stretched out across the walls like skin. The formality of the colours against the dark wood floor makes the rooms oppressive and austere and full of shadows. *Uninviting*.

The house, I decide, as I move from room to room, is like a prim governess judging me disapprovingly for my baggy jeans and sweatshirt. It doesn't help that several rooms are still unused, the air filled with dust and abandonment. God knows how long the place has been empty, but I make a mental note to get some paint samples as soon as possible. Light, bright colours will make a world of difference. Bring some joy to the place.

Along with the kitchen and sitting room that I've already seen, there's a dining room, a drawing room, another room that Freddie's turned into a games room, as well as a smaller room that must have been a library as there's a desk pushed up against the wall, maybe left by the previous occupants, and beyond that a downstairs toilet and a utility or storage room.

Past the kitchen there's a corridor leading to what was once tack and boot rooms. There's no wooden floor in those, just uneven flagstone, freezing underfoot, and narrow high windows that need a winder to open. They're colder than the other rooms too, no pretence at heating, and I guess we could use them as a pantry or storage room.

I head back to the warmth of the central hallway, where I can hear Freddie whistling along to the radio as he cooks on the Aga. I've always wanted an Aga. I get a frisson of happiness at that, a hopeful moment that once I'm used to this house, it'll be okay. I wish we'd moved in summer. I wish Larkin Lodge *felt* like it had looked in the photos. I wish I could stop being so ridiculous.

I climb the stairs to the middle floor, slowly and carefully, my right leg taking every step, the left following behind, and the creaking wood gives away my slow progress. No running up and down with no thought of danger for me. Maybe never again. One serious brush with death brings every danger into sharp focus. It changes a person. I grip the handrail tight and finally turn the corner.

From up here I can't hear Freddie anymore, only the rattling of the landing window from a breeze outside, and I tighten up the lock to quiet it before continuing. Three double bedrooms and two bathrooms. The door hinges creak as I push them open. The largest of the bedrooms is made up, the pink duvet cover a spark of brightness amid the dour, and has our things on the bedside tables, and in the nearest bathroom I find the beautiful rolltop bath I'd seen in the photos—which makes me happy because I've always wanted one of those too—and all our toiletries.

There's a steeper staircase leading up to the second floor where the primary suite is, but, as Freddie warned me, until my leg is stronger, there's no way I can contemplate going up there yet. I go back into the bedroom Freddie's allocated to us and look out of the window. The thin mist of earlier has become a thick fog, wound around the house in the darkening sky like a shroud, and if I want to see the views or garden I'm going to have to wait until morning.

'It's ready,' I hear Freddie call up from the bottom of the stairs. 'Hope you're hungry.'

As I turn my back on the creeping fog, I hear a creak from somewhere in the upstairs corridor. It's long and slow, almost deliberate. Too close to be downstairs. Has Freddie come up to get me?

The landing, however, is empty and quiet. *It's just an old house,* I tell myself, shaking away my unsettled feeling. *Old houses creak like old bones.*

4.

Emily

I'm dreaming, I know I'm dreaming because although I'm back on that narrow cliff path, I'm wearing a hospital gown and a ventilator mask on my face and not my shorts and T-shirt.

I'm walking ahead of Freddie, like I was then, annoyed at the heat of the Ibiza sun that burst through the clouds just as we'd reached the trickiest part of the hike and at the baked sandy stones that make my footsteps unsteady. I didn't even want to do this walk; I wanted to stay by the pool and have some time to myself. But Mark and Iso paid for the whole holiday, the luxury villa, the ridiculous chef, and none of us could say no. Cat is up ahead with Russell, and I know she's not struggling but she didn't want to come either. I could tell. The six of us, different coloured threads once wound tight around the spool of friendship, now unravelling, pulling in different directions.

It's all slower in the dream, as if with each step I'm being dragged through honey to the inescapable future. Freddie's close behind me, and while we're making an effort for the others, we're in foul moods with each other. We haven't had sex once since we came away and it's really starting to piss him off. I walk a little faster, trying to put some space between us—a space big enough for all my secret guilt—and a few pebbles scatter over the edge. It's not a sheer cliff edge here but maybe a fifteen-foot drop undulating to fifty in places. Far enough to kill yourself, for sure, and hearing the noise, Iso looks back at me. Iso, hair white-blond, perfectly beautiful, my oldest friend—is she even really my friend anymore or are we habit—shields her eyes with her hand to check I'm okay, but I wave her and her perfect thighs on.

'I'm okay,' I call out. In reality, I'm so very far from okay. I've done something terrible, I'm consumed by a guilt that stops me sleeping and has left me with a growing reminder of my mistake, and in moments everything is about to get very much worse.

'You don't have to, you know.' It's Russell's voice and in the dream he's momentarily there beside me, before I start to climb the incline I'm about to fall from. 'You can turn back now.' In the dream he whispers with a stale breath. 'Bad things are that way. You'll die if you go that way.' He starts to fade then, evaporating as I look at him.

'It's too late,' I answer, confused. 'I'm already there.'

The rest of the dream replays as it happened. I hear Freddie muttering behind me about going faster, close on my heels, pressuring me to speed up. I take a large stride and bite my tongue to stop me saying a million things I might or might not regret, and instead I focus on the promotion and starting my new role in ten days, and then, as I swat a fly away from my face, I stumble forward. At least I think I stumble—or did he knock into me—and as I turn to confront him, my ankle twists under me, I lose my balance, and as I tilt backward—no no no no—I stretch my arms out to Freddie, my hands grasping for him. He reaches out. He does. I know that. I see that. So do the others, turning back to see why I yelped, but his fingers don't even brush mine and I'm sure he could lean further forward, and our eyes meet and as mine plead, all I see is fear—and is that relief?—in his. And then I start to fall.

In the dream I go from the endless terrifying fall straight to the broken bones and the beeping hospital machines and the sepsis and the fever and the coma and the—

Death is cold. Even when just for a little while.

Death is so very, very cold.

5.

Emily

I wake from the dream sweating and disoriented in the strange surroundings. It's too dark. No cars. No streetlights. I'm used to the noise of the hospital, which even at night never stops. Sirens wail through double-glazed windows and nurses' shoes whisper up and down the corridors. It's never pitch-black and quiet. Not like this.

I'm trying to go back to sleep when a quiet thud from downstairs stops me. My skin prickles. After listening intently for a minute and hearing no more noise, I'm about to call it my imagination when there's another deadened thump.

I listen harder, acutely aware of how isolated this house is, of how anyone could come in with a shotgun and blast us to death before the police would even be halfway here. The kind of stuff I've read in crime novels and seen on true-crime documentaries. I put a hand on Freddie's shoulder to shake him awake but then I hear a faint caw. A loud panicked fluttering of thick feathers. Heavy wings hitting a wall. Relief floods through me.

A bird. It's just a bird.

A bird is trapped in the house.

I get up and move hesitantly to the bedroom door, my leg immediately screaming even as I reach for my stick. Freddie doesn't stir, but given that he's drunk most of a bottle of wine by himself tonight, that doesn't surprise me. We were both drinking more before my accident and whereas I've had months of enforced sobriety, he's still drinking like we used to. I can do this by myself anyway. It's just letting a bird out.

From the landing, I can hear the squawks downstairs grow more frantic, and by the time I make it to the ground floor I'm sweating despite all the physio and exercise in the hospital. In the cool hallway, I listen. A hard fluttering thud. A croak. Another thud.

I track the sound to the unused drawing room, directly under our bedroom, and after another heavy thump, open the door and quickly slip inside, pressing myself back against the wall before flicking the switch. The sudden yellow light sends the bird into a frenzy, battering itself against every deep red wall in a panicked effort to escape. I have to duck as it circuits the room, talons sharp on its feet. It's a huge black raven and has shat all over the floor in its panic, and I flinch as its heavy wings brush past me. *Germs. I bet it is covered in fleas and mites and germs.*

The bird lands on the mantelpiece, its panic temporarily exhausted, and lets out a quieter caw. It must have come down the chimney because the walls are dirty with old soot where the bird has flung itself against them, and the room smells like something awful. How long has it been since anyone lit a fire here or cleaned out the old flue?

The bird stays where it is, black eyes fixed on me, and for a long moment neither of us moves. The house is silent, and as my heart slows, I'm aware of how cold the floor is under my feet. One of us has to make the first move, so I keep my eyes locked on the bird and start to hobble to the window to let it out, staying pressed to the awful flock paper.

'It's okay,' I murmur, as much to myself as to the bird. 'It's okay. Nothing to be afraid of.'

I yank down the top of the sash window, letting in the freezing night air, and almost immediately there's the whisper of wings above my head and a joyful caw as my uninvited guest flies free. It's a wonderful relief as it vanishes into the mist. I try to peer through it for a last glimpse but the fog is impenetrable, thick and low-lying. There are other noises outside too. Creatures rustling through the unseen garden. Hunters and prey alive in the night. I close the window, locking it tight.

It's only as I go to leave the room that I realize that my bird wasn't alone.

Another raven lies unmoving in the cold fireplace, its dull eye sockets empty and unseeing. Still, I feel an accusation in them.

You didn't get here in time to save me.

The bird is withered, desiccated, dead for months, if not longer. One wing is badly scarred with feathers missing, the area around it a shocking white, maybe the result of a near miss with a farmer's shotgun at some point or a fight with another bird, and I'm amazed it could even fly. I'm torn between revulsion and sadness. Was it stuck in the chimney and died there? Did the bird I freed knock it in panic on its way down into the house, loosening it from its entombment in the walls?

Perhaps my raven had come in search of this one. I read somewhere that corvids are capable of love. And vengeance. Was all the fluttering and banging into walls grief, not panic? I can't leave the raven's corpse there, so despite my fear of germs I fetch a dustpan and brush and sweep up the dark body, opening the bottom of the window just enough to tip it out. It's barely more than a husk. A strong wind might even blow it away to dust. But at least it's back in the fresh air now.

Free of the house.

I haul myself back up the stairs, trying not to let the pain win, and in the bathroom I scrub my hands until they're bright pink with the effort but perfectly clean. I'm suddenly tired again, and this time I think I really will be able to sleep. I flick off the bathroom light and pad across the wooden floor of the dark hallway.

The pain comes out of nowhere.

It's sharp and needle-focused in the sole of my foot and I gasp, almost crumpling with the shock as I pull away. In the half light the blood on the wooden floorboards shines bright red.

Blood. My blood. No, no. No.

I lift my foot up, my aches forgotten, and the dark crimson bloom against my skin fills my vision. My worst fears confirmed. My breath hitches in my chest as the palpitations start. I can't breathe. Blood. A cut. *Oh god, not sepsis again, please not sepsis again*, and then the white heat of panic overwhelms me.

6.

Freddie

What the hell has she been doing?

The footprints run from the top of the stairs to our bedroom door, and even in the gloom of the night they're distinct, clear marks of toes and soles, a ghostly dark grey against the wood. I yawn, shivering, having been in the depth of a dark sleep when noises woke me, and crouch to look closer. Each print is made from a thick layer of sooty ash. Trod in the fireplace before coming upstairs. Did Emily knock over the ash bucket in the sitting room? Maybe she couldn't sleep and went down for a cup of tea and knocked it over and then trod in it. She's clumsier than she was, unsteady on her feet.

Unsteady on her feet. That makes me think of that day, of watching her fall, and I shiver some more. I should feel worse about what happened and what came after. But I don't. Maybe I am a truly terrible person. A monster.

There's a wash of yellow under the bathroom door at the other side of the landing, and when the sound of a toilet flushing doesn't come, I don't go downstairs to put the heating back on as I was planning but go to check on her. The door's not locked—and Emily always locks the door if she's using the toilet—so I push it open, and for a moment I can't bring myself to speak, taking in the sight. She's sitting on the floor, pressed against the wall, and she looks like a madwoman, her hair hanging over her face.

Something about the image both unsettles me and gives me a sense of relief. She looks terrified and panicked, as if something on her foot is going to harm her, and I realize that while Emily might not be fully better yet, all the worries she's left the hospital with might buy me some time. Maybe it will be good for me if she stays messed up for a little bit longer. There's no real harm in it, after all.

7.

Emily

The bathroom wall is cold behind my back, the January night seeping in through the stone, but I embrace the chill, needing it to help me calm down. Eventually, when my breathing is steady, I peel the tissue away and carefully study the cut on my foot. It barely hurts now, and the bleeding has stopped. Maybe it wasn't so deep after all. Still, I add more TCP before taping it up with a plaster. I'll need to keep an eye on it. *Just in case.*

Just in case.

Just in case of sepsis, of coma, of death.

Again.

Death is cold. Empty. Nothing. Death came before the coma, that's what they tell me. When they were battling the sepsis. I remember fever. Fear. A sense of being elsewhere. Of thinking, *This is it, oh god this is it, how can a broken leg kill me?* After that there was nothing. Even when they jolted me back to life, minutes after I'd stopped breathing, I didn't know anything about it. The long sleep of the coma lasted three months, hanging between the light and the void, holding on to life by a gossamer thread until finally I opened my eyes again.

Death trails me though, and I'm still trying to shake him off. *It'll pass*, they say. *It'll pass.* But they don't know everything.

They don't know what haunts me. I glance down at my foot again. Was the nail rusty?

'You okay?'

Freddie's in the doorway, confused to see me on the floor, my foot plastered and a bottle of TCP beside me.

'Yes.' I hold out a hand, and our eyes meet for a moment, both thinking of my accident, before he grips it tightly, too tightly, and pulls me to my feet. 'There was a bird trapped downstairs. I let it out but then I trod on a nail coming back to bed.'

'I wondered what the hell was going on when I saw the footprints. Do you need me to do anything?'

His arm feels good around my waist, handsome face full of concern. He's boyish in the pale light, almost like he was when we met. I've missed it. That all-encompassing love. I've missed him. I stand on my plastered cut and there's no pain. It's a relief. 'Pull the nail up tomorrow. And what footprints?'

In the hallway I see them for myself. Ashy black marks—six or seven of them—leading to our bedroom door.

I glance over the banister but there aren't any on the stairs. How strange.

'Is this the nail?' Freddie's crouched. 'How did it get in upside down?'

The sharp metal tip shines under the overhead light, but it seems smaller now and with only a couple of drops of rusty red around it. I was sure that my foot had spurted blood everywhere. Has it seeped under the floorboards through the tiny hole?

'I'll get that up in the morning. I promise.'

'I don't know how the soot got there.' I'm still looking at the footprints. 'My feet are clean.' I lift one to show my pink sole.

'Has to be you. Who else could it be? Did you wash your cut?'

'Well, yes . . .'

'There you go.' He shrugs. 'You washed it off. Get back to bed while I wipe it up. It's freezing out here.'

I can't shake the image of some unknown faceless figure creeping around the house while I was panicking in the bathroom and Freddie slept, and when he gets in beside me I roll onto my good side and slip an arm around him. His skin is cold, but as the warmth of the duvet envelops us he turns to face me, kissing me in the dark, and it's been so long that when we have sex it's almost like the first time all over again. We're breathless, tugging at each other's pyjamas, and I forget about the awful scars up one leg and pretend my skin is smooth and firm. We're like we used to be as we have fast and urgent sex, and I cling to him as my mind empties of sepsis and hospitals and the accident and what I did for the promotion, and I lose myself in feeling alive. When we're finished, Freddie's like a hot water bottle beside me, and I listen to his breathing as it slows into sleep.

I lie there awake for a while longer, once again alert for any sign of fever in case my foot gets infected, teased by thoughts of those sooty footprints, of a stranger's movements in our house. It isn't possible, of course. They had to be mine. It's the only explanation. My brain isn't to be trusted. Post-sepsis syndrome, that's what they call it, that's what I have to look out for. Downstairs there are several leaflets on it.

Fatigue, difficulty sleeping, muscle and joint pain, difficulty breathing, reduced organ function are among a few of the joyful physical symptoms, and then there are the mental and emotional ones: *hallucinations, panic attacks, mood swings, nightmares, brain fog, memory loss, PTSD.*

Hallucinations. Brain fog. I didn't realize my feet were dirty, that's all there is to it. As I finally drift into sleep the strange creaking comes again, quietly distant, from somewhere out in the corridor. I pull tighter to Freddie. Larkin Lodge is an old house with bad windows, I tell myself as I sink into unconsciousness. That's all.

Outside, a raven croaks, its coarse cry barking into the night sky, and it sounds like laughter.

8.

Emily

The sun shines winter-morning bright and even the heavy wallpapers and dark wood floor seem lighter as I leave Freddie rummaging for pliers to remove the nail and wrap up against the cold to go and check out the garden.

I can't believe how much outside space there is. The garden of our London flat was a tiny patio with space for a bench and a few plants, and now we've gone from one extreme to the other. At the bottom of maybe eighty feet of unkept lawn frozen by winter, there's a pond hidden by overgrown reeds, and then to the right there's a small orchard, branches skeleton bare, and beyond that what looks like a composting pile.

Down a few uneven steps to the left—that I take carefully, one at a time, my stick wedged firm on the stone—there's an overgrown path that leads to two outbuildings. A shed that Freddie's used to store our old attic boxes, and a tiny stone building that maybe once housed pigs or goats. The door is low and it's pitch-black inside. I peek in but don't venture further, the air dank and cold and musty.

I can see another run-down structure with half a corrugated iron roof and what looks like an old septic tank that's going to need removing or replacing. It's shadier here, the cold cutting through me, and I turn back with a shiver, wanting the sunlight. It's a lot of land, but that also means a lot of work. *Work.* I still can't believe they let me go. From newly appointed director of marketing leading three major campaigns and a £90,000 salary to unemployed.

It's a punch in the solar plexus every time I think about it. I've always loved working. It's something of my own that I can rely on. Have self-worth over. I was *good* at my job. My parents never had very much, and while they were happy, I've never shaken that need to be financially independent. To succeed. Freddie comes from a family of old-fashioned values—his mum stayed home and raised the children—and while I may have got caught up with thinking I wanted that too when we got together, babies and baking, it isn't really me.

In the quiet of the garden, I feel entirely alone. I worked so hard for that promotion. Did something I don't like to think about. Something with consequences that hurt me more than I thought possible.

Yet here I am, jobless, after draining the company's health insurance with my very expensive long hospital stay and with a year more's recovery to go, as if god is punishing me. Maybe the garden can be my project. Distract me from my guilt. Suddenly sad again, I turn away from the overgrown, forgotten wild and head down the side of the house.

The air is icy but so clean, and there's no wind, the sun warm on my hair, and, as I come alongside a downstairs window, I see that the dead bird I put outside is already gone. I can pretend I never found it at all. It never died. It was never here. That thought makes me sad again.

It never died. It was never here.

My leg throbs with sudden sharp pain, momentarily draining all the colour from the world. Leaning on my stick, I hobble toward the front where the entrance to the house is level, and as my breath catches at the sudden desolate majesty of the frozen moors beyond the road and the rock wall, I hear a raven cry. I shield my eyes against the low sun and make my way down to the bottom of the drive, curious to see if it's the same bird I freed last night.

'Ghastly grim and ancient raven, wandering from the nightly shore.'

The voice startles me, and as I catch sight of black wings flapping skyward, my sun-struck eyes make out the outline of a woman standing in the road.

I've reached the bottom of the drive, and the woman comes forward into the shade where I can see her. 'Edgar Allan Poe?' I ask.

'Yes.' She's slim and blond, in her late forties maybe, her hair swept up in a messy but stylish chignon. Instead of a coat she has a thick long cardigan wrapped around her, which surely isn't enough to keep the bitter cold out, watery sunlight or not, and her jeans are tucked into Ugg-style boots.

She's not looking at me but up at the house, and I can't quite figure out her expression. Wistful perhaps, but there's a wariness, a *darkness* there. I notice she doesn't come onto the drive just as I don't step onto the road.

'I heard someone had bought the Lodge.' Her head tilts sideways, her eyes still not on me. 'I had to come and see for myself if it was true.'

'Yes, we have. My husband, Freddie, is inside. We've—'

My sentence drifts to a stop. She's not listening. She's already walking back down the lane, hugging herself in the cardigan, as if she hadn't really seen me at all. *At least she spoke to me*, I tell myself wryly. That's more than you get early morning in central London.

I head back toward the house, prettier in daylight than it had been in the grey of yesterday, and while its facade is still maudlin, there's nothing a fresh lick of bright paint won't cure.

As I take it all in, I get a surprising rush of joy that this big house is ours. Away from London. Away from it all.

Up above, in the floor I've yet to see, sunlight hits the beautiful oval window, and suddenly it looks like the house winks at me.

9.

Freddie

I throw the pliers back under the sink and see Emily at the bottom of the drive talking to a woman there, both of them with halos of sunlight around them. Sometimes it feels like she's not the only one suddenly awake from a long sleep, as if we're both dreamers suddenly awake in this house without really knowing how we got here. The coffee machine bubbles, but I'm not sure I need the caffeine. I'm jumpy enough as it is.

It was easier when she was in the hospital. I could go back to the flat and have some time to deal with things, to calm myself down from my situation and straighten out. At least we're far away from everything here. A small breathing window. This house was a godsend.

It's strange. When I think back over the past few months, the move from London has been like a fever dream. Until then I'd been floundering, waiting for Emily to die, but then when they said she'd live, I needed a new plan.

I'd finally got round to charging up Emily's old iPad to take in to her, and the estate agent's page was the last thing she had looked at on holiday. There it was, Larkin Lodge, tranquil in the sunshine, the potential solution to all my problems waiting patiently for me, and the plan immediately fell into place.

She can't see me as she walks slowly back up to the house, eyes on the gravel, her stick doing a lot of the hard work. I felt her scars when we were having sex last night—a surprise I'm not going to complain about—and how she pulled away when I touched them, as if I was going to be revolted. They don't bother me. Not like that. But they do remind me of that day on the cliff. The hangovers we had from having drunk so much the night before.

What had she been doing drinking anyway? It's a thought I've had more than once since the accident, but I'm not going to broach it with her. Maybe she hadn't drunk that much at all. Maybe she'd pretended. She wasn't pretending her bad mood though, and neither was I.

I knew why I was on edge, but she'd been shitty for a couple of weeks despite getting the promotion she wanted. I guess, knowing what I do now, that she wasn't feeling great and she probably shouldn't have been out on the cliff at all. If I'd known—if she'd told me—the whole day would have been different. I'd never have let her up there. But I remember walking behind her, getting closer, both of us sniping at each other as the others got ahead, and having a sudden red-hot wish that she'd just get out of the bloody way, one way or another. When I shut my eyes at night, I still see the surprised terror in her eyes as she fell, reaching out for me.

The coffee machine beeps that it's done as I hear the front door open and she comes back inside. She looks happy, and it gives me a surprising rush of warm affection.

'Coffee?'

We need to get back on an even keel. A fresh start. I really hope those scars fade.

10.

Emily

The Lamb and Shepherd is a proper old-fashioned pub with beams overhead and brass horseshoes on the walls, and the whole building is a rabbit warren of overheated spaces.

I've had a glass of wine, which has gone straight to my head, and I'm on the verge of feeling entirely disoriented on the way to the bathroom when I peer into one alcove and there she is, looking back. The woman from the lane.

She's animated, mid-conversation with two men, one an elderly vicar, a dog collar tucked into his blue shirt, and the other a very handsome man of about her age, casually dressed in a loose white shirt, open at the neck against tanned skin, his thick hair cut slightly long. There's bright paint on his trousers, a dash of blue and a small smear of red. Artist's paint, not decorator paint. He reminds me of the all-year-rounders we met in the bars in the quieter spots of Ibiza. Free. Easy. He says something, a wry smile on his face and hand on the woman's thigh, and the other two laugh. That's when she looks up and sees me. Their conversation stops and suddenly I'm the focus of their attention.

'Sorry.' I'm awkward. 'I didn't mean to stare. I just—I saw you this morning. Outside Larkin Lodge.'

'Oh yes.' Her smile doesn't quite reach her eyes. 'I remember now. The new owner. I passed by on my walk.'

'The new owner?' The vicar is immediately on his feet, one hand stretched out, beaming cheerfully. 'How lovely to meet you. So glad the old place has people in it again. It's been empty too long. I'm Paul Bradley Carr—not to be confused with the other Paul Carr, who owns the off-licence in the high street and is known to drink all his profits. I'm the vicar at St Olaf's.' His grin is infectious, although I'm still curious about the woman and the man she's with. It didn't seem like she'd *passed by* this morning. It felt like her visit was intentional.

'I'm Emily Bennett. My husband, Freddie, and I just moved in.'

'Always nice to have fresh blood in the village,' the handsome man says, and I swear to god I start to blush. He bleeds a sexual charisma that gives him the air of some movie star. A natural charm. He's hot, really hot, and even after everything, I feel a rush of attraction.

'I'm Joe Carter. And this is my wife, Sally.'

'Nice to meet you.'

'It's a pleasure,' Sally says, before adding, looking at me thoughtfully, 'You're very beautiful.'

It's an unexpected and odd compliment, and I'm not sure how to respond. 'Oh. Thank you,' I settle on. 'And so are you.'

'Isn't she, Joe?' She looks over at her husband. 'You should paint her.'

'Maybe give her time to settle in first.' Joe smiles at me. 'My wife is my manager. Every new face is a potential masterpiece to Sally. I'm an artist.'

'And a very sought-after one,' the vicar interjects. 'All the London galleries want work from him.'

'We lived in the Lodge for a while about twenty years ago. Sally got quite attached to it but it's too big for us, and then we saw the cottage in Wiveliscoombe and the studio space and we haven't looked back. Train into London in three hours. Perfect.'

'I hadn't thought about the Lodge for years,' Sally says. 'And then there you were. Bringing it back to life.'

'Welcome to Wiveliscoombe, Emily,' Paul says. 'Heart of Dartmoor.'

'Is that a niche Conrad joke?'

'Oh, you're a bookworm? What perfect timing. We've just wrapped up our book club.' He holds up a volume. 'The collected short stories of Edgar Allan Poe. A little too horror for me, but interesting. We've just done "The Raven." Poem rather than story.'

'Ravens are drawn to death,' Sally says softly. 'Did you know that?'

'Where my imagination goes onto canvas, Sally loves books. This is her thing, not mine.' Joe gets to his feet. 'And I still have work to get done tonight, darling, so let's go.'

'My husband isn't much of a reader either.'

'Well, maybe you should join our club.' The vicar holds out the book. 'Take it and have a read. We meet in here every third Thursday.'

'Maybe.' I take the book, although I'm not sure I'm ready for some middle-aged book group in the country yet. 'And thank you.'

I watch them leave together, Joe's hand gently resting on the small of Sally's back, his movements fluid like a cat and her beauty almost ethereal, and I'm momentarily too fascinated by them to move until my bladder twinges and I'm reminded of what sent me this way in the first place.

'You had me worried.' Freddie's waiting for me by the door. 'Thought maybe you'd been sick. Too much rich food too soon.' He holds the door open for me but doesn't rest his hand protectively on the small of my back as I limp out.

'I asked at the bar about local workmen for the garden,' he continues. 'Ones with good reputations. He's going to speak to a couple of people. Thinks we should be able to get someone to start pretty soon if the weather breaks. I think one was someone called Pete Watkins? I've given them my number to pass on.'

'Great. Sounds good.'

I can just about make out Sally's and Joe's faces as a low classic racing-green sports car pulls out of the car park. I smile and wave, but they either don't see me or are too deep in their own conversation to wave back. Neither of them are smiling, their expressions intense, so different from the mood in which they left. I lower my hand, and then they're gone.

II.

Emily

I'm boiling in bed under the blanket and duvet. How can Freddie be cold? It's baking in here. He's always had bad circulation—a hangover from the chain-smoking that was one of the lesser bad habits of his youth—but this is crazy. I'm sweating in my pyjamas. Maybe I'm coming down with something. Could my foot be infected?

I creep out to the bathroom and press the thermometer against my forehead, taking deep calming breaths until it beeps and tells me I'm exactly 36.8 degrees, normal for me. I peel the plaster off to check my foot and there's barely any sign that it was hurt at all, certainly no red ring of infection. It's more of a relief than it should be, and I remind myself I'm no more likely to get sepsis again than anyone else. Probably *less* likely because I'll be so careful. I was unlucky. It isn't some bullshit punishment for what I did. There is no karma. And anyway, I've already been punished. The hollow ache inside is a reminder of that.

I turn off the bathroom light and step through the gloom onto the landing. It's a clear night and moonlight streams in from the hall window, a pool of white, and I'm almost in the bedroom when—

Scraaatch scraaaatch.

I freeze. In the quiet, the sound, like a secret whisper, barely carries to me.

Scraaatch scraaaatch.

It comes again. Not a thud or a flutter of frantic wings. Whatever it is, it's not a bird. And whatever it is, it's coming from upstairs.

The moonlight now seems to only enhance the dark shadows that fill the corners and doorways off the landing, and as I hear the sound again I reluctantly peer up to the next floor.

Maybe it's a rat. It's a grim thought. We had mice once in the flat but never a rat.

Scraaatch scraaaatch.

Definitely too loud for a mouse. In fact, it doesn't sound like an animal of any kind. For a moment I'm not sure what it sounds like, and then when it comes again it strikes me.

Fingernails on wood.

I look back toward the bedroom and then upward, caught in a no-man's-land, but I know I won't be able to sleep until I've checked it out, and I don't want to wake Freddie two nights in a row. I've got no choice. Despite the niggling irrational fear in the pit of my stomach, I grip the banister and press my good foot down on the first stair.

One step at a time I climb the steep staircase, my good leg doing most of the work, but finally, a little breathless, I reach the top and flick on the lights. A solitary bulb, no shade over it, pools soft yellow across the landing.

Dust motes hang suspended in the air against the pale green walls of the large landing, paint not paper here, and the old gloss skirting boards are chipped, as are the cupboards covering the radiators in an old-fashioned way, as if perhaps the previous owners ran out of energy or money to make it as ornate up here.

I find a bathroom on the left with a double bedroom alongside, as well as several storage cupboards lining the wall. I don't find any evidence of mouse droppings or worse, and certainly no flapping bird. The landing and the rooms off it stay silent. In the faded dusky bulb light I wonder if I heard anything at all or if it was simply my imagination playing tricks on me.

There's only one door left to open, on the far side of the staircase—the primary bedroom suite, the one we'll be moving into as soon as my leg is more manageable. From outside, the large oval window is the centerpiece of the front of the house, hinting that the space inside is something special. Facing the wooden door, I hear the very faintest *scraaatch* coming from *inside*, and then, taking a deep breath, I step forward, grip the cool metal handle, and twist.

As the vast room comes into view I have such a wave of cognitive dissonance that I can't move or think. It *is* breathtakingly beautiful, the moon hanging at the window like a perfect bauble of light, dressing the polished floor in sheets of silky white, and from the pale walls the ceiling arches up to a point, running out to where the large oval window sits in the middle.

But despite its beauty, the air is punched from my lungs as I cringe backward. What I feel is a terrifying darkness. I stare, my eyes wide. An invisible foulness covers every surface in the room like a sentient oil, clinging to it, spoiling it like rot.

Darkness.

The room is a bleak, cold space, void of anything *good*. As I stand there, my legs trembling under me, my bladder suddenly full, I'm too afraid to move. It's as if the essence of every terrible event that has ever happened has been trapped inside this one room. Has gestated here, is *still* gestating new horrors here.

I can't breathe, and I don't want to breathe in case the stench of it—because surely something this wicked must have some stench—eats into me like maggots on a corpse and I'll have to carry it with me forever.

Something bad happened in here. Someone died in here.

35

I step backward, out of the room, and the temperature rises several degrees against my goosebumped skin, the room stretching endlessly in front of me, that oval window mocking like a black eye glinting wickedness, malevolent and with purpose, and then suddenly something is *rat-a-tatting* on the outside glass and I let out a small shriek, sure my heart is going to explode.

Only the screeching caw and its large beak tapping again at the window before flying away makes me realize it's the raven, not some otherworldly creature, and I quickly yank the door shut. But not before a waft of cold air steals out after me. I look around, half expecting something—*whatever was scratching*—to physically manifest, grotesque, in a corner.

My fear of the room overwhelms my fear of the stairs, and clutching at the banister with both hands I come down sideways like a crab, one foot at a time, looking backward more than forward, afraid I might see a thick black sticky smog creeping down after me. *What happened in that room? What is in that room?*

'Why did you open the window?'

I startle when I see Freddie, irritated, standing on the landing as I round the corner, and then almost laugh with relief. He doesn't wait for me to answer before he speaks again. 'You know I was cold.'

I look up, confused. The lower half of the sash window has been pulled up, wide open. Freddie yanks it down and screws the latch up tight. 'And now this place is an icebox.'

'I haven't touched it. I heard something upstairs and went to look, that's all.'

'It didn't open itself,' he mutters, shivering. 'It must have been you. Maybe you were half-asleep. And there's nothing upstairs. The rooms are all empty.'

I open my mouth to protest, to tell him how horrible it felt in the room, but he's obviously annoyed and tired so instead I say nothing. He yawns.

'God, I need more sleep.' He heads to the bathroom, leaving the door open, calling out while he pees, 'We've got to get everything ready tomorrow. They'll probably arrive early on Saturday.'

I stare at the window. Was it open when I got up? Suddenly I don't remember, unsure of myself. I don't think it was, but I wasn't looking. But surely I wouldn't have been sweating in bed if the freezing night air had been swirling through the house.

On the other hand, if the window *was* open, then I could have been hearing noises from outside, not upstairs. Maybe that was why it felt colder in that second-floor room? Maybe.

The window wasn't open though, a little voice whispers in my head as I pull the duvet over me. *You know it wasn't. Not when you went upstairs. So then who opened it? Or what?*

I stare at Freddie's back, wishing I could tell him that the house is freaking me out a bit. I wish I felt closer to him. I wish I'd felt closer to him back then. I wish I hadn't done what I did. I'm the reason we're struggling to be normal. Hiding this guilt. Guilt I'll have to hide forever.

But what could I say now? I'm sorry I was such a bitch when we were on holiday, but I'd drunkenly cheated on you with my boss because I wanted that promotion so badly, and if that guilt wasn't enough, I'd just found out I was pregnant and didn't know if it was yours, and I wasn't even really sure I wanted *you* anymore?

God, this is such a mess. And all my own making.

As I roll away to face the wall, I touch my flat stomach and feel another stab of hollow pain. The baby died in the fall. My punishment, I'm sure. I'd been drinking when I shouldn't have been, trying to convince myself that getting rid of the baby would be the best thing, even though I knew I never could, the little life already gripping me like a small tight fist. And then, with one stumble, it was gone.

Freddie thinks we lost *our* baby. But whoever the father was, the baby I lost was mine. And it was all my fault.

12.

Emily

'Everyone should have a second Christmas in the middle of January,' Cat says as she opens up another box of books. 'It's such a miserable month.' She looks at me, trails of dark hair escaping her ponytail, over a handful of paperbacks. 'But preferably without you scaring the shit out of us and nearly dying first.'

'My hiking days are over. Not that I really liked it in the first place.' I slide some cookery books into a space on the shelves and sip my red wine, nicely warm from the glow of the fire. While a January Christmas might be ridiculous, it's good to have some fun. It's been a busy day or so getting things ready—to be fair, Freddie did most of it while I directed him—and with no more strange sounds or feelings, any misgivings I've had about something odd in the house have almost faded away. 'I only ever went hiking because Freddie wanted to.'

'I remember. I was surprised you went that day at all because you both were in such shitty moods. Hangovers, I guess.'

'Something like that.'

She looks up, curious. 'Had you been fighting?' Nothing gets past Cat.

'Not really. Just been in a bit of a bad patch. You know how it is. It's better now though, obviously. A coma will do that.'

'Maybe next time don't go for such an extreme solution.' She smiles at me. 'But seriously. I'm glad you're better. Relationships can take work, but we all know it's worth it. Marriage is team-work, after all.'

I smile back at her, half-amused that she's dragged up that saying again, but knowing that her heart is in the right place. Cat's a good person, and I'm glad to see her.

The Christmas tree is decorated and lit in the dining room and Freddie and Russell have dressed the table already, while prepping the food, the smell of cooking turkey permeating the warm house. Fires blaze in the downstairs grates and a massive icy downpour started just after Freddie and Russell finished bringing a bunch of boxes in from the outhouses so I could get my books put away. It's a proper wintry day, and the house feels almost Dickensian.

Cat scans a couple of the old paperbacks before adding them to her end of the shelves. Unlike Freddie, Cat's always been a bookworm like me. It's what we bonded over in uni. Iso was the *light*, the party life of our house-share trio, Cat was the studious one, and I was somewhere in between. Sometimes I think it's strange we've stayed friends for so long, but once our boyfriends and then husbands clicked—different as they might be too—we were locked into a six. Right now, in a new house and new life, it's comforting to have them here, and I feel a rush of affection for them all.

Given the built-in shelves either side of the fireplace, this room might have been a drawing room or library at some point, smaller than the main lounge and not as imposing as the red room or the dining room, and it's great to finally have somewhere to let my books breathe and a desk to sit at if I ever decide to write a book of my own.

'These are the last ones out of this box.' Cat hands me three hardbacks and I slot them in. All I need to make this room my own are a couple of wingback chairs and maybe some plants. I wasn't keen on the thick green wallpaper, inlaid with a gold pattern, but I'm warming to its richness now the room is coming to life.

'This place is amazing,' Cat says, flopping into my old Ikea chair, her baggy green sweater over her jeans almost matching the walls. 'So much space. And god, the peace and quiet. I wonder if there's a vacancy for a head of year in one of the local secondaries. Bet the kids are easier. I'd love to run away from London.'

'If you guys moved down here that would be amazing.' I stand back, enjoying the look of the full shelves. 'But "run away" is a funny way of putting it.'

'Just a turn of phrase. Run away. Move away. Whatever. Come on,' she says. 'Let's go get another drink and check on the turkey.'

We head out into the hallway and the click of pool balls comes from the room that Freddie and Russell have turned into a games room while we've been setting up the library.

'I'll see if the boys want anything,' Cat says, and I realize I've left my own glass behind. I turn back to fetch it, a gentle wine-and-happiness buzz making me more relaxed than I've been since getting out of the hospital.

I'm about to pick up my glass when the library door creaks slowly shut behind me.

As I watch it click closed, I feel a sudden gust of icy wind and the fire goes out.

I stare into the grate, my heart pounding in my chest. The fire isn't just out. It's cold. There's no smoke coming from the coals. No residual heat. Nothing. Rain hammers at the window, the sound my only company. *Just a blast of stormy wind coming down the chimney. That's all.* Feeling a million miles away from the rest of the warm house, I pick up the glass and force my feet to move calmly toward the door.

It's an old house and there's a storm outside. This is nothing to be freaked out by. It's only as I touch the handle, twisting it to free myself from the room, that I hear several soft thuds on the wooden floor behind me. I glance back in trepidation, half expecting sooty footprints coming toward me, but instead I see that four books have fallen off the shelves from various points, now on the rug in front of the dead fire. *Just the wind,* I tell myself again as my mouth dries. *Nothing else.* Determined not to be scared out of the room, I pick them up. *Die or Diet* by Dr Ella Jones, *Will You Love Me,* by Mhairi Atkinson, *Here Come the Clowns* by Armond Ellory, and *You* by Caroline Kepnes.

Out in the hallway the door knocker bangs loudly, and I drop the books onto the table, take my glass, and get out of the cold library, hurrying to greet Mark and Iso, who is already shrieking with delight, and to revel in the normality of our friendships.

Just the wind, I repeat like a mantra. *Just the wind.*

And I almost believe it until we go back there while giving them the tour of the house. As the others talk, all I can do is stand and stare. The fire is blazing again. The books are back on the shelves. It's as if it didn't happen at all.

It's me. I must be going mad.

13.

Emily

'Is that a fact?' Across the table in the candlelight Iso glows, her ice-white hair shining without a hint of any roots, and I'm sure she's had more Botox—but even if she has, her figure is all her own work, and I have to salute the energy she puts into staying so hot. She is *not* wearing a baggy sweater and jeans but a glamorous dress—*Well, it is second Christmas, everyone*—and a pair of very high heels. 'I think people just change,' she says. 'Most people anyway.'

'Sure, people change.' Russell shrugs. 'That's definitely part of it, but that's what we say to be kind to ourselves when things don't turn out. The essence of who we are doesn't alter that much as we age. A few people make big changes that can affect relationships—alcoholics who quit drinking or the other way around—but most of us just get calmer as we get older. Not really much different.'

Russell waves his hands around, animated as he talks, and I wonder if he's this engaged with the students he teaches psychology to at the college, or if it's an intensity he can only achieve after half a bottle of wine. Either way, it's a good distraction from my worry that I've got a brain tumour or post-sepsis syndrome or if this house is actually haunted.

'If you're a five-star beach holiday person, you're not suddenly going to become someone who wants to go camping. If anything,

43

you start wanting *more* luxury.' His look is pointed directly at Iso and she laughs, and we laugh with her. It's true. The more Mark earns—and it's an eye-watering amount for someone only just over forty—the more ways Iso finds to enjoy it.

'The fact of the matter is,' Russell continues, 'that when people fall in love the first thing they do is *lie* to each other.' He smiles at all of us, his curly hair wilder after being caught in the rain. 'And lies are hard to maintain.'

'I didn't lie to you.' Cat hasn't touched her own glass for a while, and I can see she's annoyed. Her mouth is pursed tight. Russell always ends up holding court, and the rest of us don't mind it—at least what he says is clever and interesting—but she gets embarrassed by him. 'Except perhaps pretending I liked listening to you pontificate when we should be having fun.'

'Ouch.' He blows her a kiss with a good-humoured smile. 'But are you sure about that? I lied. I came to church with you. I told you I was a Catholic to please your parents, and we both know now that I'm at best an agnostic.'

'I think he's right.' Mark refills our glasses with the expensive Barolo he brought six bottles of. 'Blowjobs, for example. Women lie about loving those. Hey, if this is extra Christmas, does that mean I get an extra one this year?'

'What is this, pick on Iso night?' She throws the end of her bread roll at her husband. 'You do better than most, darling.'

'Oh my god, Cat.' I laugh suddenly with a memory. 'You said you liked jazz. Do you remember? After your second date with Russell—the first time you shagged, I think—we had to do a quick deep dive so you could pretend to know some obscure 1970s music to impress him.'

'Okay, busted. I did. I suffered for that lie though.'

'I pretended to like skiing,' Iso says. 'To be fair, I thought I would like it. But I quickly realized I was born for après-ski not actual-ski. Those were a long few winters before I fessed up.'

'But I like that you pretended to like it. What about you two?' Mark looks at Freddie and me. 'You got together first. What were you, twenty? So, fifteen years ago? Things still the same?'

'Well, nearly dying of sepsis and spending months in hospital can change a girl.' I don't want to talk about me and Freddie. I'm not sure it would be so funny. We haven't told the others about the lost baby. Freddie said it was up to me, but I didn't want to share it.

'We agreed straight off we wanted a traditional marriage,' Freddie says suddenly. 'I've always wanted kids and Em said she did too, and I always liked the idea of the man supporting the family and the wife making the home. Traditional values and everything.'

'And I do too. But we don't have children.' I feel another flash of guilt and pain, and I'm angry at Freddie for starting this conversation. The baby would have been a cuckoo in our nest, I know that. And maybe, awful as it is, the loss has been for the best, even if my heart sees it differently. 'Anyway, we've got time to make a family.'

'Tick tock tick tock.' Iso leans forward. 'I didn't realize men's balls had a baby clock!' Nothing can dampen Iso's mood tonight, and thank god for that because it feels like the rest of us are a bit snippy.

'But yes,' I concede. 'Maybe I didn't feel as strongly about those values as you did. And I underestimated how much I would like working.'

'And you pretended to like hiking and Freddie pretended he liked books,' Cat cuts in, trying to lighten the moment. 'I bet that was as much research as my jazz panic.'

'My point is,' Russell powers on, 'that we all fall in love in part with an illusion, because we all present an illusion to someone who we want to love us. We heighten the best bits

45

of ourselves and hide the worst bits. And when looking at our partner we ignore the hints of the things that might annoy us and see only the good. The madness of first love. A successful marriage is about accepting that no one can ever be that perfect version they showed you and you chose to believe.'

'And that,' I sigh, 'was the longest explanation ever for why a couple the rest of us can barely remember from college are getting divorced. Maybe we should stop this now or it will be after-dinner divorces for us, rather than after-dinner mints.' It's a poor joke, but it's enough. 'I'm just happy to have you all here and to be out of hospital.'

'Amen to that.' Mark raises his glass, and they all join in with 'To Emily!'

'And to this lovely amazing huge fantastic house!'

'And all its weirdness,' I add, glad for the subject change, and Iso's eyes widen, delighted.

'Tell me it has a ghost.'

'I don't know.' I shrug. 'I've heard weird noises at night. Had odd feelings.' I stop there, not willing to go as far as mentioning fires going out and books flying off the shelves. 'It could just be me though.'

'It's not haunted, Em,' Freddie says, exasperated. 'It's old.'

'How do you know it's not haunted?' Iso's sharp with Freddie.

'I don't feel anything odd,' Freddie says, on cue.

'Even if you did, you wouldn't admit it,' Iso counters.

Freddie's in full disbelief mode, and I don't want to argue with him. Iso, like me, has always been fascinated by the weird. Back in the day we'd be at every fair having our tarot cards read, going to those ridiculous 'An Evening with . . .' medium shows, and all that kind of stuff.

'You see, perfect example,' Russell says. 'Freddie used to tell you it was cute that you believed in all this woo-woo stuff, but now it just annoys him.'

'Enough, Russell.' Mark reaches for the cheese. 'You never have known when to stop.'

'I don't find it surprising that Emily feels things that you don't.' Cat fingers the crucifix at her neck, thoughtfully. 'After all, she was dead for a few minutes. They had to bring her back.'

'There was nothing when I died, Cat. Literally nothing.' I don't like thinking about the nothingness. No tunnels or bright lights. One minute I was there in a haze of fever and panic and then there was only the void.

'Nothing you remember. But you crossed to the other side. If we'd been a hundred years ago or whatever, you'd have stayed dead.'

'Gee thanks, Cat.' I try to lighten the mood, but in the twinkling lights of the Christmas tree and the warm glow of the candles, a hush has settled across us.

'You know what I mean. You've glimpsed behind the veil. If there's a spirit in this house, maybe they can reach you in a way they can't the rest of us.'

'I know what we should do!' Iso claps her hands together with excitement. 'The Ouija board!' She looks at me. 'You still have that, right?'

'I don't know,' Freddie says. 'I might have thrown it away.'

'No, it's in that outhouse we got the book boxes from,' Russell says. 'I saw it.'

'Come on then.' Mark is on his feet. 'Let's go get it, Freddie. Brave the rain, then brave the afterlife.'

He makes a *bwah ha ha* sound and that's that decided. We're going to try to speak to the spirits.

14.

Emily

Freddie's face was like thunder when he came in, soaking from the dash to the outhouse in the heavy freezing rain, but he didn't say anything as he dumped the battered old box down in front of me, as if it was my suggestion we'd play it.

'Gosh,' Iso breathes quietly as I lift off the tatty cardboard lid and Cat lights the candles we've placed in each corner of the room and turns off the Christmas tree lights. 'How long has it been since we used this? Got to be more than ten years?'

'Maybe twelve.' I'd picked it up in a bric-a-brac shop when we'd gone to Blackpool of all places for a cheap weekend away, and Iso and I had shrieked and laughed till we cried with this board but we never made any contact. We'd mainly just messed around after too many vodka shots.

In the candlelight Iso's sharp cheekbones are deep shadows and she looks almost cadaverous. We all do, really, black circles around our nervous eyes making them appear sunken. Russell looks like he's about to burst into laughter again, but Freddie is still stone-faced, and a hush has fallen across the table in anticipation. Both Iso and Cat are sitting up straight in their chairs, eyes glistening. My hands are clammy. I look at the midnight-blue wood with the capital letters printed in white, curving across the middle, and the numbers in a straight line underneath. Above, at the top, on either side of the *OUIJA* are a small *Yes* and *No*, and the borders are decorated with skulls and moons and suns.

Where have you been? the board calls silently. *We used to have such fun together.*

I take a sip of wine and Iso grins. 'You and me, Emily. Like the old days.'

I feel a rush of love for her, the years of our friendship a kaleidoscope of sudden memories, placing my fingers alongside hers on the planchette, the point facing inward, the hole in it uncovered.

With my eyes closed, I take long breaths deep into my lungs and then blow them out in loud exhales. This is natural. There is nothing terrible here. The dead can't harm you. I open my eyes again. The fire has burned down, and Mark and Freddie have brought a chill back in with them from the storm outside, and the air is cooler.

'Is there a spirit present?' Iso takes the lead, and I glance at the shadows dancing behind each flickering candle. Nothing. The seconds tick by but the planchette remains still under our fingers and the flames remain steady. Someone shuffles in a chair.

'Only Jack Daniels,' Russell mutters, amused, and Freddie snorts a cynical laugh before Cat and Iso glare them back into silence.

'Ignore them,' Iso says, nodding at me to speak.

'Please answer if you're here.' The words feel stupid said out loud, and I wish it were just me and Iso without the others here, like the old days. I concentrate harder.

'Is there anybody here with us?' I glance nervously upward, but there's no sense of that oppressive presence I felt in the darkness of the room upstairs, or the sense of *otherness* in the library. I almost repeat the question, and I'm starting to feel slightly foolish, and then I feel it. The slightest tremble under my fingers.

My skin prickles. That wasn't me. I glance at Iso, but her face is tight with concentration and she doesn't look at me.

'Please.' My voice is a rasp. 'Is someone here?'

'What is it?' Cat's eyes widen, a little afraid. 'Did you feel something?'

Again a pause, but then there's definitely movement. I fight the instinct to pull my hand away as the planchette drags under my light touch, like a magnet on metal, to the top left corner.

Yes.

'Holy shit.' Iso's mouth falls open, shocked, and we all stare at the pointer. 'That wasn't me.'

'Emily did it.' Even Freddie's paying attention now.

'Emily?' Iso asks.

'It wasn't me either.' Air is stuck in my throat like food, a bubble I can't shift. I look at the planchette, still placed over the *Yes*, and think, *I was right. We're not alone.* I don't know if the temperature has really dropped or whether my fear has chilled me, but every sinew and fibre of my body tenses.

'Has to be Iso,' Mark mutters, but we ignore him.

'Thank you for answering.' Sandpaper words, my throat so dry, but there's also the slightest fizz of excitement in my belly. I am communicating with the dead. *Fuck you, Freddie.*

'Let's get it back to the middle.' Iso's eyes are wide as we slide the planchette backward away from the *Yes*. It's a different kind of pressure when we move it together, not like what we just felt. It wasn't me and it wasn't Iso either, I'm sure of it. My heart skips faster.

'Did you use to live in this house?'

No movement. I swallow hard before I ask the next question.

'Did you die in this house?'

Everything stills. I hear nothing, not even my own heart beating, as if I've been plunged into a vacuum, as if every atom has been sucked out of the world.

'This is freaking me out now.' Cat's voice is quiet, more mouse than cat. 'Maybe we should stop.' No one answers and she doesn't move. I can't stop. Not now. I don't think I could even if I wanted to.

'Did you die in this house?' My lips move and my throat vibrates so I know I'm speaking but I hear nothing. The bubble has become a pressure on my chest, the house shrinking into the vacuum, and I'm not sure I'm even breathing. I try to lift my fingers from the planchette but I can't move my hand. All of gravity is holding it there. Is there pressure in a vacuum? What is happening? Is Iso feeling this too?

'How can we help you?' she asks.

The candles glow brighter and my ears pop. I feel *distanced*. Suddenly my hand moves, Iso's too, pulled from letter to letter, getting faster and faster, so fast my eyes can't keep up.

FINDITFINDITFINDITFINDITFINDIT

'What the fuck?' Even Mark stares when our hands finally stop moving. 'Find what?'

'Stop it, you two. You've had your laugh.'

Another question comes to me, and I ignore Freddie and ask it.

'Were you murdered in this house?'

The effect is immediate. The air in front of me ripples like water, and I'm wondering if Iso can see it too when—

My arm jolts forward, out of my control. I hear Iso yelp as hers does the same, our fingers stuck to the planchette, the sudden yanking jarring my shoulder, and I know I'm being pulled to the *Yes* when suddenly—

There's a loud banging on the front door and the candles go out.

15.
Emily

'This is very kind.' The vicar, holding a glass of red wine, smiles thankfully at Freddie as he puts a plate and knife down so he can have some of the cheeseboard. 'I hope I'm not interrupting.'

'Thank you for saving me a flat battery,' Mark says. 'Left the headlights on to unload the car and was too keen to get warm to remember to turn them off.'

'We're having a belated Christmas for Emily,' Iso says, her face still flushed. 'She's been in hospital.'

'And it's nice to have surprise visitors at Christmas.' I steer the chat quickly away from having to go through the story of my accident.

'We were doing a Ouija board,' Russell says. 'When you knocked. You scared the crap out of us.'

'Russ.' Cat fires him a look and he shrugs—*What?*—although he knows exactly what. But if he was hoping to shock or offend Paul then he's failed because in fact the vicar looks delighted.

'Oh really?'

'It was getting very creepy when you arrived.' Cat passes him the Stilton. 'I don't know whether it was Iso or Emily or both who were moving the planchette, but they definitely freaked me out.'

We'd all shrieked like an axe murderer was in the house when the candles blew out at the same time as Paul banged on the door. The shrieks quickly turned to laughter as we hurriedly switched on the lights and hid the board, but it's still an odd coincidence. Did a draught blow the candles out? Was it a sign of *something*? Now that the lights are back on, it's hard to be sure exactly what *did* happen.

'It wasn't me,' Iso repeats, although I do have to wonder. It would be a very Iso thing to do. 'And it was creepy or interesting, depending on your perspective.'

'Whichever way, it was probably a good time to stop,' Mark says. 'Childish really.'

'Emily thinks the house is haunted.' Iso ignores Mark and turns to the vicar. 'She's got a *feeling*. And—no surprise—the board agreed.'

'It wasn't me, Iso.'

'The two people who believe in the supernatural are in charge of the planchette and it moved. Hardly a surprise.' Freddie's still annoyed. He's never liked any of this stuff. 'I think they were both playing with us.'

I shrug. I'm not going to fight with Freddie in front of a guest, and I don't want the vicar thinking I'm crazy. Maybe I did do it. Maybe Iso did. I rub my fingertips together. I can still feel the *drag* of the planchette under them. My head's throbbing slightly, and I wish we'd never got the board out at all.

'I suppose if anywhere was to be full of restless spirits, then Larkin Lodge is probably a likely candidate. Given where it stands.'

'What do you mean?' I sit up straighter, ignoring the awful pain in my leg that tells me I'm late for my painkillers.

'Don't tell me this house was built on an old Indian burial site,' Russell says.

'Or a *Pet Semetary*,' Freddie adds, the two exchanging a smile.

'A crossroads,' Paul says. 'It's built on a crossroads.' He sees our confused faces and leans his arms on the table, as if about to impart a secret or tell a ghost story himself. 'Ah, I take it you don't know what crossroads were used for?'

We shake our heads, and while Iso's eyes glitter with excitement, I'm not sure I actually want to know.

'Well, it was an unpleasant practice and stopped nearly two hundred years ago but harks back to when suicide was deemed a crime against both God and oneself. Those who took their own lives couldn't be buried on consecrated ground.' He takes a sip of wine before continuing. 'They were laid face down and staked through the chest to the earth. Sometimes their heads would be cut off and placed between their legs. It was supposed to tether their spirits to the earth and leave the damned souls unsure of which path to take to leave. Stuck on a crossroads for all eternity. A barbaric way to treat people.'

He sits back and drinks more wine, letting that sink in. 'I'm sure the ground must have been blessed since then.' Paul smiles reassuringly at us. 'Several times over, as there's been a house here in one form or another for at least three hundred years.'

'And no juicy murders?' Mark asks. 'No victim who could be Emily's ghost?'

'Not so far as I know.' Paul smiles kindly at me. 'And as much as I am a believer in the Holy Spirit, I'm less a believer in trapped souls. I have faith that we're claimed by one side or another after death and no one is forgotten. But if you'd like, I could bless the house again.'

'We're not believers, I'm afraid,' Freddie says. 'Your prayers would fall on stony ground.'

His attempt to use the Bible for humor makes me cringe. Freddie's never been as funny as he thinks he is.

'Well, if you change your mind, you can find me at either the church or my house. It's just a corner cut across the moor.'

'I'm sure it's just an old house making noises,' I say as if

I'm taking the potential haunting in as lighthearted a manner as everyone else.

'And I'm sure you're right.' Paul squeezes my clammy hand with his papery dry one and smiles around the table. 'Now, thank you for your wonderful hospitality but I must get home. Have a lovely evening.'

Cat goes with Freddie to see the vicar out, Russell pours more wine, and Iso gives me a half smile, and I know that even if I ask her again, she'll deny she was moving the planchette. But it must have been her if it wasn't me. That's the logical truth of the matter, whatever I feel.

I'm suddenly exhausted, my leg and my hips throbbing and my headache getting worse. I can barely keep my eyes open. As I pick up some empty pudding plates to help clear up, the thought echoes in my head. *What other explanation could there be?*

16.

Freddie

I knew something was off with Mark as soon as they arrived, and when Iso insisted we go and get that stupid Ouija board from the outhouses he started probing me with as if he *knows* something. I'd had a feeling he'd wanted to get me on my own all day and I was right. Well, he didn't get anything out of me. My secrets are still safe. Just. I should have been better at answering his recent texts though. I forget how well he can read me after all these years of friendship. He knows when I'm hiding something. I start to hide myself.

I lean against the locked bathroom door, taking a few deep breaths to calm down. Mark can't prove anything. But even if he doesn't *know*, he definitely suspects. At least it was dark and wet outside and he couldn't see my face as I tried to laugh it off. Has he shared his thoughts with Emily?

Despite the freezing cold up here, I'm overheating with nerves and my stomach clenches, threatening to force me to vomit up all that food. *Think, Freddie, think.* He can't have done. I'd know. Emily would have lost her shit. But if Mark suspects, how long will it be before Emily does? God, I've been so stupid. So bloody stupid.

I need to stop this, I tell myself for the hundredth time. I don't need it. Emily's alive and I have to look after her, get this ship back on an even keel. She's not back to her normal self yet, that's for sure. All this talk about ghosts. She moved that planchette herself, but I don't know if she even realizes it. Is her mind playing tricks on her? Post-sepsis symptoms?

Maybe it's a good thing for now. I need the time.

I have to stop. I have to.

I close the lid and sit on the toilet, my phone in my sweaty palm. Emily's never been the sort to go through my phone, but I have to delete everything incriminating just in case. And then I'll end it. No more.

17.

Emily

With a sense of trepidation, I look into the library, but the fire is still glowing hot and all the books are on the shelves where they're supposed to be. It must have been just in my head. My aching body is testament to the fact that I'm far from fully physically recovered. What sort of state are my senses in?

With the sepsis leaflets stuffed into my pocket, I go straight to the bathroom to brush my teeth, happy to leave the others drinking downstairs, but as I push open the door, I'm startled to see Freddie there. He's standing with his phone in one hand, face furrowed, as shocked to see me as I am him—we've never been a couple happy to share toilet habits, and I stumble an apology.

'Sorry, thought you were downstairs.'

'I thought it was locked,' he mumbles, pushing his phone into his pocket and then flushing the toilet. 'Got distracted by a work email. So much for the company policy of protecting weekends.'

'I'm going to bed. So tired. It's been lovely though.'

'It has.' He gives me a squeeze as he passes, and I expect him to say something about the Ouija board but he doesn't, maybe still thinking about whatever was going on at work. 'Shout if you need anything,' he adds as he looks down at the doorknob, confused, then heads back to the others. When I lock it, I rattle the handle to make sure it doesn't open again.

The toilet lid is down, which is odd. Leaving the seat up is Freddie's specialty; he never closes the lid.

Unless he was using it as a seat.

I remember his phone sliding into his pocket. Did he come up here just to do something on his phone away from everyone else?

My skin prickles with a sense of something not right, but I dismiss it. I've got enough crazy in my brain for one day. He had an email from work. That's all. It probably required some thinking about. *So why did he flush*, the small voice in my head asks, *if he hadn't used the toilet?*

Habit, I decide firmly. *What else could it be?* I'm second-guessing myself enough at the moment. I don't need to add second-guessing Freddie into the mix.

Teeth brushed and face washed, I close the bedroom door, relieved to be on my own. I flick through the leaflets, and while much of it seems scary, the general consensus is that any strangeness will pass. Sooner rather than later, I hope. Maybe I'll speak to Dr Canning. Just in case. I let the warmth of the duvet encase me, and although I don't expect to, I fall asleep within moments. With people being in the house it's like sleeping on an old boat, the occasional creak infiltrating my sleep as the others move around, but they're comforting sounds, humanly heavy and recognizable, and they pass through me like kind whispers.

When I finally do wake, in the heart of the night, it's not a bird or a haunting that disturbs me in the quiet, but a woman's murmuring. I sit up slightly, frowning to see the bedroom door is open a few inches, allowing the voices in. Freddie must have come to check on me and forgotten to close it properly. The voices come again, and a floorboard creaks as someone shifts their weight on it.

They're on the stairs maybe. The murmuring turns to urgent whispering. A man and a woman. Are they arguing? The whispering continues, getting louder but not loud enough to make any sense of it, and then the deeper tones of quietly spoken words. A man. Placating. Then a gentle laugh. Something else. A wet sound. Is that kissing? Maybe Mark and Iso on the way to bed. They get annoyed with each other sometimes after too much wine and then are all about the making up.

I lie back on the pillow as their whispering drops to almost imperceptible. Outside, the raven scratches the night with a series of caws. *Ravens are drawn to death.* That's what Sally had said. As I drift back into sleep, I hear the echo of my own voice—*Were you murdered in this house?*—and feel the sharp tug of the planchette, and it pulls me into such a heavy sleep that I'm almost back in the empty void again, so much so that I don't even feel the mattress shift when Freddie finally creeps in beside me.

18.

His mate is dead. The raven knows that.

But still, he picked up her desiccated corpse from the edge of the house, so light he could lift her by her scarred wing as if she were a winter twig, and carried her up to the tree by the wall, forcing her husk between the trunk and the branches so she wouldn't fall. He sleeps close to her, plumping his feathers for both of them, keeping out the cold.

In daylight, he leaves her and scavenges for food, picking at the carcass of a dead rabbit on the road before the foxes claimed it. Taking the eyes of a dead sheep far across the moor that the farmer hadn't yet found. He brings morsels back for her even though he knows she can't eat. She's dead. He left her to die, panicking in that dark void, as he raced back toward the sky. Perhaps that's why he can't let her go. He should leave and roost at night with the others, but instead he stays in the branches of the old tree, watching the house, now with light in the windows and warmth coming through the walls.

The air is getting colder, not only at night. He can feel the threat of more snow and ice hanging in it, sharp and friendless. He wonders if perhaps he should move her and roost on the roof near the chimneys for warmth. Perhaps he will not fear the house so much now that there is life and heat in it.

He looks to his mate for answers, but her eye sockets are dull and empty of anything but reproach.

19.

Emily

'This is such a beautiful house.' Russell's ready to leave first, always the most organized. While he waits for Cat to finish getting her stuff together, I stand with him on the drive by the front door, drinking coffee. The air is crisp and cold but clean and the sun is bright.

'And you have all that right here on your doorstep. Unbelievable.'

'I don't miss the bus fumes, that's for sure.' The moor does look wonderful in a barren, austere kind of way, craggy outcrops and wild land littered with hardy shrubs built to survive.

'I saw a massive raven on the wall this morning,' he continues. 'Through the window on the top floor when I went upstairs to have a proper look around. The views from there are incredible. And that main room is as big as our flat. It's gorgeous.'

He obviously didn't feel anything horrible up there. It must have been my imagination.

'And,' he goes on, 'if me and Cat don't stop sniping, then maybe I'll rent it from you.'

'You guys are okay though, right?' We turn our backs to the front door and take a couple of steps from the house. 'Is this what all the 'people change' stuff was about last night?'

'I don't know.' He stares out over the moors but isn't really looking at them as he pushes his glasses up on his nose. 'I'm irritating her, I think. She's definitely irritating me.'

'Everyone irritates their partners. Look at Iso and Mark. Always fighting but they adore each other. That's marriage.'

'I used to love that she was religious. Weird, I know, because I can't buy into it, but I loved that she had that level of ability to have faith. Now I find it's her excuse to be holier than thou. I guess familiarity breeds contempt.'

'Maybe that's where being forgiving comes in. Nobody's perfect, whatever illusion they create at the start.'

'You and Freddie are always happy.'

'No one's always happy.' I stare at the ground as a gust of chilly wind whips round us. 'And there are plenty of things about Freddie I used to find charming but now annoy the shit out of me so much I could strangle him. But marriage is teamwork, and so I ignore them. And you and Cat are a great team.' I squeeze his arm. 'And you will be fine.'

'Yeah.' He stands taller and grins at me. 'Thanks. Oh, and well done on the Ouija board last night. You and Iso made it seem so real. Totally creeped us all out. You planned it, right? That *Find it* over and over. Inspired. Find what?'

'I don't know.' It's my turn to look over the moors so he can't see my discomfort. There's no point in denying it again because he won't believe me, so I lie. 'Just came to me.' My unease is back. We hadn't planned it. And if it wasn't Iso, why would I have moved the planchette to spell that? Such a random thing to say and yet so urgent. 'I'll stay up later next time you visit.' I change the subject. 'I was so knackered.'

'You didn't miss anything. The rest of us weren't long after you.'

'Oh, I thought you'd carried on for a while.' I'm slightly confused. Freddie wasn't in bed until late, and if the two people I heard weren't on their way to bed, then who was talking so quietly on the landing? Bumped into each other going to the

64

bathroom maybe?

When they've piled into their cars and left us alone in the quiet of the countryside, I go up to bed for an hour and find that Iso has left a beautiful Moleskin notebook by the bed with a note. *I thought you'd maybe like to diarize your new life! You always kept one at uni!* It gives me a rush of joy as I relish the feel of the expensive paper inside. There's a pen there too—a Montblanc—and the thoughtfulness of it gives me a rush of sudden warmth toward her. I open it to the back and write in small, careful letters *Find it*, before putting it in my bedside drawer and lying down on the soft mattress.

20.

Emily

It's boiling in the house when I wake up, the day already darkening into afternoon. I've been asleep for hours. My mouth is dry and I'm disoriented as I come down the stairs. The thermostat is up at twenty-six. No wonder it's like a sauna in here. I can hear football on so head to the sitting room.

'Jesus, Freddie, you're going to burn if you're not careful.' Freddie's so close to the fire that his hands are almost in it. 'And it's boiling in here.'

'There was a draught.' He doesn't look at me, still leaning so far forward he's blocking the fire with his torso.

'You came to bed late last night.' Maybe it was him I heard on the landing. 'Who stayed up with you?'

'No one.' He's irritated. I can hear it in his voice. 'In fact, I went upstairs but you'd opened that hall window again and it was freezing. So I came down and stoked the fire to warm up.' He looks at me now and I see something in his expression I've never seen before. A slight *darkness*. As if he's holding back a deep rage. It unsettles me. Freddie's never looked at me like that before. Does he know? Or suspect?

'Why do you keep doing that? You know how cold this house gets.'

'I don't keep doing that,' I protest. 'I didn't open it the first time and I didn't open it last night. I went straight to sleep. It must have been one of the others.' There's a long pause before he finally speaks.

'I guess it must have been.'

He leans back and my eyes widen as I see what's burning.

It's the Ouija board.

'That's mine.' I stare at him, astounded that he'd have the audacity to destroy it. 'You can't burn it.' I watch the *Yes* being consumed by the crackling flames and it suddenly feels like a bad omen.

Were you murdered in this house?

'I should have thrown it away before we moved. It's a stupid thing. And it's not good for you.'

'It's just a game.'

'I know you, Em. You *believed* it. Even though everyone else was sure it was Iso moving the planchette.'

'I was caught up in the moment.' My face burns red with both denial and the truth of his words. I *did* believe it. Maybe I still do a little. 'It was creepy. That's all. But I know you're right. She must have been doing it.'

I glance again to the blackening wood. It's taking a while to burn given how hot the fire is. As if it's fighting it.

'Maybe you should speak to Dr Canning.' He's watching the flames rather than look at me.

The fire spits loudly at us in our awkward silence and finally the board succumbs and bursts into a blaze of light. It was damp, that's all. Nothing supernatural about it.

21.

Freddie

More frost comes overnight, hardening the earth like concrete, and my breath hangs in crystals as I hurry to my car in the midnight blue of the early morning, the moon still bright in the sky overhead. In front of me the moor could be an ocean, it's so dark.

I didn't wake Emily to say goodbye, instead leaving a note in the kitchen. She's still pissed off with me for burning the Ouija board, even if she wouldn't come out and have the argument about it, instead just giving me the silent treatment. Always the victim, Emily. How she loves playing that role. Even though I lost a child too.

There are plenty of things about Freddie I used to find charming but now annoy the shit out of me so much I could strangle him.

The front door hadn't been closed properly when she and Russell were talking outside, and when I brought Cat's bag down for her, it creaked open in the breeze, carrying Emily's quiet sentence inside. I didn't hear more, Cat and Iso clattering down the stairs too loudly, but the words stung, and as she went back to bed to sleep the day away, I was left alone in the cold of the old house and had plenty of time to think about all the things I used to find sweet about her that if I'm honest drive me mad now. My thoughts were bees buzzing in my head. And what was that *Find it* business? Did she suspect something? I don't even remember fetching the Ouija board to burn it, but god it felt good pushing it into the flames and knowing how much it would piss her off.

I pull out onto the road, relieved to be leaving Larkin Lodge behind, and as the miles go by my head clears in the morning air. When I finally reach the motorway, my mood toward Emily has lifted. I was stupid to react so badly. She didn't say anything too terrible, and she's right—people do end up irritating each other. I shouldn't have burned her Ouija board, however stupid I think it is. Aside from anything else, I can't risk annoying her too much right now. I don't want her getting suspicious of me.

That makes me turn my thoughts to the much more pressing situation I've got myself into. Despite all my promises to myself to stop it, I somehow got in deeper at the weekend, and I can't even understand why.

The only thing I do know is that I need to get myself out of this shit one way or another.

22.

Emily

I wake up to a text from Freddie apologizing for burning the board and being so shitty and wishing he could be here to look after me, and I fire one back hoping he has a good few days in London and to enjoy it while he can before the Exeter transfer is finalized.

Still in bed, I stare out at the cold day and wonder how I'm going to fill mine once I've done my physio exercises. I have a pang of missing work again but quash it. At least I'm alive, I remind myself. And at least they paid me for the year, and given how long I've been in hospital my bank balance is pretty healthy. We've got the profits from the sale of the London flat too, so all in all, we could be in a lot worse situation. Who knows, maybe when we've got the grounds sorted and modernized a little inside, we may even make a profit on this place when I've persuaded Freddie to sell it.

I'm thinking about dozing for another hour when a racket from downstairs startles me upright, goosebumps immediate on my skin. It's the library, I know it is, and with my heart thumping and nerves on fire, I force myself downstairs.

When I reach the room the door is wide open and I gasp slightly, stepping backward. The books are on the floor. *All* of the books, scattered as if thrown in rage around the room. There are only four volumes left on the shelves. I know exactly which ones they'll be, but still I pick my way gingerly over the mess until I reach them to confirm it.

It's as I expect. The four that came off the shelves before— *Die or Diet* by Dr Ella Jones, *Will You Love Me* by Mhairi Atkinson, *Here Come the Clowns* by Armond Ellory, and *You* by Caroline Kepnes.

I take photos of the mess on my phone, proof to myself that it's real, and then look back at the four books. What have they got to do with anything? Is *Find it* to do with these? I flick through, wondering if there might be messages scrawled in them, but they're just ordinary books. I put them down on a coffee table and start picking up the rest to reshelve. I can't see any gaps in the wall or wood that might cause some crazy wind, nor any slope that might have made them fall, nor anything else that would prove a logical—if tenuous—reason for my books to have been thrown around the room. There is no reason. It wasn't me, I'm sure of it.

I consider calling Dr Canning to talk it through, but I don't have any of the main symptoms listed for post-sepsis, and thinking the house is haunted doesn't make me crazy. This isn't something he can help with. Plenty of fully functioning healthy people believe in ghosts and hear weird things in buildings. I know that absolutely this mess wasn't me, and until I can find something concrete to explain it, I'm going with what my gut believes.

Were you murdered in this house? The planchette was moving to *Yes*, I could feel it. It wasn't me and it wasn't Iso. Something is haunting this house.

Find it. Find what? And where to start?

I close the door on the library and go back upstairs to get dressed. When I get to the landing, the window is open again. I didn't open it. I'm pretty sure Freddie didn't unless he's trying to drive me insane, and why would he do that?

I close it carefully and then stare into the quiet hallway, my mouth dry with nerves, but I stay calm. I feel tasked with a mission. A way to fill the day. I'm going to research the history of the house. Find out who died here.

At the kitchen table, with the warmth of the Aga behind me, and the front door close enough that if something happens in the house that really frightens me I can get out as fast as my damaged body will let me, I'm disappointed at first that all I can find from a search on Larkin Lodge is an old Zillow listing and something to do with a place in America. But then, after a second coffee, I go into the library website hub for the area and find that a trove of local newspapers have been uploaded and archived.

Before long I've zoned out everything around me as I dip into history, scanning from one report to another as I search Larkin Lodge. I can't get even so much as a hint about any murders, but I do find some information about the house.

There's an obituary from 1864 of Christopher Hopper, the man who bought the house after the previous building was gutted in a fire. He was quite a famous surgeon in Exeter who opened missionary hospitals in Indian slums, so when he died in 1887 there were several print obituaries. They stated that he'd rebuilt the house, but within a year he and his wife had left to start their missionary project. He died fifteen years later, and his wife, Hannah, died of a broken heart only two months after him.

There's nothing more until an article from 1958. 'Actress Fortuna Carmichael buys country retreat.' This one does have a picture. A glamorous woman, all curves and lipstick, lies across the bonnet of a fabulous car parked in Larkin Lodge's drive, with a tall, handsome man standing casually beside her, smoking a cigarette. The caption underneath says, *Fortuna Carmichael and husband Gerald, the fiery couple as famous for their spats as for their romance, settle in to country life at Larkin Lodge.*

I scan the piece. She was a theatre actress who'd done a couple of B movie thrillers, and he was a producer. In the picture they both look completely fabulous and certainly not haunted. The Lodge in the backdrop is almost exactly the same as it is now, except there are flowers bursting from beds around the drive and some creeping plants clinging to the stony facade. I look at the grainy top-floor window, a dark blot looking down on this picture of joy.

I move on, the years skipping by in seconds, but there's not much else other than an entrant to a village garden flower show in the eighties, and then it just mentions the name, not who was living here. I search for murders in the village and only one comes up—a drunken domestic gone too far on a local farm in the seventies—but other than that the locals of Wiveliscoombe seem remarkably murder-free. I'm stumped. Could there have been a killing that was brushed under the carpet? Someone who went missing perhaps?

A search of missing persons brings up far more results but none that really gives me any information I can use. Over the years several young girls and a couple of men and two elderly residents suffering with dementia have vanished, but as far as I know—aside from the old pair—they could have just jumped on trains to escape the rural life or marriage or family or any of the awful reasons young people run away from home. Nothing.

I'm stumped, and then I remember. Sally and Joe from the pub said they'd lived here but not for long. Maybe they'd felt the haunting too.

23.

Emily

Wiveliscoombe is larger than a village but still only a small grey-stone Devon town with narrow streets, and the woman in the general store-cum-post office merrily points me in the direction of Joe Carter's art studio as I pay for a box of chocolates and a bunch of flowers. I find it—a stylish one-level barn conversion—a few streets away. There's a beautiful large thatched cottage alongside, with the house number in the same brushed steel as the sign saying *JC Artist*, so it must be their home. There's music coming from the studio, so I go there first.

Sally opens the door, her blond hair thick and long over her shoulders, a loose sweater over leggings, and her feet bare apart from a silver toe ring and perfectly painted nails.

'Emily!' Her face lights up. 'Come in, come in. Joe's working through there but is always happy to have a break.' She waves me inside. 'And I'm packing up canvases, which is my least favourite job, so this is perfect.'

With white walls and white painted floorboards the room should feel cold and austere, but there's a bright Moroccan rug, several beautiful large potted plants, a couple of blue sofas with colourful scatter cushions, and a stylish art deco red floor lamp that's taller than me. There's also a very modern and sleek desk with paper littered all over it and four paintings in bubble wrap leaning against it

'This place is gorgeous.' I was expecting something quaint given the locale, but everything here oozes style and cool.

'Thank you. The art is Joe's, obviously.' There are three large modern canvases on the walls. One is a portrait of Sally, and the other two are nudes, both women, one very old and one much younger.

'Joe's fascinated by the female form.' She looks up at the painting, almost wistful but in awe. 'Come on, let's let him know you're here.'

I follow her through a connecting door into a second space that reminds me of drama studios at school, the walls and floor black, the complete opposite to the stark white of Sally's office area. Several lights of different brightnesses, like a photographer might use, are dotted around the room, creating a mosaic of light and shade. It's humidly warm, and the air smells sweet, and it takes a moment before I recognize it as weed. There's so much to take in, I don't know what to say.

Two young women—the dark-haired one I'm sure I recognize as a waitress from the Lamb—are naked on the large sofa, their perfect bodies entwined in each other, on the verge of a kiss, and on the table in front of them is an open bottle of wine, two glasses half-drunk, some white powder, and a rolled-up twenty-pound note. I don't know if they've consumed any of it or if it's part of the setup, but my skin heats with the wildness of it all.

'That's beautiful, Jess. Can you keep your mouth open like that?' Joe's behind the easel, holding a joint in one hand and moving the brush in quick strokes with the other. 'Perfect.'

He looks up to see us there and puts the brush down and smokes the joint, adding to the pungent air.

'Well, this is a nice surprise.' He smiles, all angular cheekbones, and there is such a rakish handsomeness about him, I feel suddenly awkward. It doesn't help when behind him the girls start kissing and giggling, touching each other for real. I don't realize I'm staring until Joe laughs gently.

'Youth will youth. Let's leave them to it.' He takes my elbow and leans in, adding softly, 'It's the aftermath I want to capture anyway. The languid glow. All that contented joy.' He sees the chocolates and flowers I'm carrying. 'Are those for us? That's very sweet.'

'I wasn't sure what to bring.' They seem ridiculous now, prudish, but back in the brightness of the office area, I put them down on Sally's desk anyway.

'Peonies are always a delight.' She takes the joint from her husband, draws on it, then holds it out. 'Do you?'

'No thanks.' I shake my head. 'It was never my thing.'

'I'm intrigued.' Joe perches on the desk and nods me to the sofa. 'What brings you here bearing gifts?' Despite the drugs, his blue eyes are clear and thoughtful, and I find the word *mesmerizing* coming to mind. Sally is beautiful but Joe has so much charisma he could have been a movie star.

'It's about Larkin Lodge. You said you'd lived there. And I wondered if you knew if the place had any—well, history.'

'History?' Sally's on the other sofa, knees under her chin. 'That sounds ominous. Like mass murders or something?'

I shrug. 'One murder at least, I guess, yes.'

'A murder? Not as far as I know. But I only owned the house for a few years and that was nearly twenty years ago.' Joe takes another toke on the joint and then points at me with it. 'But I'm curious as to why you ask.'

'I know most people don't believe in ghosts.' I shrug, uncomfortable. 'But I do a bit. And there have been strange noises. A weird sensation. That kind of thing. I wondered if you'd noticed anything when you lived there.'

'You think it's haunted,' Sally says, gleeful.

'Or perhaps it's simply an old house with old bones.' Joe stubs the joint out.

'That's what my husband, Freddie, would say. He's always very rational. But I thought I'd ask.'

'Well, I wish I could help, but I'm afraid I don't remember anything odd about the place.' He looks to Sally. 'Do you?'

She shakes her head. 'I only lived there a couple of months before we got married and sold up.'

'Must just be me. But thank you for not laughing at me.'

'Not at all,' Sally says. 'I'm fascinated by that kind of thing. Women are more perceptive anyway.' The hem of my jeans has ridden up and some of the long red shiny scar tissue like a shallow valley the length of my limb is visible. I tug the bottoms down.

'Is that from your accident?' Joe asks. 'You fell off a cliff, is that right?' I look up, surprised.

'Sally does yoga with the estate agent. There are no secrets in this town.' He smiles. 'But you shouldn't be embarrassed about it. That scar is a symbol of your survival. And all bodies are beautiful. We're lucky to have them.'

'That's a good way to look at it. Thank you.'

'And as for the house, even if there is some dark secret in its history as yet to be discovered, the past is the past and invariably a mystery. It's *your* house now. Enjoy it.'

'I'll try. And thanks again.'

'And if you need anything, we're here.'

The door to the studio opens and one of the girls, flushed and in a loosely done-up robe, peers around the corner, the wineglass in her hand answering my silent question as to whether the booze was a prop. Sally and I might as well not be there, as she smiles coyly at Joe. 'Are you coming back?'

'No rest for the wicked.'

He floats a soft kiss over my cheek and then the girl takes his hand, leading back into the darkly decadent room, and her giggle dances out to us before the door closes again. I glance at Sally as she comes with me to let me out, but there's not a hint that she finds it at all uncomfortable, whereas I'm flustered for her. And for me. I'm not really a prude, but it was so flagrantly sexual and surprising.

'If you feel something, you should trust it.' Sally leans on the doorframe as I step back into the cold January day. 'Women have far more intuition than men. Maybe you should try the parish records at the church.' She's thoughtful. 'That's where I'd look for the forgotten secrets of the dead.'

As we say our goodbyes, I figure it's worth a try.

24.

Emily

The graveyard is beautiful in an eerie way, not quite overgrown but not too tended either, with trees that must dapple sunlight beautifully on the graves in summer. I'd tried to get into the church but the door was locked, and despite knocking I got no answer, so instead of browsing parish records I found myself wandering among the gravestones. Some are so old they're worn back to nothing, and others are shiny new marble with gold inlay and fresh flowers. I loiter and look at the names and imagine all the stories I'll never know between the birth and death dates of each one.

I trace my fingertips across one uneven stone, battered by the elements and green with years of moss, and wonder about the person it belongs to. All this death is making me gloomy but also making me think more rationally. Sally and Joe didn't have any weird experiences in the house, and the graveyard and memory of my time in the hospital, and the clinical loss of the cluster of cells that was the baby, are very much reminding me that when you're dead, regardless of my supernatural leanings, you're probably just dead. There probably are no ghosts. And given that I'm the only one experiencing anything strange in the house, which option would a sound mind believe—that Larkin Lodge is haunted or that my recovering mind is playing tricks on me?

It's only as I head back along the narrow path to the gate that I recognize a name on one of the newer stones, a shiny marble built to last. *Gerald Carmichael. 1938–2004. Most beloved perfect husband. Loving and kind.*

I pause and stare at it. Gerald Carmichael. That handsome man who used to live in the Lodge. I look to the grave beside it, expecting to see Fortuna's, but there's nothing. Was she buried somewhere else?

'Well, hello.'

It's Paul, the vicar, pulling his earbuds out.

'I didn't realize you were here. I knocked.'

'Sorry, I was listening to an Abba marathon while sorting out the store cupboard. Didn't hear a thing.' He pauses. 'Is everything okay?'

'I was just curious to see the parish records. I wanted to dig around in the past of the house. That sort of thing.'

'Ah, so you *do* think there is a ghost.' His face crinkles with a smile, but it's a gentle expression; he's not laughing at me.

'Not really. I'm just curious about who's lived there before us. I figured it might be fun to put together a potted history of the place. I saw Sally and Joe, and she said to try here.'

'Did you go to the studio while he was working?'

'Yes.' There's a pause and our eyes meet, and we both burst into laughter.

'Quite the avant-garde couple, aren't they?'

'I'm not going to lie,' I say. 'I didn't know where to look when I saw his models. And Sally's so chilled with it. They're very nice though.'

'They are.' He looks down at the grave. 'You found an old resident then?'

'I recognized his name from a newspaper article. I'm surprised his wife's not buried here too.'

'I'd be more surprised if she was,' Paul says. 'She's in her nineties but she's still alive. She's in Willow Lane House—a retirement home—about ten or fifteen miles from here. I think she moved in not long after Gerald died. I obviously didn't know them when they had the Lodge, and then they lived in London for a long time. Didn't come back here until Gerald was sick. I'd only just taken up my post and she would come and sit in the church occasionally, but we weren't friendly as such. She just found the church comforting.'

I look back down at the stone. 'All these graves. So many stories.'

'And every one a unique blessing.'

Clouds are forming overhead and an icy wind suddenly blasts, unexpected, through the barren branches of the trees around us. My leg throbs and I pull my coat tighter before leaning heavily on my stick, the pain immediately exhausting me. It comes like that, in waves, and I feel as if I'm made of lead.

'You should get home.' Paul takes my arm and helps me toward the gate on the slightly uneven path. 'Get warm. As for the parish records, there's some online but nothing that goes back too far. Most were lost in a fire. Electrical one around 2005. We had to get half the interior rebuilt. But at least it's not so cold in there now.'

I'm just starting the engine when he trots over and knocks on the window. 'Oh, and I meant to say. The Lodge is a big house and if you need someone to help with the cleaning I can send Mrs Tucker along. She's very reliable. And the vicarage is just at the next turning down on the lane from you. On the corner. You can probably see it from your house. She cleans for me twice a week and could come after.'

'Great. I'd love that.' It is great. Freddie's rubbish at staying on top of stuff and there's no way I can do much more than wipe down the sides and do the laundry. Plus, however much I try to rationalize away the strangeness in the house, I'll be glad of the company.

25.

Emily

I'm feeling calm and rational and determined to stay that way even though the afternoon is turning dark as I pull into the drive where Larkin Lodge waits, unwelcoming in the gloom. Behind me the moors are already being swallowed up by cold mist. I wish we'd moved in spring. Everything is better in the spring. Spring is all about the joy of life. Winter is death, and right now, in this freezing January, we're caught tight in its grip.

Inside, I turn all the lights on, and after eating a leftovers sandwich I swallow some painkillers and go up to bed, needing to take the weight off and lie still for a while. The book of Poe short stories is on the table and I read the first, 'The Telltale Heart', a dark little story of murder and guilt, before opting for my Kindle and something cheerier as day descends into dusk outside.

After a couple of hours, the pills are thankfully taking the edge off the pain. I stand to stretch and then go to the window to look out, hoping to maybe see lights on at the vicarage, beacons of life to ease my silent isolation, but all I can see is the claustrophobic mist spilling over the wall from the moor and making its way up to the house.

I'm going downstairs to get something else to eat before calling it a night when a noise stops me in my slow tracks. It's quiet at first, and I listen for several seconds before it comes again. A creaking sound. *It's an old house*, I tell myself again like a mantra. *Old houses make noises.*

But these noises are coming from the second floor.

Reluctant but unable to ignore it, I peer up to the darkness of the next landing. The sounds come again. A click followed by a pause, and then a long creak. Another pause, then a creak and a click again.

Click. Creeeeak.

Pause.

Creeeeak. Click.

When I swallow my throat makes a quiet click of its own. There's a moment of silence and then it comes again.

Click. Creeeeak.

Pause.

Creeeeak. Click.

My body chills, my breath caught in my chest as I listen. I know what it is, I realize as it comes again—*Click. Creeeeak. Pause. Creeeeak. Click.*

It's a door slowly opening and then closing. Over and over.

I don't want to go up there—I don't want to go up there *at all*—but I need to see for myself. I turn the landing light on and take the stairs slowly to a point where, if I stretch, my eyes can just see above the floor of the upstairs landing through the balustrades.

In the gloom, the round door handle of the primary suite twists slowly—*click*—and then the door opens a few inches—*creeeak*—giving me a glimpse of an ominous darkness beyond, and then after a moment's pause creaks and clicks shut again. I stare, not trusting my own eyes. How can the handle be turning itself?

I watch as it repeats, my palms gripping the wood until they're slick with sweat, and then it repeats again.

On the third time, in the pause between the door opening and closing, the scratching starts. The scratching I heard before. *Scraaatch scraaaatch.* Like nails dragging on wood.

As if something is trying to crawl out and is being pulled back into the room.

26.

Emily

I do not go back to bed. Instead, I scurry as fast as I can down to the ground floor, convinced something awful is following me, and go straight to the sitting room, closing the door and pushing the old occasional chair under the door handle. I pant, sweating and terrified, my heart pumping so hard I think it will burst, but the handle doesn't move.

Still, I don't take my eyes off it as I eventually curl up on the sofa, a blanket around me, and put the TV on loudly on some old comedy channel to save me from the terrible silence. I don't watch the show; I watch the door and try not to think about the darkness of the night and the mist outside that's suffocating the house. At some point, my mobile phone, still upstairs, rings out, Freddie calling to say goodnight, but I let it ring till it stops. Then finally, after hours of staring at the door, my eyes grow heavier than my fear and I drift into a disturbed sleep full of vivid nightmares.

In my dream I'm asleep on my bed and I wake with a start. Something's woken me. A noise. A heartbeat. It's coming from under my bed, pulsing the mattress as if it's made of skin.

I sit up and the first thing I see is that there's ice covering the bedroom window and icicles on the furniture, but I'm still warm. The heartbeat gets louder; what was a gentle pulse now shakes the entire bed, thumping at it from underneath, demanding attention until the whole room vibrates and I have to cling on as if on a raft in a storm. Suddenly it stops, quietening back down to a steady gentle prod from underneath, and dream-me plucks up the courage to peer under the bed.

Freddie's there, clinging to the bedsprings like a mountain climber, fingers hooked in around the metal. He looks my way and smiles, his grin stretching too wide, cutting across his face ear to ear, and his eyes shine in the gloom.

Don't touch the floorboards. They'll suck you in. *He shivers.* I told you it was cold in here, didn't I? I told you. Why do you keep opening the windows?

He opens his mouth wide and the gaping yawn takes on the shape of the second-floor window, and I look into the void and am terrified it's going to swallow me up and then—

I wake up for real, gasping and sweating on the sofa, my body screaming in pain. To my relief, as my surroundings settle into place, I see it's morning, sunlight streaming in around the corners of the curtains, and the house is quiet and calm.

When I carefully open the sitting room door, everything is normal in the hallway and there are no strange sounds coming from the second floor. Still, I don't want to linger here today alone if I don't have to, and after I've texted Freddie to say I'd slept through his call and all is well, I have a quick shower, take some pills, and then head out. There's one more person I can ask about this house. I just hope she'll speak to me.

27.

Emily

Willow Lane House could easily pass for a quiet spa hotel with its long drive, manicured lawns, and ivy-covered Cotswold stone wall. Whatever else happened in Mrs Carmichael's life after Larkin Lodge, she definitely didn't go broke, because this is not a beleaguered NHS residential home. I rang ahead and explained that I'd bought a house Mrs Carmichael once lived in and was now exploring the history of the building and would love to meet her as she used to be a friend of my grandmother's. The receptionist didn't give me much in terms of response but told me to ask for Mrs Marshall when I arrived, which I duly do and smile at the young woman at the desk whose voice tells me she's the one I spoke to on the phone barely thirty minutes earlier. She doesn't smile back.

I wait in the reception area, a beautiful open space with bright light windows, and hear laughter as two nurses walk by wheeling chairs into the garden. No, definitely no poverty here.

'Emily Bennett?'

I turn to see a woman maybe in her fifties in a trim trouser suit, clearly a manager or administrator, coming toward me.

'Mrs Marshall?'

I lean on my stick, and I see her instant shift to sympathy. I may hate this stick and everything it represents, but it brings out the best in other people.

'Thank you so much for letting me visit. I know it's probably unusual for someone to want to spend time with a stranger.'

'You'd be surprised.' She smiles and nods at me to follow her. 'Since the boom in those *Who Do You Think You Are?* style programs, people are finding relatives they've never heard of before in homes across the country.' She leans in slightly as she waits for me to catch up. 'I expect most of them are hoping for some lost inheritance.'

'Well, I'm certainly not after anything like that.'

'So I gather. You said your mother was a friend of hers?'

'My grandmother actually. They worked in the same theatre for a while. And now my husband and I have bought the house that was Fortuna's home in Devon.'

'Oh, how wonderful. The circle of life. And yet it happens often, I guess. So many people travel away and then return home, don't they? Even after all those years in London, Fortuna and her beloved Gerald moved back to the South West when he was sick.'

'I saw his gravestone in the local church.'

'Cancer, sadly. Left it too late to get checked out. You know how men are. Always stick their head in the sand. Fortuna was broken-hearted, poor thing, when she moved in here.' She slows her pace down to let me hobble alongside her more easily. 'Anyway, she doesn't get any visitors these days apart from staff. We try to keep her in good spirits, but she's very elderly and starting to have some muddled moments and gets anxiety attacks very easily. So don't expect too much. And probably twenty or thirty minutes will be enough. She gets tired quickly.'

We come to a stop outside a room, and Mrs Marshall pushes the door open and sweeps in, introducing me loudly to the neatly dressed elderly woman seated in an armchair by a set of patio doors.

28.

Emily

Mrs Carmichael has a face like a withered walnut, but her silver hair is set nicely and her clothes are clean and bright. I expected her to be stick-thin, but her middle is wide and her heavy bosom rests on the waistband of her skirt. She looks like a retired schoolteacher and it's hard to see the woman from the newspaper report, so glamorous and daring, in this old woman in front of me now sitting in an armchair by a large window.

'Hello, Fortuna. Thank you for seeing me.'

She doesn't answer or even look at me.

'The gardens here are lovely.' I look out of the window as she's doing. 'Do you go and sit out in the summer?' Her dark eyes, raisins in her elderly face, don't move and her mouth stays firmly shut. Sweat prickles at my hairline. Is this what it was like for Freddie and my friends when they visited me when I was in a coma? Did they sit beside me, talking inanely until the words—very quickly, no doubt—dried up? 'Can I get you anything maybe? A glass of water?'

She still doesn't answer, but her eyes turn to me, suspicious, and I look around, awkward.

On the shelf and table are several framed photos. There's one of her when she was maybe in her late sixties, still beautiful, with a man I presume is Gerald, who looks thin and vaguely ill. It looks like they're on a cruise. In another, maybe a decade earlier, they're sitting at an outside table in a restaurant, tanned and smiling and happy, on holiday.

Behind it, I see the photo that was in the news report, taken on the drive at Larkin Lodge. It's sharper and crisper, and they're both absolutely gorgeous in it. He's dark and handsome with a devilish smile and she's in a kimono looking entirely bohemian with a scarf in her dark hair as she lounges on the bonnet of the car he's standing beside.

I hold up the picture. 'You must have loved him very much.'

There's another picture of Gerald placed on top of a wooden batik box at the back of the display. It's an odd photo to have framed, and I take a closer look. He isn't smiling but staring, angrily, into the distance. The kind of photo that's taken without the subject's knowledge. I lift it up and the lid of the box comes away with it. Superglued together maybe. Why would anyone do that?

It takes me a moment to realize what I'm looking at inside. *Mementos.* But it's a collection of the strangest mundane objects. A tie. A comb with hair on it. A tennis sweatband. Is that a scrunched-up pair of underpants? What kind of things are these to keep? A watch or a wedding ring I would understand. But this stuff? It's not even clean. I can see a sweat stain on the wristband and I dread to think the state of the Y-fronts. Why would anyone choose these things to remind them of a husband?

'I don't know you,' she says suddenly, staccato words like tiny dry twigs snapping. 'Why are you here?'

'I'm Emily. I live in a house you used to own. Larkin Lodge. I wondered if I could ask you some questions about it.'

'Larkin Lodge was a long time ago.' Her wary eyes don't move from my face.

'I know. But I didn't have anyone else to go to.' I hesitate for a moment and then bite the bullet. 'This will probably sound stupid, but sometimes I feel like the house might be haunted. I wondered if you ever experienced anything strange there too? Noises? Smells? A bad feeling?'

Her eyes widen enough for me to see the cracks of tiny pink veins in the yellowing whites. One hand flutters to her throat.

'There are no ghosts at Larkin Lodge.' Her expression hardens. 'Gerald died of cancer.'

'Oh, of course. I didn't mean him. I just wondered in general if you ever heard anything strange.' I pause. 'Especially coming from the top-floor bedroom.'

Her expression hardens, unfriendly, but not before I see a flash of surprise, and then something else. Secrecy? Guilt, perhaps? Whatever it is, she shuts down.

'You need to leave.' She's suddenly cold. 'I don't want you here. There are no ghosts in Larkin Lodge.' One hand goes to her throat again, then pulls at a strand of her hair, an anxious tic.

'I'm so sorry if I've upset you.' She won't meet my eyes, looking back out of the window, and she's drawn back into her chair as if to put as much distance between us as possible. 'That wasn't my intention.' Is it me that's upset her? Or was it the mention of the upstairs room that did it?

'Go away now,' she snaps, and her hands trembling against the arms of the chair, her fingers tap ping at them, as if she's building to some sort of episode.

'I'm sorry,' I repeat, backing away to the door. 'I'm sorry.'

I'm almost out of the room when she speaks again. Quietly. To herself.

'I found it, but I didn't use it. I put it back.'

'What did you find, Fortuna?' I look back at her, my heart thumping. *Find it.*

She's staring through the window with such dread I feel awful for coming here even though my skin is prickling with the electricity of what she's just said.

'Gerald died of cancer,' she repeats, and then sinks back in her chair, and I can see she's closed down. I won't get any more out of her unless I push hard, and that would most likely cause an anxiety attack as Mrs Marshall warned and I don't want to upset her like that. I also might want to come back another time.

There are no ghosts at Larkin Lodge. Her words echo in my head as I get back in the car to drive home. So why do I feel like she meant the exact opposite? And what did she find and put back? And the way she reacted to the mention of the upstairs bedroom. She had a bad feeling about it too, I know it. Despite her upset and having no clear sense of what's going on in the house, the visit has given me a sense of validation. There *is* something wrong with the top floor.

29.

Emily

The first thing I do when I get back to the house is write up what I can in the notebook, summarizing the events of last night and my visit to Fortuna, and then look at the first two words I wrote on the back page: *Find it.* The words from the Ouija board that everyone thought I'd spelled as a joke.

I found it, but I didn't use it. I put it back.

That's what Fortuna Carmichael said. It's too much of a coincidence. There's something hidden in Larkin Lodge, and I don't know what it is but I have to look. I cook some quick noodles and then start in the freezing boot rooms at the end of the kitchen corridor. The search is quick. I test the flagstones for any that might come free to reveal a hiding place underneath—they don't—and then check in the few cupboards. Nothing.

I move methodically through the downstairs of the house, the radio with me for company. I'm not really listening to the music as I lift rugs, check behind doors, and look in unused cupboards and under the sink, but the familiar drive-time show reminds me of London and normality and life in the buzz of the city, making me feel less alone. Every so often, I turn it down and listen out, but the house stays silent.

I leave the library for now as it was empty until I put the books in there and so I've seen the shelves bare, and instead start checking each stair on the way to the first landing, but there are no loose floorboards or secret drawers. What am I looking for?

I found it, but I didn't use it.

Is it the weapon used to murder whoever is haunting the house? A knife? Will its discovery finally allow the spirit to be at peace? Or somehow prove who the killer is or was? If the house was haunted back when Fortuna Carmichael was here, then the murderer is probably dead too by now. Maybe Fortuna stumbled across a weapon and then left it where it was in case someone thought she'd killed someone with it?

I'm sweating by the time I've finished in our bedroom and the bathroom, the lights all on now that it's dark outside, but I've found no evidence of anything unusual hidden away or any secret hiding places, and I'm not really surprised. If there's something hidden in this house, I know in my gut it's going to be on the top floor.

I stare up the stairs but can't bring myself to move. I don't want to go back up there, especially not in the dark. Should I wait until morning? Or maybe when Freddie's back I can find some excuse for both of us to go up there—measure for curtains or something—and do a search then. I can't go up there alone. I can't.

I'm still hesitating on the stairs when the door knocker sounds downstairs, and I'm flooded with relief. Whatever is hidden up there can wait another day.

It's freezing outside and now that it's dark the night mist has spilled over the barrier wall and flooded the narrow lane, barely any visible road left at all.

'You drove here in this?' I hold the door open for Sally and she comes inside.

'I'm used to it. Everyone is around here. I know all the lanes and bends and passing points. It's not as if we get many strangers, not off the main roads anyway. We're all careful. More likely to hit a badger or deer than another car.' She smiles at me. 'Welcome to rural living.'

'It's going to take some getting used to.'

She hands me a bottle of wine and takes off her coat, hanging it on the banister. 'Hope you don't mind me just showing up. Joe's painting, and I was bored. And then I thought of you up here and . . . well, here I am.' She looks around at the hallway. 'Strange to be back. So different now. The wallpaper definitely wasn't ours.'

'It won't be staying. I prefer bright, light colours.'

'Houses are funny like that, aren't they? Made new by new owners. All the history wiped away. Sometimes I wonder how much the buildings remember though. In the bricks, you know what I mean? Something must soak in. All those lives.' She smiles as if she means it half-heartedly, but I find it hard to smile back. There's something in the bricks of this house for sure.

I follow her into the sitting room, watching as she takes it all in, fingers trailing on the banister as she goes by and then get us both a glass of wine before joining her again. I'm tired but happy not to be alone.

'Does Joe often work into the night?'

'When he's in the zone, yes. I'd say I pity those poor girls, but they love it.' She leans back, relaxing. 'I'll be glad when these paintings are done. He's been working too hard. I mean, I absolutely respect his artistic process, but I long to have him back.' We're comfy at either end of the sofa, me awkward with my bad leg stretched out on the coffee table, and Sally like a languid cat, settled in against the cushions.

'Isn't it weird? For you?'

She frowns, puzzled. 'How do you mean?'

'The girls. Are they always nudes? Don't you worry? I mean, if the process is that intense, that he might, well, you know . . .'

'Oh god, no, it doesn't bother me at all.' She sits up straighter, amused by me. 'Joe loves women. That's part of who he is. And it's art, isn't it? Our connection is so much deeper than that, so why would I worry about a few beautiful young things with crushes on him?'

I laugh. 'Because they're beautiful young things with crushes on him?' I remember how entwined the girls were in each other and how they'd kissed. It was male fantasy one-oh-one. Had they been performative for him, or was it pleasure for themselves? Either way, I wouldn't want Freddie watching. 'I'm not sure I'd be so cool about it is all I'm saying. I wish I could be, but I don't think I could.'

'People get so heated about sex. But it's only love that really matters.'

'I guess so, but I'm a bit old-fashioned on monogamy. I hope it works as much for you as for him.'

'Of course, he's all about freedom, polyamory even, but I've never wanted another man. You've seen Joe, right? Why would I?' She looks over at a wedding photo on the mantlepiece. 'And where's your husband? Freddie, isn't it? Shouldn't he be here looking after you?'

'Oh, he's in London for work, but he'll be back tomorrow. They're transferring him to the Exeter branch, which will be great, but he's got a few days more to do before that.' He'd texted earlier to say he'd be home tomorrow night; I wish it was tonight, but at least it's only one more night alone here.

'You guys should come to lunch this weekend. I love to cook. Or at least throw dishes together. I call it Mediterranean but it's really just a melee of flavours.' She smiles again. Everything about her is *easy*, and I wish I could be like that. Relaxed and happy. 'And Joe loves meeting new people.'

'We'd love that.'

'So.' She pauses and studies me. 'You really think there's a ghost at Larkin Lodge?'

'Oh, you know how it is.' I sip my wine, hiding behind the glass. 'Old house and everything. It was just a silly moment.' I'm embarrassed. But since told her I add, 'I mean, you lived here, didn't you? And you weren't haunted.'

'It was so long ago. We were only just together. I barely remember it. But there's no such thing as ghosts, Emily.' She puts her glass down. 'When you're dead, you're dead. All that energy vanishes.' She gets to her feet. 'And I should leave. I feel like I've got a migraine coming on. Need to get home before it hits. Can I use the loo before I go?'

'Of course. Migraines are awful. Will you be okay?'

'Yes, it's only five minutes. And you look exhausted yourself.' She's right, I am exhausted, emotionally and physically, after last night and today.

I take the glasses and bottle to the kitchen and swallow some painkillers with the last of my wine, my leg throbbing after being still for a while. When I go out to the hall to see her off, she's leaning on the door to the library, slightly wistful. 'You've made it lovely in here. Cosy den.'

'I love books. Freddie not so much. Figure this'll be my reading room.'

'Very posh.' Her smile falls as she looks puzzled. 'Odd selection to have out.'

She's looking at the four books on the table, the ones that flew off the shelf. 'Just haven't finished putting them away.'

'Creepy though.'

'What do you mean?' It's my turn to be puzzled.

'Don't you see it? Look.' Sally points. 'Read the first word in each title downward through the stack.'

I do, and as she laughs, my blood chills. I read down the stack again. *You* by Caroline Kepnes, *Will You Love Me* by Mhairi Atkinson, *Die or Diet* by Dr Ella Jones, and *Here Come the Clowns* by Armond Ellory. The first words are perfectly lined up.

YOU WILL DIE HERE.

You

30.

The rooftop is better than nestling in a barren tree in the freezing night, but the raven wishes the man would come back. There were more fires when the man was here, and the extra heat in the tiles would make him feel less uncomfortable about being on top of the house.

He puffs his feathers out and settles down, pressing his head into the dry husk of his mate. She is closest to the bricks, and as her feathers warm slightly from the heat it's almost like she's alive again, except for the fragile hollowness of her frame. He can't press his head too hard for fear he'll break her.

His mate is dead. He knows this.

He drifts into sleep for a while, only the lights of the car leaving and the movement of the woman within the walls waking him, but when the house falls silent and dark, and with his talons clinging to the roof, he dreams of the day his mate flew inside. Her frantic caws and the angry sweep of her wings as she became trapped in the flue. His own drive for sunlight, wings close to his body, propelling upward, leaving her behind, not wanting to get trapped himself. He never liked the house. She never listened.

Even as he perches beside her, his beak lost in her dryness, he's not sure how much he ever liked his mate. Not fully. Not after that first summer. She was quick to anger. Quick to rage. She pecked him. *Peck peck peck* at his face and the underside of his wings where the skin was thinner, sharp stabs of annoyance if her mood wasn't good, if the twigs of the nest weren't pliable enough. If he hadn't hunted well enough.

What is it that keeps him with her, he wonders, as he wakes in the stretch of the long night, when the woman within the walls turns a light on below, a glow of yellow startling him awake. Is it love or guilt?

As he presses himself closer to her, his dead lover doesn't answer.

31.

Emily

I can't sleep, my head a whirlpool of dread dragging me down. I stare up at the ceiling, trying to calm my thoughts, but I can't. All I can see is that stack of books, a message from whatever— whoever—is haunting this house.

You will die here.

Is it a warning or a threat? Or just a random unfortunate collection of titles? *There are no ghosts at Larkin Lodge.* I repeat Fortuna's words in my head even though I don't believe them. There's something wrong with this house. Alone in the middle of the silent night, it's starting to suffocate me as I lie still under the covers, trying to ignore that pressing urgency of my bladder, until at last I can't.

I'm alert for that terrible creaking and clicking sound coming from the second floor, but there's nothing but silence as I hobble to the bathroom. I left the hall light on when I went to bed, so I'm spared an awful moment of darkness when leaving the bedroom, and the landing is warm, lingering dregs of heat still escaping the radiators even though they've been off for hours.

The smell comes when I'm washing my hands. At first, it's just the hint of something rotten in the air, but as soon as I step back into the landing it assails the back of my throat, making me almost gag and only pressing my clean, scented hands pressed onto my mouth that stops me. It's a thick unpleasant dampness, sweetly *wrong*. I automatically glance up, fearful, but it's not coming from the top floor.

The smell gets stronger as I head toward the bedroom, and I wonder if maybe there's a dead rat in the drains. As I reach the place where I trod on the nail, it gets so bad I can't move any further forward without the real threat of vomiting. Could there be something dead under the floorboards?

I open the window—*Yes, Freddie, this time I did open it*—letting freezing air in. I do the same in the bathroom and grab the can of air freshener, spraying liberally throughout the middle floor as I open every window and wedge open every door to get some air flow through.

When I'm done, I take a few deep breaths that cling icily to the wet flesh of my lungs and stare out at the endless night until my skin is cold as death and I'm shivering.

I go back to the hallway, hoping the wind tunnel of breeze I've created will clear out the stench quickly. Where has it come from? What is it? If a rat or something had died under the floorboards it wouldn't have rotted so fast, surely? Not in the middle of winter. The smell would have crept in slowly, gradually building up now that the house is warm again. But there's nothing subtle about this. It's got to be something bigger than a rat. A large dead thing under there somewhere.

The stink is still strong, a sludge coating me, creeping between each strand of my hair and coating every pore of my skin, and I'm starting to feel a little faint when suddenly there's an almighty crash as all the windows slam shut at once.

I shriek and stumble backward, crouching on my haunches in the place the smell was strongest, protect my head, my heart pounding. *The breeze. It was a breeze. It's only a breeze.*

The doors around me slam shut in unison, the sound like the crack of thunder, and while I don't cry out this time I curl in smaller, as if the ceiling might fall in on me. After a moment, I straighten up in the silence. *It was just the breeze*, I try to tell myself again, but I don't believe it. The windows closed first, so there was no breeze to close the doors. Certainly not enough to make the doorstops come away first.

It's only after a moment, waiting for my racing heart to slow, that I realize the smell has gone. I lean down closer to the floorboards, but there's nothing but the scent of old wood.

It's then that I see it.

A bent nail is sticking up through the floorboard, with rust red decorating the end of the metal. It's the nail I trod on, the one Freddie told me he'd pulled up. I stare at it in disbelief, the madness of the last few moments almost forgotten as my anger at Freddie overwhelms me. It's a sudden visceral rage that takes me by surprise, and in my head I call him all the names and foul words I can think of.

He told me he'd pulled it out. He *knows* how much I worry about cuts and injuries now and with good reason. He knows I'm doing my best to get well. How could he do this? Be so casual about something that worries me?

It's the same nail. I know it is, and I realize, knowing Freddie, what probably happened. He probably couldn't get it out and then got distracted and figured he'd try again later and then never got round to it. That's Freddie all over. Thoughtless. Careless. Stupid. Always trying for an easy life. I used to like that about him when we met, his *laissez-faire everything will be all right* attitude. It was a great counterbalance to my need to have everything under control, but I realized a long time ago, after all that shit at uni that nearly finished us, that he just *hopes* everything will be all right because he's lazy and has no self-control. Freddie's *it'll be fine* is shorthand for *I can't be bothered.*

I stare at the nail for a long few minutes before I haul myself to my feet. Well, this time I'm not letting him get away with it.

32.

Freddie

'It must be a different nail.' I've finally got a word in as she pauses for breath, her anger exhausted, after ranting at me like I'm some difficult child she needs to discipline.

'Because I pulled out the one you trod on.' I stay calm and reasonable, in part because one of us has to, and in part because I know it will irritate her more. 'You saw me go up to do it. And it's one o'clock in the morning, Em. Why are you calling me now?'

I wasn't asleep when she rang. I'd been on my phone, lost in the screen, tapping away despite all my promises to myself. Seeing her name come up on the screen out of the blue so late jolted me into such a guilty panic I almost didn't answer.

'Because the nail is there.'

She's sullen now, annoyed that I haven't capitulated and apologized, but too passive-aggressive to keep pushing. But in this instance I've got nothing to apologize for. 'Don't you believe me? Why would I lie?'

Lies, lies, lies. I don't want to think about them. *I haven't lied*, I tell myself. *Not yet.* But that doesn't make me honest. I'd lie if she asked the right question. *I'll stop. I will. I have to.*

I feel sick and dirty, and even her unusual anger isn't tempering that. Maybe this is all part of the post-sepsis thing, and the grief from the miscarriage, because she's never been a quick-to-rage person before and neither have I. I was angry with her when I burned the Ouija board, but now that I'm here, in Johnny from work's spare room—I couldn't stay with Mark and Iso after his probing questions—I can't remember exactly why.

'If I hadn't taken it out, I'd tell you. I'd have told you at the time. I mean, why would I lie about that? What would be the point?'

'I'm sorry,' she says, eventually and reluctantly. 'If you say you got it out then I believe you.' *If you say* . . . What she really means is *I don't believe you but let's not argue anymore.* She's like that, Emily. She always has to be right. I used to like it about her. Now it just irritates the shit out of me. I think back to what she said to Russell.

There are plenty of things about Freddie I used to find charming but now annoy the shit out of me so much I could strangle him.

Yeah, well, that goes both ways, Emily.

'It's this house,' she continues. 'It freaks me out.'

'It's just a house, Em. And a beautiful one.'

'Did you get a survey done? When you bought it?'

'Why?'

'There was an awful smell just now. It was like rotting meat. Coming from under the floorboards. Where the nail is. Anyway, it was so horrible I opened all the windows and was nearly sick.'

'If you're thinking it's the drains, get a plumber in.' I avoid the mention of the survey. I cut that corner, but there's no need for her to know that.

'The windows all slammed shut. And the doors.'

'The house is on a hill on a moor. There's always a breeze there.' My head is starting to ache and I want to sleep. I've got too much other shit to deal with.

'Yeah,' she says, defeated. 'Yeah, you're probably right.'

'There's nothing else it could be.' She doesn't say anything to that, and I realize what she's thinking. I *knew* she'd believed in that Ouija board and I'm glad I burned it. 'And please, for god's sake, don't tell me you think our new house is haunted.' I rub my hand across my face. And she had the nerve to talk to me like I was a child. 'Think about it logically. You've been told that post-sepsis syndrome can affect your senses. Which is most likely, that or a ghost?'

'I guess.' She doesn't sound convinced, but then she's always had her beliefs in ghosts and mediums and the paranormal, as if that is somehow superior to wanting proof.

'Is this because of what the vicar said? About the house being built on a crossroads? The suicide victims buried under it?'

'No.' She's indignant. 'God, no. I wasn't thinking about that. It's just weird, that's all. Weird shit happens here.' She's getting irritated again.

'Do you want me to drive back now?' I ask. 'I can if you want. I'm sure work will understand.'

'No, it's fine,' she answers eventually. 'You're back tomorrow anyway.'

We say our goodnights and hang up and I ignore the next notification that pings up, turn my phone on silent with Emily on cut through, and put it on the other side of the room to avoid more temptation.

I have to stop. I *will* stop. This mess can't get any bigger.

I imagine Emily alone in that big house, all the lights on, afraid, and then think about all the things those post-sepsis brochures talked about. Paranoia. Sensory hallucinations.

Maybe I should speak to Dr Canning.

33.

Emily

I finally drift into sleep as night turns to day, and I'm dead to the world when the phone rings, dragging me blearily back into reality, and when I glance at the clock it's already ten.

'Hi, Dr Canning.' My mouth is dry but I try to sound as peppy as possible. 'How are you?'

There's nothing wrong with sleeping until ten, especially for someone just out of hospital. But I don't want to share. I don't want to explain that I was awake all night raging at my absent husband over a nail. Now, in the beautiful daylight, I can't really understand why I was *so* angry. Why did the nail bother me so much compared to the awful smell and the slamming windows and doors? They freak me out way more.

'Emily?' Dr Canning's been speaking and I haven't been paying attention. I sit up and flinch as my hips spasm slightly.

'Sorry, the signal's not great. You cut out.'

'I was asking if everything was okay? No problems?'

'No, I'm good.' I sit up straighter, not sure why, but suddenly alert. Something in his tone. Something worried. 'A bit tired but I'm actually doing better than I expected.'

Outside a thick dark cloud spreads across the sun, washing the room in a cool grey. Maybe it's not such a nice day after all.

'Okay, that's good.'

'You sound surprised.' He does. Why does he? He has no reason to.

'Oh, it's just not uncommon for there to be adjustment issues. Migraines. Visual abnormalities. You'll be dealing with a lot of sensory overload after such a long time in hospital on top of the illness itself.'

'Well, nothing to report but tiredness here.' I'm cheery as the first heavy splatters of rain hit the window. The hairs on the back of my neck prickle. He's not due to call me today. A little coincidental that Freddie and I fight and I tell him about the smell and then my specialist calls the next day. It's ten in the morning. If Freddie rang him first thing, that's about right for them to have spoken and then for the doctor to be calling me. I don't feel that awful strange rage I felt in the night, but something else. Something hollow. Sadness maybe? A sense of betrayal. Freddie talked to my specialist without even telling me.

'I'm fine, honestly.' I have to give him something. If I'm too effusive that everything is perfect and Freddie's rung to say he's worried about me that's going to be odd, and it won't be me he believes.

'I've had the occasional strange smell but nothing lasting,' I say, reluctantly. 'If I'm honest, it was a bit freaky in the moment, and I probably overreacted, but like you say, these things will probably happen for a while.'

'Ah yes, that's quite common.' He sounds relieved. 'But try not to get too worried about it or let your imagination run away with you. You've not only been through a health crisis, you've also moved house. Your brain is sorting everything out, but there will be glitches in the matrix for a while.' Freddie must have mentioned what I said about the smell. Maybe he's mentioned the haunting stuff, but Dr Canning's obviously not about to bring that up.

'Yes, I need to think of it that way. But honestly, I'm good.'
'You certainly sound well. And call me anytime, Emily. Okay?'

We say our goodbyes and I toss the phone back on the side, staring out at the smeared grey. The sunshine I've only just woken up to has been swallowed up by a heavy rain that's almost hail, landing icy sharp against the windows. The weather seems to change in an instant on these moors, the wild land's moods swinging violently from one extreme to the other, and it's so gloomy that I don't bother getting dressed but go downstairs, take some pills, make a cup of tea, grab more pills, and head straight back to bed. My whole body aches from too much activity and I refuse to feel guilty about crawling back under the covers, especially when the world outside is so uninviting.

I found it, but I didn't use it. I put it back. I should go up to the top floor and search, but I can't. I just can't. I don't want to think about that, and I really don't want to think about those awful words, *You will die here.*

I stare at my phone again. No texts from Freddie. Is he annoyed at me about our fight? I can't remember exactly what I said, but I know I was mad, the events of the night now like some hazy dream. I remember feeling rage though. I guess fear brought it out in me. Seeing that nail again.

The wind races around outside, whistling through any tiny gaps in the bricks as the rain lashes the building, and I feel like I'm on a boat on stormy seas, but the sounds are soothing, reliable, and known, not creaking doors or the thud of moving books, or doors slamming shut by themselves. Today, everything is perfectly normal in the house.

My eyes are heavy and after barely a few sips of my tea, I pull the duvet up close around my chin even though the bedroom is toasty warm and find some old episodes of *Modern Family* on my phone to play in the background so I don't think about ghosts or poltergeists or ominous threats.

No wonder Freddie is worried about me, and he doesn't even know everything. I wish something would happen around him. Just so he'd know I'm not imagining it all.

Just so *I'd* know I'm not imagining it all.

34.

Freddie

Emily's car is in the driveway but the house is quiet—*and freezing, why is it always so bloody cold?*—so I light a fire in the sitting room and then get the tools from under the sink to see about this nail. Now I'm back in the house, I feel my irritation with her returning. How many nails can possibly be sticking out of our floor? And why was she so quick to disbelieve me?

She probably hasn't forgiven me for burning that Ouija board. I've been feeling a bit bad about calling Dr Canning and not telling her, but that guilt is vanishing. After all, she was going on about bad feelings and smells. The doctor *needed* to know. Also, I'm starving after work, and I wasn't expecting a three-course meal or anything, but I thought she might have at least thrown some pasta in a pan or be here to welcome me.

The irritation is like bees buzzing in my head. I don't know where it's come from and it's not like me, but I can't shake it off. And it certainly isn't helped by what I see—or more accurately, what I *don't* see—when I get to the middle landing.

It's only as I swear out loud in a burst of annoyance that there's the rustle of bedclothes and she appears, still in pyjamas, in the doorway. I look up at her, surprised.

'Have you been in bed all day?'

'I was exhausted.' She's barely awake but glances down at her watch. 'You're home early.' She gives me a half smile but then it falters, my irritation obvious.

'What's the matter?'

'Look.' I point down at the floorboard. At a single tiny spot on the floorboard. At the small hole tinged at the edges with a stale red. The hole where the nail used to be.

'I told you I'd taken it out,' I snipe as she follows my gaze. 'I don't know what you saw, but it wasn't *that* nail. In fact'—I scan across the rest of the landing to double-check—'there are no nails.'

She frowns. 'There has to be. I *saw* it.' She flinches as she tries to crouch, awkward and obviously in pain with her leg. Her eyes dart across the wood. 'It was there. It was.'

Her sudden insecurity—her terrified self-doubt—gives me a flash of victory. *Not always right, are you, Emily?*

'It doesn't matter, Emily.' I'm softer. 'Maybe it was a splinter you saw. It was the middle of the night.'

'It *was* the nail. It was right there.' She looks up at me, suspicious. 'Did you take it out? Just now?'

'Of course I didn't.' My irritation rises again. 'Look, it was probably just a trick of the mind. Dr Canning says—'

'You called him, didn't you? He rang this morning, asking questions about if my senses were working properly.'

'I was worried about you, that's all. I was going to tell you.' An icy draught slinks like a cat around my legs. No wonder it's always so fucking freezing in here. 'I'm your husband, Emily. I'm allowed to worry. And he's not just *your* doctor. I spent days with him by your bedside. Days and weeks you don't remember. I have a relationship with him. He helped me too.'

She can't argue that and instead shrinks back toward the bedroom door, as if afraid of my snippy tone. Always the wounded party. 'But honestly, Emily. What's more likely?

That you imagined the nail due to your post-sepsis, or that I snuck up here when I got home to quickly take it out before you woke up? Do you want to check my pockets?'

She doesn't answer but looks down once again at the tiny hole in the wood. 'I don't understand it, because it was definitely there. And there was that awful smell.'

It's so typical of Emily to never admit she could be wrong even when all the evidence points that way, but there's no point in continuing to argue with her. I'm freezing, and I want to get down beside the fire to warm up with a nice glass of wine. I've got enough bullshit on my plate to sort out.

'There's no smell now, is there?' I reach out and touch her arm.

'No. But there *was* one.'

'I'll take a look under the floorboards tomorrow if you want.' The smell is the clearest indication that she's been having a post-sepsis syndrome moment, but I'm not going to spell that out. She must know it even if she won't admit it.

'And as for the doors and windows slamming shut, it must have been the draught that's always coming through. No wonder I'm always freezing.'

'Maybe we should go upstairs and check the rooms there. See if that's where the draught is coming from.' She's almost hopeful as she looks at me. 'Or the smell.'

'Not tonight, Em. There's no smell now, and I'm shattered. Why don't you have a bath and I'll sort out food?'

She opens her mouth as if she's about to push it, but then doesn't. Finally she nods. 'Okay. And thanks.' I guess she wants a truce too.

She's still concerned, glancing down at the floorboard, not trusting herself, but she looks up at me, grateful and nodding, and I have a pang of how scary it must be for her to not trust her own senses. And then I'm awash with guilt again. *I'll stop*, I think as I head to the bathroom, happy to warm my cold hands under the hot water tap for a bit as the bath runs. *I'll stop tonight.*

But first I need to get by the fire and get rid of this awful cold in my bones.

35.
Emily

I lean over the sink to spit as I brush my teeth, exhausted. Yesterday was a quiet day, Freddie working from home, and I thought I'd sleep better, but I managed only a few hours' sleep, and they were filled with awful dreams of Freddie standing in the library holding a dead baby covered in blood and looking at me with such horror, moaning, *There was a cuckoo in my nest*, as books hung in the air around him. When I turned to run I was back on the ridge on the hike, with Freddie telling me to go faster, and then in my dream I felt his hand on my back and I was falling all over again.

In the humidity of the bathroom, full of steam after my too hot shower, I feel like I've been run over by a bus, and we've got lunch with Sally and Joe today. I swear I never felt this bad in the hospital. I splash cold water on my face. It didn't help that the bedroom was so hot all night; I must be dehydrated. The only cold thing in the room were Freddie's feet, ice blocks under the covers. Maybe *he* needs to see a doctor.

I straighten up, leaning my hands on the sink, and look in the mirror. My reflection is invisible in the steamed-up glass, as if maybe I'm the ghost. Maybe I died back there in the fall and this is all a dream.

You will die here.

Just book titles. Just coincidence. Just a breeze knocked them out. There's nothing to find. There was no nail. You cannot trust yourself.

I repeat the sentences over and over until in my tiredness I very nearly believe it. I don't like this house, whether it's my condition or something else. I only went on about how great it was back then because it had popped up on Rightmove after Freddie and I had been sniping at each other. I didn't even remember setting an alert for country homes. I didn't really want to move here. Not really.

God, I wish we were back in London and going for lunch with our old friends. I could turn up in sweatpants and a hoodie with them.

I'm still staring, lost in thought at the blurred mirror, when a scratching comes from behind it. No, not a scratching. A squeaking. My eyes widen as letters start to spell out in the condensation, writing from the *other* side. *No no no, what now?*

Ǝ . . . Я . . . Ⅎ . . .

The three letters have been written in the wetness, but as if from *inside* the mirror, each one backward, right to left, not left to right, scrawled by a finger pressing from the other side of the wall behind. The shapes are shaky, as if they've taken a huge amount of energy and effort to write, but the letters are clear. *F . . . R . . . E . . .*

Freddie. Is it trying to spell Freddie? No sooner have I had the thought than another *E* is shakily and slowly scrawled. It's thinner, as if the effort of communicating has become too great a struggle.

F . . . R . . . E . . . E

No, not Freddie. Another letter starts, so faint I almost can't see it at all.

F . . . R . . . E . . . E . . . M

It fades before the bottom of the last stroke, but I know it's an *M. Free me?* Surely that's what was being written before it stopped.

'What's the matter?'

Freddie's voice is so unexpected that I gasp and stumble backward, my legs banging into the bath. 'You're white as a sheet.' He's in the doorway, phone in hand, looking at me, concerned.

'Look.' I grab his arm and drag him in. 'Look at the mirror.'

'What am I supposed to be seeing here?'

'The letters.' The words are out before I see what he's seeing. The letters are gone. Just drips of waters smearing down the glass as the steam cools. My heart sinks and my head spins momentarily. It can't have vanished. It can't have. But it has.

'Letters?' His disbelief is clear on his face. Disbelief. Pity. Annoyance.

'I saw something.' My words are hollow. There's nothing there. Just like the nail.

'Can you see why I called Dr Canning?' He wipes the mirror clean with a cloth, both our reflections clear now. 'You're seeing and hearing and smelling stuff that just isn't happening.'

'It was there.' All I can see now are our reflections staring back. I look like shit. An exhausted, pale mess next to my healthy husband.

'It was steam and your imagination, nothing else.' He looks around, distracted. 'But we need to find where that draught is coming from. It's driving me mad. Why do you keep turning the heating off when it's so bloody cold?'

'Because it's baking in here,' I bite back. 'And I'm *not* imagining that—just go and look at the thermostat. It's about twenty-five degrees everywhere in the house because you keep turning it on *and* lighting fires. And there isn't a draught.' I pause. 'Maybe *you're* imagining it.'

'I'm not.' It's his turn to be unsettled. 'I can feel it around my ankles. It's like ice.'

'So if you're feeling something that I'm not, it's real, but the other way around, I'm having some post-sepsis episode?

Maybe the draught is part of whatever weird shit is going on in this house. Something messing with you. Have you thought about that?'

'There's no such thing as ghosts, Emily.' He goes past me and out into the corridor to head downstairs. 'Listen to yourself. I could strangle Iso for playing that prank with the Ouija board.'

'You know a cold draught is how most people feel a presence in an old house, don't you?' I follow him down, annoyed that my slow pace makes me look weak.

'Old houses have draughts.' He doesn't slow down but goes straight to the kitchen, angrily pulling out slices of bread for the toaster, not asking me if I want any. In his pocket his phone flashes up through the fabric, vibrating, but he ignores it.

'Some really odd stuff is going on here, Freddie. Look at this.' In the heat of my anger I pull up the photo of the library. 'I heard noises and found it like this. The first time there were only four books on the floor. This time, the same four were the only ones left on the shelves amid all this mess. And those four books, look what they spell. *You will die here.* And you wonder why I'm freaked out?'

I'm so busy talking while shoving my phone under his nose, I don't see his expression change. There's a long pause before he eventually looks up from my phone screen. He's appalled. 'Jesus, Emily. When did you do this?'

'I didn't.' I stare at him. 'Of course I didn't. It was like that and then next time I went in it was all back to normal. Whatever did it, it wasn't me. Maybe it was your icy draught.'

'I think we need to speak to Dr Canning about this.'

His phone flashes again through his pocket.

'What are you doing on your phone all the time anyway?'

'Work stuff. A lot of email round robins. One of us has a job.'

'Wow.' My spine stiffens. 'I'm sorry my near-death experience stole my dream promotion. But I'm still getting paid for the year, so what do you care? And on the subject of caring, I don't *care* if you believe me or not. I saw those letters in the mirror.'

'Just like you saw the nail in the floorboard?'

His words ooze casual venom, and we stare at each other like enemies across battle lines. We might as well be strangers. I get so hot in my anger it feels like every drop of blood is boiling metal in my veins. Looking at Freddie, I'd say that he's feeling exactly the same. He opens his mouth to say something and I know it's going to be awful, that it will *end* us, but just then the doorbell goes, startling us both, and suddenly the rage vanishes as quickly as it had come. The heat floods from me as I look back toward the front door.

'Oh god. The vicar's cleaning lady. I forgot.'

I hurry as best I can to answer it, and when I glance back Freddie's looking down, confused, at his toast, as if his anger has also left so suddenly he's feeling hollow and unsteady.

Something's up with him, and it's not me and whatever post-sepsis thing is or isn't going on. Just as I pull open the door, I'm sure I see his phone flashing bright again, and it must be buzzing because his face darkens. My stomach tightens. Maybe there's trouble at work.

'You must be Emily. I'm Mrs Tucker.'

I stare at the tiny old woman on the doorstep carrying a bag of cleaning products and wearing a housecoat like something out of a 1970s sitcom rerun. 'The cleaner? The vicar sent me.'

'Sorry. Of course. Please, come in.' I step back to let her in. She's far older than I was expecting, and I feel bad thinking of her mopping and scrubbing after us. What was Paul thinking hiring someone so *ancient*?

'I didn't know what you had so I brought my own things, if that's all right?'

'That's great.'

'Would you like a cup of tea before you start?' Freddie's in the kitchen doorway, all charm and light as if we hadn't been snarling at each other moments ago. 'I'm Freddie. Emily's husband.'

She nods, birdlike, as she puts down her bag. 'Good to meet you. And that would be grand. I'll drink it as I work. Milk and two sugars.' When she smiles her tiny teeth are stained from what must be years of smoking. Her hair is still dark, with streaks of silver, and it's pulled back in a tight bun.

'I won't get in your way.'

'We're going out for lunch in a bit, so you'll have the run of the place.' I wonder if she'll *find it*, whatever it is.

'Don't worry about the top floor,' Freddie says, sorting a mug out for her. 'We're not using it yet.'

My heart sinks. I'll have to try harder to find it myself. I need to prove my sanity to myself, let alone to Freddie.

36.
Emily

We'd just arrived at the cottage when Sally's text came in—*Will be ten mins, just let yourselves in, the door's never locked. Help yourselves to drinks*—and the oddness of it goes some way to clearing the tension between Freddie and me.

The only thing he'd said in the car was quizzing me about getting a cleaner, which in turn pissed me off because it felt like he was expecting me to do it all like some 1950s housewife even though he insisted that wasn't the case. We'd sat in silence after that, and I'd wondered what was really at the bottom of our constant annoyance with each other. I have the guilt in the empty space in my abdomen, but what does he have?

'I guess we go in then,' Freddie mutters, and opens the door.

As I follow him inside, we both gasp, our bad moods fading slightly with our shocked surprise at what greets us in the hallway. A vast canvas painted in pinks and browns, maybe five feet high and wide.

'Wow.' Freddie glances at me askance and then looks back at it, tilting his head. 'Is that a vagina?'

'I think so.' I look at him and pull a face. 'Very 1970s though.' And then we both laugh and for the next few minutes, once we've found the wine in the kitchen, we're like schoolkids again, exploring the glorious artistic eccentricity of the cottage. While from the outside it's a gorgeous thatched country home, the internal decor is almost Moroccan in style, large cushions for lounging rather than sofas, terracotta pots, low mosaiced tables. All gorgeous, but all secondary to the artwork on the walls.

'He really likes vaginas,' Freddie says wryly, and I snort another laugh.

'And boobs.'

The paintings aren't only nudes but several more like the big one in the hallway, close-ups of female anatomy in bright and vivid colours, and they're amazing, but it's an onslaught of physicality wherever you look.

'I hope they get back soon,' he says. 'I'm starving.'

'The art making you hungry?'

We laugh again, like kids, our bad moods melting away, and when Sally and Joe arrive our moods only get better. Joe is a charming host, and the tapas-style food Sally's prepared is delicious. Once we've eaten our fill and are lounging on the large cushions, it feels like we're Romans after a feast.

This time, when Joe rolls a joint and holds it out, I find myself taking it, caught up in their bohemia, but I immediately cough after the inhale.

'Oh god, that'll do for me.' I giggle, the thick smoke making my head buzz, and then Freddie takes it, inhaling deeply.

'So all these are from live models?' Freddie hands the joint back, gesturing at the walls.

'All local models.' Joe reclines, and I can make out the muscular tautness of his torso under his soft shirt. He's at least fifteen years older, but in way better shape than Freddie. Joe is hot, I think again. Super hot. There's no denying it.

He sees me looking and, stoned himself, smiles. 'I probably know them more intimately than their doctors.'

'Women love Joe,' Sally adds. 'They always have. It's how he captures their essence in his work. They relax around him. And he's a genius, of course.'

'Let's not get carried away.' He leans over and kisses her, and she looks at him with such love it makes my heart ache. Freddie and I were like that once. Where did it go?

'Is that your daughter?' Freddie points at a framed photo of the two of them with a woman maybe in her early twenties.

'No, my niece. She lives in New Zealand. My only niece, so we try to get over there every couple of years to see her. Children didn't come along for us and we're okay with that. But what about you two?' Sally asks. 'Larkin Lodge would make a great family home.'

'I've always wanted kids,' Freddie says. 'A wife and a family. Old-fashioned maybe, but we've been working toward that.' He looks down and I think for a moment that he's going to tell them about the miscarriage, but he doesn't. 'Although getting Emily over her horrific accident has been our main concern.' He squeezes my knee and I take his hand, feeling a sudden rush of affection for him. I don't want other people to know. I can't bear their sympathy messed up with my own guilt.

'Speaking of horrors,' Joe says. 'How's the house? Any more strange feelings?'

'Oh, let's not talk about that, please.' I don't look at Freddie as my neck prickles with embarrassment. 'I feel silly. It's my imagination, I'm sure. Apparently odd things can happen after sepsis. The brain chemistry inside needs to settle down or something.'

'I don't believe in ghosts myself.' Joe's looking into the last of his red wine. 'Other than the ones we carry with us.' He looks up and smiles, as if it's a joke, but something about it makes me shiver, even as Freddie and Sally laugh.

'The house needs some life, that's all. You should have a party,' Sally says. 'The vicar knows anyone worth knowing; he can help you invite people. Cheer the place up.'

'That could be fun,' Joe says from behind a cloud of smoke. 'I don't believe in going back to previous homes, but I could make an exception in this case. I'm curious to see the Lodge again after all this time. And never let it be said that Joe Carter says no to a party. My professional reputation is at stake.'

'Could be a nice idea.' Freddie nods.

'We can invite our London friends too.' I'm not sure I have a party in me, but now that Sally and Joe have suggested it, it feels like a done deal, and if I'm going to meet a bunch of new people I want my oldest friends around me.

'So what's the magic of such a long and happy marriage?' Freddie asks when we've finished our coffees and straightened out a bit. 'You two seem to have it nailed. How do you stay so close?'

'It hasn't always been perfect,' Sally says. 'I had to get used to Joe's work, so many women. But suddenly it all clicked and we've never looked back. I can't imagine life without him. He's my world.'

'And Sally is the perfect wife.'

'True love, huh?' Freddie smiles.

'Something like that. You have to be prepared to work at it.'

My thighs prickle against my seat, and I'm sure Freddie feels as uncomfortable as I do. The way we've been so snipey at each other hasn't been good. So what if he doesn't believe me that there's something odd in the house. I haven't really given him any proof, and of course he's going to worry about the sepsis stuff. The other way around I'd be the same.

'Marriage is teamwork,' Freddie says, looking my way, and we smile at each other. I do love him. I do. I love him very much.

37.
Emily

'I'm really sorry about this morning, Em.' As we get in the car, I can tell from his face that he means it. He's almost forlorn. Ashamed of himself. 'And last night. I don't know why I was so shitty. Whatever is or isn't going on in the house it's obviously freaking you out a bit and I need to be more respectful of that. Especially as you've been on your own there for a few days.'

His hand reaches across for mine and I take it. This is my Freddie. This is my husband. My heart lifts again, and I feel as bad as he does. 'I'm sorry too. I know you worry about me. And I know you called Dr Canning with the best of intentions.'

Away from the house, full of great food and with a warming wine buzz, once again I'm second-guessing myself. Were there letters in the mirror? Was it my imagination? Maybe I *should* go and see Dr Canning. Get *more* pills.

'But is everything okay with *you?*' I hold his hand, enjoying the familiar feel of him. 'You're not normally so snappy.'

'Stuff at work. The new boss is constantly in my inbox even though I'm moving branch.' He looks the other way as we pull back onto the lane. 'I need to manage it better. Especially at weekends. I shouldn't take it out on you.'

I look at the passing moors, so barren even in the sunshine. I can't warm to them, and I don't think I ever will. The isolation and unforgiving nature of this place frightens me. I miss the city, I realize, with its constant noise and people. Safety and freedom of numbers. I miss my friends too. Before my accident, Cat, Iso, and I were constantly WhatsApping one another. If not every day, then never more than a couple of days without a ping. But I guess that fell by the wayside for them when I was in hospital and is hard to pick up again. Especially with me just hanging around at home so far away. No drinks after work, no gossip, no *buzz*.

Ahead the house looms into view, alone on its hilltop, patiently waiting for our return. 'They're very happy, aren't they, Sally and Joe?' Freddie adds from nowhere, thoughtfully.

'They certainly look that way. And she doesn't seem at all bothered about all those women's vaginas everywhere.' We laugh again and I squeeze Freddie's hand.

'We're happy too, aren't we?'

'God, of course, yes. Always.' He sounds so surprised that I'm even asking. 'Especially now that you're home and well.' He grins at me and winks. Not the Hollywood star style of wink that Joe probably has, but it has a charm of its own. 'And when we get inside, Mrs Bennett, I'm going to show you just how happy I am.'

'Oh really?'

'Really.'

Suddenly it's like the old days, the *early* days, way back when we first met and impulsive afternoon sex was something we thought we'd never stop doing. Back when we couldn't get enough of each other. We are okay. We will be okay.

There's nothing wrong with the house, I tell myself as Freddie unlocks the door, and I follow him in over the threshold, already eager to get upstairs and get our clothes off. It's just me. It's all in my head.

38.

Emily

It's a perfect weekend.

The weather has the edge of winter crispness to it but is dry and bright enough to fool you into thinking that spring might be on the way regardless of it being February, and it raises my spirits. We spend Saturday afternoon upstairs, and even with my fragile body we still manage a couple of bouts of sex, which we follow by watching a cheesy action movie on Freddie's laptop and eating oven pizza in bed.

Nothing wakes either of us in the night, and when we do finally roll into each other's arms at around eight on Sunday morning, I'm not sweating from overheating and Freddie's feet aren't like ice blocks.

'Good morning.' He kisses my nose.

'Good morning.'

'I'm starving.' He sits up and yawns. 'And thank fuck, at last this house feels warmer.'

I have such an overwhelming rush of love for him and, more than that, affection. After a few years of marriage love lingers on as a matter of habit, but the affection fades. The affection is the magic. That warmth and wanting to be near someone. To touch them. I sit up and snuggle into his back. 'Warm croissants.'

'Your wish is my command. As long as you bought some.'

We cuddle a little longer before I shove him toward the bathroom, and then I lie back on the pillow happier than I've been since before my accident. Since a while before it, if I'm honest.

It's not just the surprisingly good day yesterday but also a little hope inside me. A chance to put something right. We had sex three times over the course of the afternoon and evening, and not once did either of us even pause to reach for a condom. I touch the soft skin of my belly. Maybe a spark of life is already happening inside me. A baby to assuage the guilt of my infidelity and all that came after. The guilt of Freddie mourning a child that might not even have been his. I can pretend none of it happened. It had been a terrible mistake, I knew as soon as I was sober, even when I got the promotion, and I'd thought the pregnancy was my punishment. But karma got me. I got the job but never got to do it, and I nearly died. And I'd lost a baby I hadn't even had time to realize I wanted. I know Freddie has lost one too, but he hadn't known I was pregnant—when I woke up in the hospital I pretended I had been planning to tell him after the holiday—so it wasn't the same. I had known there was a baby growing inside me for two weeks by the time we went, and I'd spent a lot of that time wishing it wasn't. I have guilt over that as much as guilt over the stupid infidelity that led to it.

When Freddie heads down to the kitchen, I go to shower and pause to glance up to the second-floor landing. There are no sounds or creaks. All I can see up there are floorboards bright in sunlight. I need to pull myself together. Throw away those books downstairs. Ignore any strange noises. It's all in my head. It has to be.

It's me, not the house. I don't like the idea that I could have pulled the library apart and then tidied it without remembering any of it, but maybe I did. No one else would have done it. And if there's no such thing as ghosts, then there is only that

Sherlock Holmes quote: Once you eliminate the impossible, whatever remains, however improbable, must be the truth.

I touch my stomach again and once dressed, I go down the stairs more confidently than I have since we've been here. Even my leg isn't hurting as much today.

We eat croissants warm from the Aga while sprawled across our sofa together, reading the newspapers on our iPads, and then we cook a roast chicken dinner, pour some lovely red wine as the afternoon darkens, and play cards in front of the fire as the night turns darker.

Freddie doesn't look at his phone once all day. None of that tense, furrowed expression I've seen when I've interrupted him answering emails. With his phone ignored, he's my Freddie again. Chilled. Kind. Funny.

'It's been a perfect weekend, hasn't it?' I whisper when we're finally in bed again, dozing off in the quiet calm of the still house, not even a raven's caw to disturb the peace. 'Just the two of us.'

His mouth twitches into a smile. 'Perfect.' He's bleary, already nearly asleep. 'If only it could be the two of us all the time. Forever.'

We sleep entwined in each other and I relish the smell of his warm skin and even the staleness of him in the morning before he creeps out of bed early to leave for London, promising me with kisses that he'll come straight home as fast as he can.

I hear the front door closing and the faint sound of his engine purring off down the drive, then lie in bed wary for creaking doors or falling books or awful smells drifting down from the second floor, but there's nothing except for the clicking of the radiators as the heating comes on. I curl back up under the covers and stay cosy, one hand drifting to my stomach. I still want us to sell this place. I still want us to move back to London. But for now, even if just for a year, maybe we can find some happiness here.

39.
Emily

Merrily Watkins, an earthy, rosy-cheeked, cheerful, solid woman in her early fifties, and her husband, Pete, a no-nonsense, quiet man, tanned and weathered from a life working in the fresh air, turn up mid-morning on Monday in a battered old Land Rover with mud-splattered tyres.

'There's a lot of work to be done.' I'm stating the obvious as they've already trampled round the wet ground and measured up spaces and taken photos and so have seen it for themselves. The garden is massive and a mess.

'That's how we like it. I love a project.' Merrily has her camera out, constantly snapping different areas. 'And Pete's happiest when he can get the digger out.' They both seem impervious to the cold. Pete's only in a T-shirt and jeans despite the rapid drop in temperature this morning, and while Merrily has a jacket on over a jumper, I'm in three layers, wrapped up in my quilted Uniqlo coat and still shivering.

'Obviously we want to keep the orchard, and we want it to still look like a countryside garden,' I say. 'But it would be great to do something with those outbuildings. A home office in one or a gym. A summer house maybe. And the paths need levelling. A patio and barbecue area would be wonderful. And a fence around the pond.' Even if we don't stay here for very long, we've got the profit from the London flat and getting all this sorted will add value, I'm sure.

'It's big enough that we can make four separate areas, each with its own style, don't you think, Pete?' Her husband nods, the quieter one in the couple.

'Not sure how much you want to spend though?'

'I know it's not going to be cheap, but if you send me a quote I'm sure we can figure it out. If it's too much I guess some bits will have to wait.'

'I'll get some designs over to you, then we can decide the level of cost for the materials. Don't worry.' She smiles, already head in the project. 'We'll get this space looking amazing.'

'I'll get that septic tank emptied out first,' Pete says. 'Fill it in and level the ground. Then dig out the paths. But leaving the two buildings aside, I reckon we could bring it in at around twenty-five grand. Going with middle price options for paving slabs and decking. I'd go composite. It looks as good and you won't slip. A lot of places I end up laying new lawn but yours just needs some refreshing.'

'Sounds great. Will we have to wait long?' Even in the bitter cold with my toes going numb I'm feeling fired up about the changes. We can redecorate inside too. Get rid of the suffocating flock wallpaper. I might even try to get up to the second floor this week. Take some air fresheners and dispel my fears. Face them at least. If I can get through a few more days without any strangeness, then maybe I'll fully relax. I'm already looking forward to Pete and Merrily starting work. I won't be alone here.

'A week or so? Depending when Merrily gets you a quote you're happy with.'

'I'll send that over to you tomorrow. Doesn't take me long.'

'Great. And how do you work? Upfront or . . .'

'No, weekly. You pay at the end of each week's work. It's a small town. We rely on trust.'

Before they leave Pete brings in a stack of logs and Merrily builds a fire in the sitting room to make sure I'm cosy even though I'm capable of doing it myself, and it's not only the flames that are glowing. As I wave them off, I am too. I check the library a frisson of nerves in the pit of my stomach, but the books are on the shelves apart from the four I threw away, and everything is normal.

A warm, normal, beautiful house. That's all it is.

Still, I hope Freddie hurries back.

40.

He leaves for longer in the days now, takes to the skies and cries out to the heavens as he races across the moors, scavenging among the dead things hidden in the frozen gorse and moss between the craggy rocks. Sometimes he sees another raven watching him. She pecks at a lifeless rabbit, lying half in and half out of a stretch of bog, and then perches on a stone several feet away, giving him space to approach.

When he strips the dregs of meat from the carcass she lets him be. Her feathers shine. There is no broken wing. They dance like this, around each other, for hours, and then as the bright canopy becomes a blanket of night, she heads away to where the others all roost, warmth and comfort in numbers. She caws an invitation to him, and although he wants to follow, he finds he turns and his wings take him back to the strange house on the hill where his dead mate waits.

Her dark dead eye is full of venom. *You can't leave me. You left me alone. You fled and left me to die. You murdered me.*

He shuffles in closer and drops a morsel of rotting mouse in front of her that he knows she won't eat. She can't eat it. His mate is dead. He knows this. He settles down beside her to sleep.

But this night he dreams of earlier long hot days, many cycles gone past, when they were young, before her wing was damaged, before she pecked at him, before he *chose* to leave her in the chimney, before he fled up and away not only from the danger but from her—*You left me to die. You murdered me*—when they existed only in the joy of each other. Before, before, before.

And nevermore.

In the morning, the new raven, Bright Wing, as he thinks of her, alive and vibrant, not like Broken Wing beside him, is on the wall. Waiting patiently, beady eyes alert and sparkling. He doesn't look at his old mate as he flies off, letting out a caw that comes from deep inside him and speaks to freedom and imprisonment and wanting what cannot be had.

As the wind cuts cold across his beak and Bright Wing comes alongside him, and they circle and dash like he has before, he can't help but think—*before, before, before.*

Maybe not nevermore.

41.

Freddie

Emily's accident replays in my sleep, the nightmare a vivid assault on my senses. The heat of Ibiza on my back. The salt in the dry air. I follow her on the stony track and wonder why she's been so shitty all holiday, not letting me touch her. It's me who's got the problems. She's got her dream promotion when we were supposed to be concentrating on my career, and she's still bitching at me. She's hiding something, I know it. I guess that makes two of us. I'm sure she's walking slowly on purpose. Why can't she speed up? Get this stupid hike over with.

When it really happened, I got up close, irritatingly close, filled with an urge to have a really big fight, the kind that makes you honest, no matter what the consequence. I wanted to shove her, I really did, and maybe I was too close, and maybe I brushed her, but I didn't push her. But in the dream it's different. In the dream I push hard and watch with glee as she turns toward me, ugly with irritation, before her ankle twists and that anger turns to surprise. This time when I see that awful dread on her face I grin so hard my face is in danger of tearing in two, and as she falls and her hand reaches out for me, my smile turns to laughter. When her body breaks on the rocks below, I laugh harder.

I'm free, I think, standing there on the rocks. I don't have to stop at all. But then the sky clouds over, suddenly cold and heavy with rain, and in the distance I hear sirens, and I know I'm not free and

I'm going to prison and suddenly I'm thinking of all the things I'll never have again, like a cold beer on a sunny day and a Sunday roast with good red wine and watching movies on a whim, and this is all her fault and god, why did I kill her? And then, just as the panic overwhelms me, I wake up.

I stare at her, a lumpen shape in the darkness asleep beside me, and my heart jackhammers as I swallow hard. *She's alive. I'm not going to prison.* I take a deep breath to calm down. Fuck, what a dream.

My feet are almost numb with cold and my bladder's contracted, leaving me with a fierce need to pee. This bloody freezing house. My good mood from a great day at work was ruined when I got home and felt that draught again and then Emily told me how much the garden work was likely to cost. I told her that the money from the flat was tied up in investment accounts and rather than lose the interest, maybe she could pay for it from her insurance salary. She's got a chunk that has accrued during the months she was in hospital. She agreed, which was good. And of course Cat, Russell, Iso, and Mark have already said yes to the party. The thought of Mark back here makes my stomach clench. But if he *knew* anything, he'd have told Emily and confronted me directly.

I get out of bed, my toes painful with the cold, and hobble to the bathroom. The landing window is open again, the net curtain blowing with the night breeze, and the temperature is a few degrees below freezing out there. I close it, angrily. Why does she keep doing this? She knows I'm really feeling the cold here. She'll deny it again, but it's not me, so it has to be her.

I hear a faint creak and look up into the sombre void where the second floor is an ocean of darkness. Somewhere up there a door clicks shut. I shiver and make a mental note to order a bunch of draught excluders from Amazon. Of course we probably wouldn't need them if my wife didn't keep opening windows at night. My irritation blisters some more.

I use the toilet in the dark, not caring if I splash, and then head back to bed. It's five-thirty. If I can shake off my annoyance I can get another hour of sleep before heading to the London office. It's my last week there and thank god for that because between the mess I'm in, Emily, and the travelling, I'm exhausted.

'Shit.' I feel a sharp prick on the sole of my foot, thankfully before I've put all my weight down, and when I crouch I can't believe what I'm seeing. I left my phone downstairs to avoid temptation in the night—*You're in enough trouble, Freddie*—but the moonlight from the window makes it easy to see.

A nail with a bent tip.

It's sticking out the wrong way up, from a splintered hole with black drops that in daylight would be rusty red dried blood on the edges. I stare at it. It's not just any nail. It's *the* nail. How the fuck did it get back in the floor?

Emily.

I look up, through the open bedroom doorway, and for a moment I think she's waking up, but she lets out a small moan and rolls onto her side, and then half back again, twitching, restless in whatever dreams she's having.

I pull at the glinting nail, expecting it to be firmly embedded, but it slides out of the wood with ease. Did Emily find it in the rubbish and put it back? Why would she do that? The bees are buzzing in my head again, discordant, as I sit back on my heels, an answer coming to me. Emily likes to be right. She always has done.

Instead of getting back into bed, despite the cold, I sit on the end of the mattress, my back to her, and stare at the sliver of moonlight coming through the gap in the curtains. The bees buzz louder. Did she open the window on purpose? So the cold would wake me and take me out into the corridor? Was it a lure so that I'd stand on the nail? So she could say, *Look, look, I told you so!*

Another thought comes to me. Does she even know she's done it? She wrecked a room downstairs and put it neatly together again and doesn't remember it. Dr Canning says it will pass. But what if it doesn't? Is she going mad? Outside, a raven caws, the first birdcall of the dawn even while it's still pitch-black outside.

I should get back into bed. I should try to sleep for another hour. I'm so tired. But the bees are buzzing too loud in my head, *buzz-buzz-buzzing* with irritation at Emily, devouring any sympathy I might have. Ghosts and nails and windows. The madness of Emily, my beloved wife.

Maybe if she went mad, that would save me.

42.

Emily

At first I'm sure it's a ghost sitting on the end of the bed.

Startled, I half sit up in the gloom, staring at the stiff figure, and then I realize who it is. Not a ghost at all.

'Freddie?'

He doesn't answer. He doesn't even twitch. His back is straight, his hands resting on his thighs. He's sitting perfectly still with his back to me, staring at the streak of pale moonlight slicing through the gap between the curtains. It's cold in the bedroom, as if the window's been left open again.

'Freddie?' I'm louder but he still doesn't move, and my voice in the quiet and his stillness disturb me. A quarter of his face is visible, and he looks empty. Not like my Freddie at all.

'Go back to sleep.' His voice is as hollow as his expression. Maybe he's half-asleep himself. Maybe he's been sleepwalking. I lie back down, expecting him to climb in beside me, but he doesn't.

When the alarm finally goes off an hour later I pretend to stretch as if I've just woken up, and Freddie gets quickly to his feet as if *he's* just got up, but we're both liars. As he heads into the bathroom, barely glancing my way, I try to cling onto the dregs of the joy I'd found yesterday in the new quiet calm of the house, but Freddie's foul mood since he got home yesterday has drained it out of me. As the shower bursts into life, I get my dressing gown and hobble downstairs, not wanting any awkward conversations while he's getting dressed. The closeness of the weekend feels like a dream. When did our marriage become this pendulum of instability?

The kettle's boiling when I see his iPhone sitting on the kitchen side. He didn't take it up to bed. Why? We always take our phones with us. He normally charges it by the bed. Freddie—like everyone these days—is never far from his phone.

My heart picks up pace. Freddie's been so moody. Up and down. Are there secrets in his phone? Things I don't know about? It makes me feel sick—I don't want to even *think* the word *affair*. That would be some irony, wouldn't it? All the guilt I've been feeling over my awful one-night stand with Neil at work, and what if Freddie's having an actual affair? Neither of us has ever been the jealous type, and I've always figured it's because neither of us is the cheating type, but it turns out I was—if fleetingly. Maybe he is too? Does fidelity change over the years? Have I been smug and complacent?

Sex with Freddie had been sparse for a while before my accident because of my own guilty secret, and then I was in hospital for months. Freddie was alone for a long time. I stare at the black screen, my body fluttering with temptation. I have never *once* gone through Freddie's phone. I've never been that person. I take a deep breath. I'm not that person. But I've never been so confused by him either. These strange moods. The business with the nail. The window. Something's going on with him. I need to know what.

The pipes are rumbling so I know he's still in the shower. It'll be at least fifteen minutes before he's downstairs. It's now or never. When will I get the chance again? Before I can change my mind, I turn on the phone and then put in his passcode, relieved that he hasn't changed that. *He wouldn't,* I remind myself as his home screen comes up, a photo of the two of us sitting behind the icons. *Because he would never believe for an instant that you'd look at his things without asking.* Phones are so personal. Private. That doesn't stop me looking.

There's nothing unusual in my scan of his texts. Then his WhatsApp. Again, nothing I don't recognize. And when I click into the threads from his work colleagues I've never met, wondering if maybe he's disguised a lover with a different name, the messages are all about meetings and nothing interesting let alone clandestine. I check the archive; nothing there either. His Facebook messages and his Instagram and then his email are free of anything suspicious. It's all normal.

I'm stumped and beginning to feel ashamed of myself when something niggles me. I think back to finding him in the bathroom, on the night of the Christmas dinner and Ouija board, so focused on his phone when he said he'd had to answer a work email. I go back into his inbox—there's nothing for that night. Nor is there anything in his sent items. He doesn't delete emails, I know that because he tells me off for deleting stuff I might need later, and why would he delete just one? I look through last weekend and this and there are no work emails at all. So if he hasn't been emailing work, what *has* he been doing on his phone? And whatever it is, why has he deleted it?

I'm so lost in my thoughts I don't realize he's out of the shower until I hear him at the top of the stairs. With fumbling fingers I quickly turn off the phone, put it back where it was, throw a couple of slices of bread into the toaster.

He's got a girlfriend somewhere. My stomach knots. It's the only explanation. I was in hospital for months and he got close to someone. These things happen all the time. Freddie's not used to being on his own and he's never liked it. There was temptation and he gave in to it.

'Do you want a coffee?' I'm amazed at how normal my voice sounds when inside I feel like my heart is in a vice, being crushed to implosion.

'No, I should head.' He's already pulled on his coat. 'I'm so glad this is the last week of this commute. I'll be back Thursday. Got my leaving drinks on Wednesday. Shouldn't be too wild. It's not like I'm leaving the company.'

'Okay, good. The others'll be here Saturday morning. I'll get the party stuff organized.' I'm desperate for some kind of reassurance, but he doesn't even look at me. Was that why he was up in the night, sitting on the bed? Thinking about his affair?

'I'll see you Thursday then.'

'Drive safely.' I should confront him. But with what? That I just went through his phone without his permission and found nothing suspicious but I still think he's having an affair? I'd sound like some paranoid jealous wife. And I'm not that. I don't want to be that, even as my heart is breaking with fear. Karma's coming for me again. I slept with someone because I was drunk and stupid and had always had a little crush and thought it might get me a promotion. It was so mercenary that it must be way worse than if Freddie met someone he liked when I was in a coma. But still, the jealousy stabs at me. The idea I could have been dying and he was in bed with someone else.

He opens the door, cold air sweeping through the house, and then, as if it's blowing away his mood, he turns back. 'Call me if anything worries you. Love you.'

'I will. Love you too.'

And then he's gone.

The toast pops up, but I can't even think about eating. Could Freddie really have cheated on me? I take my coffee and go through to the sitting room, dropping onto the sofa. I can't imagine it. But then I can't imagine what he was going through when I was in the coma. Maybe it was a one-night thing with someone from work like I had? Or at least a short-lived fling. Some comfort that got out of hand?

A thought strikes me. A glimmer of hope. Maybe he's been trying to end it. My heart lifts suddenly. Yes, maybe that's it. Maybe that's why he's been having such odd moods. He's never been good with pressure. Maybe he's told her it's done and she's hurt and he's trying to smooth it over? Hiding in toilets and messaging and then looking guilty. That fits. He still loves me. He must do. Otherwise why would we have moved here to start afresh? He's moved to the Exeter office away from London. *If* there was an affair, then he's left her, not me. I sit back, a jangle of conflicting emotions.

I know Freddie. I know him better than anyone. We've had a terrible year, and anything that's happened in it—and I have to remind myself that I don't have proof that anything has happened at all—as long as it's over, I have to let go. After what I did, I have to.

Invitations. I'll distract myself with the invitations for the party. But as I carefully climb the stairs to shower myself, my spirits are low and my heart aches. In the bathroom I stare into the mirror where the steam from Freddie's shower has become running drips of water, looking like my face is melting in the reflection, turning me into someone I don't quite recognize. I have changed a bit since my accident, I can't help that. Maybe Freddie can't either.

43.

Emily

The weather has definitely turned. There's no hint of sunlight in the ash-grey heavy sky, the day barely a perpetual gloom that permeates the house, making the shadows longer and the flock wallpapers darker even with all the lights on. I try working in the sitting room, making lists of drinks and food, but I find myself staring out the window at the leaden countryside, once again thinking about Freddie. I can't stop thinking about Freddie and what he might have been doing while I was hanging in the balance between life and death. It sticks in my craw that I might have been dying while he was sleeping with someone else. *Maybe* sleeping with someone else. The understanding of his situation I felt earlier is fading now he's gone and I'm here alone again. Who cheats on a desperately ill wife?

You don't know anything for sure, I tell myself over and over as I add sausage rolls to my list. *You have no evidence of anything.* My evidence is the *lack* of things. An email that wasn't there. That's it. So ridiculous when I think of it that way, but still I can't let it go.

I'm constantly plagued by the opposite of evidence, ever since I've been in this house. Even when Fortuna Carmichael told me *There are no ghosts at Larkin Lodge* I took it as evidence there were. A message telling me to *Find it* and I've found nothing.

After my shower I updated my notebook with the events of the mirror and added in about Freddie always feeling cold here, and I kind of wish I hadn't because with the bleakness of the weather outside, a purgatory of grey, it's hard not to feel creeped out in the big house on my own. My eyes keep darting to shapes in the wallpaper that seem like they're moving in the corner of my eye, but when I look at them directly, everything is normal. It's disconcerting if not frightening, and I'm tired of second-guessing my own imagination. I'm doing it with Freddie and I'm doing it with the house. It's as if either everything is wrong or nothing is wrong and my brain can't decide which, leaving me in limbo and going round and round in circles.

By midday I feel like the rooms are shrinking around me, and unable to bear the oppressiveness of my own thoughts any longer, I get my coat and keys and head out to the car. I'll go mad if I stay here alone all day. Freddie will be home on Thursday and I'll talk to him them, I decide. Have it out. Evidence or no evidence.

'They're quite something, aren't they?' Paul says with a smile, seeing me look up, aghast, at the stained-glass windows. The dull yellow lights in the church turn every crease in his face into a crevice, making him look almost threatening, as if he's a different person underneath, but even that is preferable to some of the images in the glass.

'I know I'm not an expert, but I thought stained church windows were supposed to depict saints doing good deeds?' There *are* some saints in the images, but they're surrounded by demons in reds and blues with pointed tails, sharp teeth, leering and grinning, aiming tridents at the naked figures of terrified humans trying to flee, running them into raging fires.

'Modern ones, maybe. But this church is hundreds of years old. And the fifteenth century was not kind to this part of the world. Plague. Smallpox. Famine.'

'Surely people would want comforting images while they prayed.'

'Want and need are different things. Good and evil live in us all, and those years of hardship and fear brought out the worst in people, including, sadly, a lot of those in the Church. They blamed all the misfortune on supernatural forces, and that created panic and hysteria. A fair number of men and women in this part of Devon were hanged or drowned as witches. People believed in demons, and so these pictures were designed to remind them of the punishments awaiting those who strayed from the path of good Christians.'

'No one ever thought to change them?'

'They're part of the nation's heritage now. The past teaches us about the present. And in the summer we get a lot of tourists coming through and popping a pound or two in the collection box to see them. How do you think we got the new roof?' He sits down on the front pew and pats for me to sit alongside. 'Now, what brings you out to me in this dreich day?'

'Well, Joe and Sally suggested we have a party to get to know some local people. I was going to invite the people I know, you, the Watkinses, and Mrs Tucker as well as a few London friends, but I wondered if there was anyone else who might be nice to meet? I don't mean in a useful way, just locals who are nice or are maybe on their own or lonely? Maybe four or five more people?' I hold up my little stack of cards. 'If you wouldn't mind?' I feel embarrassed, but Paul looks pleasantly surprised.

'Consider it done,' he says, taking them. 'But let's get into the vestry. I've got some hot chocolate in there and both bars of the fire on. Can't have you getting cold.'

I follow him through to the back of the church as he talks about a few neighbouring farmers I should invite, and despite the worry in the pit of my stomach about whatever Freddie may or may not have deleted from his phone, I feel slightly warmed to be becoming part of a small community.

Maybe we should stay here for longer. If Freddie's affair has been in London, suddenly I don't want to rush back there. But do I really want to stay in Larkin Lodge? It's not the kind of place I want to stay forever.

44.

Emily

By Wednesday it's minus four outside and the cold traps me in the house. Even though I can't see any ice, I haven't even been out to the woodstore for logs or coal for fear of slipping, instead keeping the house warm with the central heating and all the lights on to try to dispel the grey gloom. I still haven't been up to the second floor, and even though the house has been quiet I can't shake the foreboding that seems to come from within its walls, and I know I won't be able to until I've faced the primary suite again. Every time I tell myself I'll do it, I find an excuse or a reason to delay. The truth is that I don't want to go up there while I'm alone in the house. I'll wait until Freddie's back tomorrow.

It's his leaving drinks tonight, so I don't expect any texts from him—we've never been in each other's pockets—but as evening rolls around I can't help wondering what he's going to be doing and with whom. If she's someone he works with, even if he's ended it, will there be some last booze-induced moment?

I browse his Facebook looking for women from his work and evaluating them against myself. Women whose bodies didn't break and who didn't spend months in hospital. Fully functioning women. In the end, my head is throbbing so much that my suspicions burn themselves out in the pain. He'll be back tomorrow. I can talk to him them. Hopefully he will just be shocked and laugh at me. Maybe he deleted an email because it was sensitive information for work. Maybe he's not lying to me at all.

I cook fish and chips from the freezer but I can't find much enthusiasm to eat more than half, so I put the rest out the front in case of birds and wildlife who might want it. Maybe my raven will come for it. I haven't heard him for a day or so. I hope he does. The air is icy and I bolt the door closed and wish we had a cat or something so I didn't feel quite so alone and morose.

45.
Emily

The nightmares come for me again.

In the dream, Larkin Lodge is folding in around me like origami paper. I'm standing on the middle landing and the window there is a mouth, opening and closing, mist coming into the house like exhaled smoke.

In the gloom I hear a moan, and I look behind me through the bedroom door to see the vicar, Paul, sitting on the bed, the awful demons from the church windows clinging to him, their claws digging into the flesh of his cheeks, dragging his skin downward, his jowls tearing.

Good and evil live in us all, *he mutters at me.* Even in you, Emily. You did a bad thing. You tell yourself it wasn't your fault and you didn't have a choice, but there's always a choice. You did what you wanted. You always do what you want.

The claws reach his mouth and eyes, and as they start to tear him apart the bed bends in around him and he vanishes just before the whole room does. I'm left staring at a blank wall.

Need and want are different things, *a voice hisses and, as the window folds and vanishes, a light overhead comes on, the bulb swinging violently from side to side on the cable. I see Freddie then, crouched, crab-like on the wall leading up to the second floor. He's facing downward, head turned to look at me, as he scuttles backward, up into the gloom, his feet and hands clacking against the plaster.*

I told you not to touch the floor, *he hisses as he moves jerkily back a few more paces until only his head is visible in the blackness upstairs.* I told you.

My feet are suddenly cold, and I look down, shocked, to see the floorboards, all *with nails sticking out of them, snapping over each other,* clack-clacking *as they bend. Before I can move, they're over my feet, trapping me, and with each further fold, I drop suddenly a few inches, my legs disappearing. I'm being eaten up by the house.*

You'll never get out now, *Freddie says, with that awful dream grin that stretches his face wide.* Never, never, never. *As he disappears backward into the void of the second floor, the pressure around my legs increases and I start to scream, but my voice is a raven's caw, louder and louder, and I can understand what it's calling—*YOU WILL DIE HERE—*and then—*

I wake up with a start, the nightmare and reality blending as I can still hear the grating bark of my dream scream, and then I realize that there is a real live raven cawing loudly somewhere outside the bedroom window.

Downstairs, I check outside while the kettle is boiling, and even though my heart sinks at the sight of the damp, freezing mist that's clinging to every outside surface, heavy and ominous, there's no ice and the fish and chips left outside have all gone. I hope it was the raven who fed, cawing his thanks when he woke me. It's a small moment of joy in an unsettled morning.

I can't shake the nightmare, and in the quiet, the house once again feels strange and darker, and I'm constantly glancing this way and that, things shifting in the corners of my vision, like there are worms under the wallpaper, rippling and wriggling just below the surface. Every corner is filled with threatening shadows no matter how many lights I put on, and in the end I take my tea and toast into the sitting room and wish I had the coals to light a fire. I want the comforting crackle and the glow of the flames.

The only book I can read without going into the library is the Poe collection on the coffee table, and with a perverse curiosity to see if I can look at it without my imagination running away with me, I read 'The Murders in the Rue Morgue'. It's a heavy-going piece, for me at least, because I'm out of practice at reading anything but modern books, but I still feel a shiver when a body is found up the chimney and there are broken nails in windows. It all feels a little close to home, and I end up cheating and googling a summary before putting the TV on and filling the sitting room with the cheerful voices of morning chat shows.

Outside the mist refuses to shift, and I text Cat and Iso to say how much I'm looking forward to seeing them again at the weekend and not to worry about dressing up for the party. Iso can get quite *out there*, and I expect the locals will not be turning up in five-inch heels and skin-tight dresses. Neither of them answer, both busy at work, and once again I feel like I'm still somewhere in limbo between life and death out here in the Lodge by myself while everyone else is caught up in the cut and thrust of big-city industry.

In a sudden bout of self-pity I get a craving for crumpets and head back to the kitchen to top up my tea and toast. Maybe I'll find a comedy on Netflix. Have a sofa day. Sod even doing my physio. Anything but think about Freddie and missing emails and my own unreliable brain.

I'm in the downstairs hall, heading to the kitchen, when the smell hits. That same awful, rotten stench that choked me upstairs. I take two steps forward and it clears. Then I take two steps back and it returns. I go up two stairs and it thickens like the blanket of fog outside and my mouth dries, ready to gag. It's coming from upstairs. *Or is it? Maybe it only exists inside your post-sepsis brain, crazy Emily.*

I stand, wide-eyed like a rabbit, alert and unsure. Even if it is just in my head, that doesn't take the stink away. I'll burn some toast maybe. Get the posh coffee machine on. Then open the front door. Drown out the bad smell with other strong ones. Confuse my damaged brain. I have to stay sane. Focus on what's real. I'm about to turn away when I hear it.

A creak.

My heartbeat immediately picks up. Not a creak. This isn't the door upstairs opening and closing; this is something else. The sound comes again. It's a *tread*. A heavy foot on the stairs, and I feel the banister tremble under my fingers where I'm gripping it. Another footstep, and then another, closer together, *four, five, six,* and I stand back, alarmed. Something's coming down the stairs. With each tread, the noise is louder. I back away. Whatever it is—*whoever* it is—must be nearly on the middle landing by now, and the vibration that was coming through the banisters now shakes the walls of the house.

I hear the thud of unnatural footsteps closer overhead, threatening to come through the ceiling, and once again I'm sure the walls are closing in on me, the fronds in the awful flock wallpaper, rippling like ivy, ready to tear away from their place on the walls and wrap around me, trapping me here until whatever is coming down from the second-floor room reaches me and I'll die of fright at the sight of it.

As the thumping footsteps turn into a run above me—*thud thud thud*—racing for the last flight now, I can't take it anymore, and I grab my keys from the side table and yank the front door open before slamming it behind me and running, no longer caring about ice, into the enveloping mist.

46.

Emily

I'm not even sure where I'm running to. I stumble down the drive, my face burning despite the freezing mist that scalds my lungs as I gasp. When I glance back the fog is so thick the house is barely even visible, and for all I know the front door is wide open and whatever was coming down the stairs is about to reach out and grab me.

My leg screams at me to stop but I push onward, the white fire of panic fuelling my adrenaline, and I wonder if I can get to Paul's house before whatever or whoever it is catches me. I hurry down the lane, not caring about cars or even looking out for headlights, little half moans of fear escaping me as I manage some shambles of a run as far away as I can get from Larkin Lodge.

I barely see the figure coming the other way until I collide with him, and I let out a shriek of surprise, almost falling backward, my balance gone. I probably would have crumpled if he hadn't grabbed my arm and kept me upright.

'Woah there, you nearly gave me a heart attack.' It's a thick Devonian accent, and as my panic slows and he comes into focus I see a rough but concerned weather-hewn face looking back at me.

'Sorry, sorry,' I mutter, getting my breath back and taking him in. He's wearing a red fleece and hat and has a bag slung over his shoulder. A postman. 'I didn't see you.'

'Can't see a thing in this. Worst mist this mist. You need to take care on the lanes. I left the van at the last turn, otherwise I might have knocked you down.'

I apologize again, my heart slowing. I glance behind me but can see nothing. No monster. *But who knows*, my rebellious brain whispers. *Maybe it's waiting for you further back. You can't run forever.*

'Were you coming down to check the postbox?'

It takes a moment before my brain, still focused on what may or may not be chasing me through the fog, recognizes what he's said.

'What postbox?'

'You're the new woman at the Lodge, right?'

'Yes, Emily Bennett.'

'You've got a mailbox on the lane. Just twenty yards that way. I'm happy to come to the front door, of course, but your husband told me to put the post in there.'

'Oh, of course,' I say, breezily, as if I already know this. 'I forgot. So much going on in a house move.' Freddie never told me about the postbox. And why would be put himself out when the postman would easily deliver it to the house? I look down at the keys in my hand. 'I guess it's one of these keys to open it?'

My heart's thumping hard again, but this time with a very real-world fear. A truth in my gut that Freddie's hiding something from me. And I'm starting to think I might know what it is.

'That small one looks like it. Do you want me to walk you back? It's right against the wall just up there. Or are you going to carry on with your run?'

'No,' I say with a smile. 'No, you're right. It's probably not safe in this weather.'

'I'll keep putting it in the box then?' he asks. 'Like your husband said.'

'Yes. Thank you, yes,' I mutter, already walking back the way I came. 'That's great.'

I stand at the open postbox for a long time, staring down at the collection of letters there. I'm aware of the caw of a raven overhead, and then the answering cry of another, and while the breath is knocked out of me from what I'm seeing, a small part of my brain wonders if the raven I released from the house has found a new love.

Maybe I need to find a new love.

My heart is heavy as I head back to the only place I have to go, home to Larkin Lodge. There are lights on inside—lights I'm sure I didn't turn on—and now I can see it through the mist from the lane, guiding me back.

Oh, Freddie, I think, once I'm through the front door to find the smell vanished, the house warm, and no awful footsteps sending me running from the house. *Oh, Freddie, what have you done?*

It's only later, when my mug of tea is cold and I'm staring at the pieces of paper around me, all the evidence I need, that I realize that if the house hadn't terrified me so much that I ran out into the lane to collide with the postman, then I'd never know about the postbox and all of *this.*

Maybe the house wanted you to know. I curl up, hugging a cushion on the sofa, holding it protectively against my stomach. *Maybe it was protecting you.* There's no affirmation from the Lodge around me. The other alternative presents itself again— that maybe it's all in my head—and this time it makes more sense. Maybe Freddie mentioned the postbox to me ages ago and I forgot. Maybe my subconscious drove me out of the house to find my answers. Right now, I don't even care *how* I found out. I lie there, staring at the walls, waiting for Freddie to come home.

47.

Emily

I wait for him in the sitting room, choosing the wingback chair in the corner that's always been more for decoration than use. All I can think is, *How could you, Freddie, how could you?* I haven't lit the fire, and with only one lamp on, I'm sitting in the shadows, barely visible, as if I'm a ghost myself. I can hear my heartbeat. The tick of the clock. I don't look at the walls. I don't want to see the grey lines on the blue flock wallpaper pulsing like veins. I don't want to see anything *ripple* in the corner of my eye. When I've dealt with this I will damn well go up to the second floor and put the *find it* to rest once and for all. I can't think about the ethereal right now. The physical world—and my husband—are what's screwing me over.

'Emily?'

The noise of the front door and a gust of cold air heralds Freddie's arrival, and my stomach instantly tightens with nerves. I've never been good with confrontation. The last time we had any kind of major row was nearly twenty years ago, and it was the same row we're about to have again. The same subject matter, the same lies, the same weakness.

'Sorry I'm late.' He appears in the doorway and my mouth dries. He looks so normal. As if he hasn't been lying to me since I woke up in that hospital. As if everything is fine. 'Traffic was shit.' He frowns, spotting me in the corner. His eyes narrow, the first hint that he's realizing something is wrong. 'Don't you want the lights on?' He doesn't wait for an answer before flicking the switch, flooding the room with brightness.

'What's this?' He comes forward, staring not at me but at the coffee table and the few pieces of paper laid out on it.

'You promised never again,' I say, eventually, as he picks up the final demand and the overdue credit card payment letters that I found in the postbox. 'After uni. After you nearly destroyed us. And this is worse than that time, isn't it? One of those credit cards is in my name, Freddie.' The heat of my anger and disappointment and *hurt* burns into my face and tears fill my eyes, threatening to spill. 'I knew you were keeping something from me. When I walked in on you in the bathroom when the others were here. You were on a gambling site, weren't you?'

He slumps onto the sofa while I sit in the chair, my back ramrod straight, the stronger one despite everything I've been through.

'Oh god, I'm so sorry.' He lowers his head into his hands. 'I'm so sorry.'

'How bad is it?' My voice is sharp. I know it's bad. The final demands show that it's bad. But still I've been clinging to some joke of a hope that we're not completely ruined.

'I wanted to get the money back so you'd never know. But it just got worse.'

'How bad, Freddie?' I repeat, my stomach churning so much it sends bile burning up my throat. He shrugs, not wanting to answer. Oh god, can it be worse this time? The last time he gambled away his entire inheritance from his parents and was working his way through our savings when he finally confessed. I'd told him ever since we'd been together that I hated his love of gambling, but he'd always told me it was just a casual thing, like men who go out and get pissed once a month or whatever, but he did it with cards or racing. Until his parents died. Then I realized the hobby went *way* deeper and was an addiction. An every day thing. A secret thing.

'I told you I'd leave you if you ever did this again.'

'I know. I know. And I'm so ashamed.' He looks up at me, hopeless and forlorn. 'It's a disease, Emily. You know that.'

'That's what you're going with? That's supposed to make it okay?' I want to punch him in the face. 'Yes, it's a disease. But there are doctors for it. You go back to Gamblers Anonymous. You talk to someone. You don't gamble away all our money.'

'I thought you were going to die.' His eyes fill with tears. So that's his excuse. Poor, hapless Freddie. I used to think he was sweet but actually he's just weak. More fool me.

'Everyone thought you were going to die. It broke me. I couldn't imagine life without you.' He sniffs, loud and snotty. 'At first it was just once. Just once, and then I didn't do it for ages. I hated myself for it. Then when you got the sepsis and were in the coma—I—well, it all went to shit. It was worse. Way worse than before.'

'How could it be worse than before?' I feel sick. 'Just tell me, Freddie.'

'It wasn't just the apps.' He takes a deep, shaky breath. 'Before the holiday, the guys from work, they'd been to some late-night unlicensed drinking den after a dinner. I hadn't gone with them, because I hate that drinks and strip club shit they do, you know that.' His words are coming out fast, as if now that he's been caught, it's a splurge of a confession. He wipes his nose with the back of his hand as he continues. 'But the next day they said they'd gone to some poker night thing in a place in Denman Street, and obviously I was doubly glad I hadn't been, and honest to god, Emily, I didn't think about it again. Not for a long time.'

'But then you did.' I take a sip from the wine beside me, but it tastes sour. How could he do this to us? To me? Suddenly I feel better about my own guilty secret. At least I only did it once and it didn't wipe out our savings.

'Not until after your accident. I was trying to hold it together, working even though you were getting worse and worse and . . . and I could see in the doctors' faces that nothing was positive. It was like one minute there was you and me, and then the next you're nearly dead and the doctors are telling me you'd been pregnant and everything I'd wanted had been so close to reality but had been snatched away. Like a 'here's what you could have won' moment. Everyone thought you were going to die. I thought you were going to die. One day after work I couldn't face going home, so I went out on my own and got drunk. I don't know how I found the place, to be honest. The addict part of my brain must have taken me close to the street and then, well, there I was. Denman Street.' He looks at me and pauses as if this is enough explanation, but it isn't *nearly* enough.

'And? That was it? You were straight back down the bookies and in the apps?'

'No. Worse than that. It was like I'd pushed a self-destruct button. I was going to the card game most nights. Started off small. But every time your situation got worse I would gamble harder. Bigger. I ended up owing money—a lot of money—to some people. Not the sort of people you ever want to owe money to.'

'Jesus, Freddie.' I don't know what I was expecting, but it wasn't this. For me, the coma was an empty sleep that lasted both a second and an eternity, but so much was happening while I was in the void. 'How much did you owe them?'

'A lot.' He's shrinking into the sofa, becoming smaller in front of me. I'd thought he was glued to my bedside, holding my hand for weeks, but no, he was off getting himself in a huge mess. Did he think of me at all, or was he totally preoccupied with how to save his own skin?

'Oh god.' Suddenly it dawns on me. Everything falls into place. The enormity of his lies. 'When you said we should sell the flat to move here, that wasn't about me at all, was it? You used the profits from the flat to pay off your debts to these gangsters, didn't you?'

He says nothing for a long moment. 'I'm so sorry, Emily. It was the only way. I was going to meetings by then—I hadn't gone to any games, not since they threatened me, but I was on the apps. I convinced myself I could win enough back to then have the one big win. To get everything back before you realized there had been anything wrong.'

'Are you fucking insane?' The swear word comes out of me like a bullet and it stuns Freddie into silence. I don't swear much, it's never been my thing, but my rage formed it like a weapon in my mouth. 'When has that ever worked for anyone? How much of a cliché are you? Like a character from some shit British crime straight-to-DVD film?' I reach forward and grab some of the final demands, holding them up in his face. 'Clearly your plan didn't work. You've got thousands of pounds of credit card debt here, according to some of these letters. All from after the move. Is there any money left? Anything?' I sit back in my chair, the truth of it finally hitting home. We're broke. We've got nothing. If there was any money he'd have paid off the cards.

'Only whatever you have.'

'Why did you let me get the people around about the garden?' I'm beyond anger and into exasperation. 'That's twenty-five thousand pounds of gardening work I've just said yes to.'

'I thought—I hoped—I just . . .' His mouth opens and closes like a drowning fish. There's nothing he can say. He hoped it would just go away. That some miracle would come along.

'I thought you were dying,' he says again, as if this explains everything, all his weakness. 'After that last time, I never thought I'd ever gamble again. I thought I was past it. I thought one or two card games wouldn't matter.'

'It was me who was in hospital, Freddie. It was me who nearly died. And now that somehow makes it my fault that you couldn't stop yourself from gambling away all our equity?' I stare at him as he cries.

'You know, I keep thinking about what Russell said that Christmas night about how we're never with the people we fell in love with. I thought you were so sweet and kind when we met. It was refreshing that you weren't trying to be alpha all the time. But now I see that was just hiding how weak you are at heart. It's why you wanted a traditional marriage with a wife at home with the children, so you'd always have someone to need you. But it's why you've never been promoted too far. Why do you think I wanted *my* promotion so badly, Freddie? Because one of us had to succeed. It wasn't just for me; I wanted it for us.' I say it so convincingly I almost believe it, and maybe it's in part true, but I wanted it mainly for me. That doesn't change his weakness though.

'You just had to be strong this *once* for me. But you weren't. And then you lied. Acted like everything was normal. If you couldn't be strong, you needed to be honest. And you weren't that either.'

'I was so glad you were going to be okay. I couldn't tell you. I couldn't. I was so afraid you'd leave me. Or the shock would make you sick again. I love you so much. I was so scared. I didn't want to lose *us*, Emily.'

I can't help but half laugh, shocked and heartbroken at everything I've heard. 'Us?' I finally say. 'Oh, Freddie. I'm not sure there can be an *us* after this.'

48.

Freddie

We talk until late, a second bottle of wine opened as I beg forgiveness and we both cry. I hold onto her tightly when she lets me, as if I'm drowning and she's keeping me afloat, and she veers between anger and heartache, but I can tell she's starting to relent. There's nothing Emily likes better than having the moral higher ground, and she's not going to let that go quickly. She can talk about how she misread me when we met, but that goes both ways. I thought she was the most forgiving person I'd ever met, but she's not. She stores it all up like weapons while acting like Mother Teresa. She'd lose her shit completely if she knew that I'd been gambling a couple of weeks before the holiday. That in fact it started again that first night out from work.

Do we still love each other? Are we a habit? Is it a tired mixture of both? She's not the only one who wonders, and she still hasn't told me why she was so weird before her accident. Maybe I'm not the only one who had a secret.

She hasn't mentioned divorce yet. Our marriage still has a chance. There can still be an us. When we finally head up to bed, sometime around two, I go to the spare bedroom. She doesn't tell me to come back but instead says, 'Maybe it's for the best. Just until I get my head around all this.'

Her eyes slip away from me like she's a coy victim, and when I feel that draught coiling once again around my ankles as we say goodnight, I feel the first hint of annoyance at her. I close the spare bedroom door, shivering, and stand by the radiator for a few moments. It's still hot, the thermostat only turned down moments before, but the warmth is swallowed up by the icy breeze cutting through the gaps in the windows and the old floorboards.

The bed creaks, complaining about having company, and under the thin duvet I suddenly feel like a child again, sleeping over at my grandmother's house, in the cold loft room that she converted for her grandchildren but never bothered to make feel lived in. A room that was happy being left to itself. I have that same feeling here, where the shadows are different from those I'm used to, and the heavy blue walls could be night itself crowding round me.

It's cold as night in here too, the draught wheedling through the mattress under me, and I pull the duvet tighter. I want to go and turn the heating back on but I daren't with Emily now knowing how much debt we have. As if a few quid keeping the house warm is going to make any difference.

Downstairs, I was distraught at the thought of her leaving me, at the possible end of our marriage, consumed by how much I *need* her, but now that I'm up here and alone, I'm getting more and more irritated at being painted as such a terrible human being. There were so many *How could you lie to me like that?* And *You should have been honest with me's*, as if she'd never done anything wrong in her life. She *knows* gambling is an addiction. A disease. She knows it isn't easy to stop. Why couldn't she see that I only kept going because I was afraid of losing her? It was love. I thought she was dying and I went into self-destruct. I didn't lie to her anyway; I just didn't tell the truth. I was *protecting* her. She doesn't know how difficult it was for me during those months. She wasn't even awake. But still, I'm the big disappointment.

The curtain flutters, like the rustle of a panicking bird's wings, sending shadows and shards of moonlight in a kaleidoscope pattern across the room, more evidence of the breeze Emily insists doesn't exist, and I sink deeper beneath the covers. It's almost a joy to have a whole bed to myself again. It took ages to get used to sleeping alone while she was in hospital, but then, quietly and guiltily, I began to love it. It's been odd having to share the space again. That's what Emily doesn't get. Her accident and coma have been hard for me too. I've been the one on the outside.

I'm drifting into an emotionally exhausted and wine-drowned sleep when a creaking tread on floorboards drags me out of my doze. I listen blearily. The creak comes again. And then again. Footsteps. Is that the stairs? I have a moment of panic that maybe the people I still owe money to—the sort who don't send polite letters in the post and who I've told Emily I'm clear of when in fact there's ten grand outstanding—have come down to Devon to break my kneecaps, but realize it must be Emily. What is she doing up at this time?

I half sit up and frown. Has she been upstairs? It definitely sounds like she's coming down from upstairs. The steps are even and surprisingly heavy. I've got used to Emily's feet being out of time as she limps, dragging her bad leg carefully behind her, but this doesn't sound like that. There's a pause and then the footsteps come closer. *Too heavy for Emily*, I think as my heart starts to race. Could it be a burglar? The space between treads feels almost too long as they get louder and closer. *Unnatural.*

The curtains tremble once more, and I peer through the shards of moonlight to stare at the closed door. The footsteps are getting closer. It has to be Emily. It has to. No burglar would make so much noise, surely?

167

Finally, the feet come to a stop outside my room, and the last step is so impossibly heavy I'm sure it makes the bed tremble. I wait, my breath held, the air around me cold from the draught but my skin burning with an irrational fear, but there's only silence. The pause goes on for so long that I'm starting to question whether I heard anything at all or if it was just a hangover dream, when suddenly the round handle starts to turn. I stare in horror as it twists slowly one way and then back again before falling still. The door doesn't open. No one comes in. But I can feel in every fibre of my being that there is a presence on the other side watching me through the wood. I let out a small moan and the noise adds to my fear as my mouth dries and my palms clench. I'm sure I'm going to have a heart attack, this burst of terror the final straw after months of stress and debt.

I don't know for how long I sit there staring at the door, but eventually I get pins and needles and so I prop the pillow so that I can lie down and still watch it, but the handle doesn't turn again and there are no more footsteps. Eventually, my eyes drift shut and I'm half-convinced after so much silence that it was all my imagination. Or Emily. It must have been Emily. Maybe she was going to come in. To make up properly. Get us back to us.

I remember how strange the footsteps sounded. Maybe she won't even remember she was up. Maybe she's going mad. All those things she's imagining. What she did with those books. I sink deeper into sleep as cool air settles on my face. My last thought is a gossamer thread of sticky webbing in my subconscious.

Maybe it wouldn't be such a bad thing if she did go mad. It might help me.

Maybe, in fact, I'd quite like it.

Us

49.

Emily

The hubbub downstairs fades as I grip the banister and climb the steep flight of stairs to the second floor, breathing shallow in case of the awful smell, but there's nothing but warm dust. I've waited until the party's fully started and the guests are mingling, Freddie in full host mode, before going up to finally finish my search of the house. There is safety in numbers, and Cat is still getting ready in their room on the middle floor, so it's now or never. If I don't find anything, then I can put this madness out of my head and focus on the very real predicament Freddie and I are in and what I'm going to do about it.

The landing is quiet, and despite my heart beating faster than normal, I'm pleased I'm not panicking or filled with dread. I'm a grown-up. I can do this. The double bedroom just has a bed in it and Iso and Mark's overnight stuff, and no built-in cupboards, but I do a circuit, scanning the walls and floor, but there's no spaces where something could be hidden. The same goes for the bathroom, and after checking the storage cupboards, I'm left with only the primary suite to check.

My palm sweats slightly as I grip the handle, but I take a deep breath and push the door open. I brace myself, expecting the awful onslaught of horrific dread I felt last time, but there's nothing, just quiet, no strangeness at all, and when I flick on the light, it's just a large, empty, beautiful room, the glorious feature window at the other end. It is innocuous. Normal. I look down at the floorboards and there's no sign of the scratching I'd been so sure I heard.

I'd still happily turn and rush down the stairs, but I've come this far, so I wedge the door open and hesitantly go further inside. I'm half expecting the door to suddenly slam shut and trap me in here forever, so I hurry across to the bathroom and quickly search it before going to the dressing area at the other side. The longer I'm up here, far away from everyone else, the tenser I get. The sudden normality is unsettling me as if it's a mirage.

The quicker I move, searching the drawers and cupboard spaces, the closer my panic comes to the surface. And then I hear it. The creak of floorboards in the bedroom. Footsteps coming closer. Eyes wide, I press myself back against the cupboard, sure that I'm going to have a heart attack—*you will die here*—my breath coming in gasps, and then I hear—

'Emily?'

Relief floods through me and I let out a mildly hysterical half laugh. Joe. It's Joe. That's all. I come out of the walk-in closet, my face red.

'You scared the shit out of me.'

'I wondered where you were.' He's casually dressed in jeans and a shirt, but as ever, he looks great. There's something of Jeremy Irons in his heyday about him. 'You can't hide at your own party. What are you doing up here?'

'Just taking a moment.' I don't have any valid reason, and that's the best I can think of. 'You know how it is.'

'Shame it's so dark.' He's at the window. 'Strange being back after so long. I'd forgotten how good the view is. Quite stunning. Isolating but stunning. Don't you think?'

'I haven't seen it. The stairs are tricky with my leg.' Right now, all I can see is mist and darkness. 'I'll come back up in daylight.'

He leans on the windowsill and turns his attention to me. 'You don't have to answer and can tell me to mind my own business, but is everything all right with you and Freddie?'

'Why do you ask?' Our closest friends haven't noticed that maybe we're having problems so I'm surprised Joe's picked up on it.

'You're up here when the party's downstairs, for one thing.'

'Oh that. I just . . .' I blush slightly. 'If you must know, I was dispelling the last of my ghosts. This is where I heard the strange noises coming from. The horrible smell. I wanted to come up and check it out for myself, and I figured when there was a houseful of people was the best time.'

'Your ghost was in here?' He looks around the room, thoughtful, alert, as if maybe he does believe in the super-natural a little after all. 'I can't sense anything.'

'Me neither, now. It's fine. Obviously was just my mind playing tricks on me.'

'Maybe we should get back downstairs, just in case. Don't want to invade their space.'

I go first, and he pushes the doorstop away, turning the light out and shutting the room up again, and after he looks back at the primary suite door for a moment, I can feel him watching as I hobble slowly and carefully back down the stairs.

'I really would like to paint you, Emily. Such beauty in the face of adversity.'

Happier now that I'm on the middle landing, I laugh. 'I don't think Freddie would be too keen. Your art is amazing, but it's very intimate.' Remembering how shocked Freddie was when faced with the first canvas in the cottage, I have a pang of affection for him despite all the shit we're in.

'I'd paint you in a silk dressing gown, your leg stretched out, the rest of you relaxed in a chair. All the curves and none of the nudity. How about that? The sexuality you'll have to allow me. Although you're perfectly safe. I won't try to sleep with you. I don't have sex with all my models, whatever the gossips say. Of course, if you wanted to I wouldn't stop you either.'

Everything about Joe should be creepy, but instead he makes my heart beat faster, the upstairs room totally forgotten. He makes me feel like a woman. A living breathing woman who is raw and real and perfect *for* her flaws rather than despite them.

'But come on, we should get back to the party. I can feel the pool table calling me.' He matches my pace on the way back to the melee below, and I turn off the upstairs lights before pausing to say hello to Mrs Tucker, and Joe disappears down the corridor. I like his calmness. It's infectious. I feel better for having finished my search. I didn't find anything. There was nothing to find.

The party seems to be going well. In the library Mark is giving financial advice to Ron Cave and his wife, Elsa, the farming family who own most of the nearby land on one side of us, while Alex and Dom, a younger couple who are very involved in the parish activities, listen, wide-eyed. I know how they feel. When Mark starts talking about his work to me, he might as well be speaking Japanese.

In the sitting room Russell is cross-legged on the floor in the corner laughing with the Watkinses on the sofa, and it's good to see them all chatting so animatedly. Turns out Merrily's sister is head teacher at the local secondary school and Merrily used to teach part time at Exeter College, so they're sharing amusing horror stories of rabid teenagers and school politics.

Over by the fire, Freddie, my poor woeful Freddie, is with the vicar and Cat, and I think despite having religion in common with the vicar, Cat is a bit bored because she keeps looking to the door, maybe wondering where Iso's wandered off to. She's not making any move to come and talk to me, but I don't mind.

It's hard pretending everything is fine, and I think Cat is the most likely to see through my veneer. Iso never looks beneath the surface of people really. She's very busy *being* Iso, but Cat has always been more interested in others. It's the quality that makes her such a good teacher. When she asks *How are you?* she's not looking for a cursory answer. And if she gets one, she'll dig deeper.

Looking at Freddie, I'm not sure how I feel. I'm shell-shocked. All our equity gone. We're running on empty, and he still has some debts to clear. I love him, I'm sure I do, but I wish I could respect him more. He's always been prone to weakness under pressure. He's always been prone to weakness full stop. It's the part of him I've always ignored—the part of him that makes him agree with other people's opinions because he'd rather not say what he actually thinks, and I let him call it diplomacy rather than an inability to stand his ground. The part of him that lied to me rather than tell me what's really been going on. The part of him that blames my accident for his weakness. I feel so conflicted. How can you love someone but not like them very much all at once?

The thought makes me feel bad because it's not as if I don't have my own secrets and shame. He's been truly apologetic and stayed out of my way yesterday, popping into the Exeter office to give me some thinking time. If everything I'm experiencing here is coming from my post-sepsis syndrome, then I'm amazed the house didn't fall down around my ears. It stayed standing and silent and most of the time I just stared out of the window, watching two ravens whirling around in the sky over the moors. I like to think it was my raven. I like to think he's found a new love.

Maybe I should find a new love. Freddie looks over at me and smiles, all hangdog and adorable. Someone like him but who isn't so weak. Maybe I should leave him. There was a part of me that was thinking that before the holiday. The part of me who had cheated and wanted the promotion and wasn't sure I wanted to be a stay-at-home mum to a baby I could only be sure was mine, not Freddie's.

I touch my stomach, a new hope maybe growing there, and pick up my glass, heading toward the kitchen, where I tip out my wine while no one's looking and get a glass of tonic water and add a slice of lemon. I can't make any decision about Freddie yet. Not until I know. My period was due yesterday but so far there's no sign. A day late doesn't mean anything in and of itself, but I can't shake this tiny feeling, a small certainty that something's changed inside. I'm becoming *two* again. And this child would definitely be part Freddie too. Could I manage as a single mum? Would I want to? And could I do that to Freddie? Keep him from being a proper dad? It's what he's wanted all his adult life. It could be the making of him. Of us.

I head back toward the sitting room, but as I pass by I notice that the upstairs hallway light is on again. There's someone on the middle landing, their shadow casting long down the wooden stairs.

'Hello?'

I take a couple of steps up, then pause. It's Sally, her back to me, facing the landing window. She's standing so perfectly still that I wonder for a moment if she's on the cusp of some kind of medical event. 'Sally?' I go up one more. 'Are you okay?' She doesn't answer. I keep climbing, my good right leg doing all the work, and even with the sound of my approach, she doesn't look my way.

'Sally?' I repeat as I reach her, and finally she startles and turns to me, eyes wide and confused, one hand fluttering up to her throat.

'God, I was lost in my own world, sorry. I think I'm getting another migraine.' She looks back to the window even though

176

there's nothing but darkness and mist outside. She does look pale though.

'I've got loads of painkillers downstairs,' I say. 'A smorgasbord of them, in fact.'

'Ah, great.' She smiles, that vague expression fading. 'And sorry. Maybe it's a hangover from the last one. They can be like that.'

I nod at her to take the stairs first, and as I'm going to follow, I see her glance backward. An odd look. Wary. A look she doesn't want me to see. I glance to where she was looking. The landing floor. As I follow her down, I know exactly the spot.

It's where the nail had been sticking out.

50.

Emily

'Sally.'

Merrily Watkins comes in to refill her wine glass—her flushed face, red jumper, and burgundy wine clashing and yet making her a portrait of earthy joy—as I'm getting Sally some painkillers and a glass of water. 'You're looking well.'

'I wish I felt it. Awful headache.'

Laughter comes from the hallway, followed by Joe and Iso tumbling into the kitchen, Iso leaning her head against his arm, before they high-five each other.

'We beat Freddie and the vicar three times. Shots for shots,' she says, breathless. 'They have had to drink a lot.'

'We didn't beat them, we annihilated them.' Joe grins at Iso. 'You don't look like a pool shark, but you have the moves.'

'All that wasted time at university had to pay off somehow, right, Em?'

'I guess so.'

Iso's glowing, her eyes sparkling, in a much better mood than when she arrived, and I'm sure her flush is as much about Joe as it is from wine, and when he winks at her I have a sudden tiny twinge of surprising envy.

'I'm not feeling so great.' Sally puts the glass on the side. 'I think I'm going to head home. Do you mind? Sure you can get a lift back from someone.'

'Hey.' Joe's immediately all concern as he comes closer and studies her face. 'You do look pale. Come on, I'll get our coats.'

'You stay and have some fun.'

'No arguments.' He kisses her forehead. 'I'm taking you home.' He looks at me. 'It's been great, Emily. Thanks for having us.'

I help them with their coats and see them to the front door, wondering if Sally will glance upward as we go past the stairs, but she doesn't, instead leaning into her husband, as if she's suddenly exhausted. There's something so touching about it. They may have an unusual relationship, but the love between them is clear.

I stay in the doorway to wave them off, and I'm sure I hear her mutter something about how strange she feels, or how strange it was to be in the house, or maybe something akin to both.

They're getting in the car when Merrily joins me, holding out a mug. 'I saw you weren't drinking,' she says. 'Thought you might like a cuppa.'

'That's so kind. Thank you.'

She lights a cigarette and I hug the warm mug and we watch as Sally and Joe drive away.

'Me and her were best friends when we were young. For a bit. Hard to believe, looking at us now. And it's hard to believe that those two are still together, with the way she was at the start. I've heard of mellowing with age,' Merrily says, exhaling smoke and misty breath, 'but she'd have had your pretty friend's eyes out just for looking at Joe back then.'

'Sally?' I'm surprised. 'But she's so chill about the girls he paints.'

'She might be now. She pretended to be, sure. She *wanted* to be. And maybe at first, when he was adoring her, she was cool. But she was too naturally insecure. And it's not like he was promising monogamy. Love, maybe. I think he did—and does—emotionally faithfully love her. But sex? You've seen him. That's like breathing to men like Joe. Sally couldn't deal with it. God, she would lose her shit. Get jealous of every woman he spoke to.'

'That bad?' I ask. After finding her upstairs I want to know everything there is to know about Sally.

'She even got jealous of me once.' She snorts a laugh. 'Mad as a hatter. I could never talk her down. Got fed up of trying. It got to the point where women stopped talking to him and he stopped talking to them, around her at any rate. And then there was that lovely Georgina Usher.' She leans against the wall of the house and sniffs in the cold. 'Sally drove her out of town completely. She just up and vanished one night. She was an artist. Taught in the school part time. Very different from Sally. Sally back then anyway. Very sixties. Wild. Free. Dark eyes, dark hair.'

It's freezing outside, but I don't care, absorbed in this glimpse into the past. 'Was she close with Joe, this Georgina?'

'Georgina had been to a couple of the art classes Joe ran here at Larkin Lodge, but as far as I know, nothing more. But that was enough for Sally. She was convinced they were doing *something* or that Georgina was trying to seduce Joe. I know she threatened her at the school. And then she told whoever would listen that Georgina slept with married men and danced naked in a bar in town on weekends. Ridiculous accusations, but the intent was to cause just enough gossip to get her sacked. When none of that worked to get rid of her, Sally saw her in the off-licence in the village buying beer and was convinced it was for Joe. For some clandestine meeting. I'm pretty sure Sally had taken to following her by then. Our friendship was pretty much over because it was all she talked about, and Pete and me were getting serious. I remember Sally looked terrible by that point. Thinner than ever. Not sleeping. It was eating her up.'

'What happened?' I hear a scuttering sound overhead, birds in the eaves, maybe as impatient as me to hear the rest of the story.

'She walked straight into the shop. Took the beer bottles out of Georgina's hands, put them back on the shelf, and said very calmly and coolly—in front of Peter Lamb, the shopkeeper—that if Georgina didn't leave Joe alone she'd slit her throat.'

'Wow.' I stare at Merrily. 'That's quite something.'

'Yes, it is. But that was enough for Georgina. No one saw her again. She dropped in to say goodbye to Joe—and probably tell him to get rid of his crazy girlfriend—and that was that.'

'Did she move to Taunton to be closer to the school?'

'Oh, they never saw her again either.' She stubs her cigarette out on the gravel and pockets the butt. 'Vanished in the night. I thought that fiasco would be the end of Sally and Joe—because who'd stay with her after that?—and I wasn't the only one who thought it would be the best thing for both of them. I think Sally's mum was ready to pack her off to her aunt over in New Zealand to start afresh, she was so worried about her. But we were all wrong. Within two weeks they were engaged, and maybe he got her some professional help because she stopped with all that jealousy stuff as far as I could tell. Never showed it again, that's for sure. I guess they figured their shit out. But I never wanted to be friends with her again. Leopards and spots.' She looks at me, wry. 'She'll always be crazy Sally Freemantle to me.'

She turns to go inside, but I don't follow her. My head is a whir as I watch the mist spilling over the wall, a tide creeping in to drown the house in the night.

Vanished in the night. Last seen in this house. Did Sally kill her? Did she kill her in this house?

Don't do it, I tell myself. *Don't go back down that path. The room upstairs is fine. There is no ghost. You've got bigger problems.*

And I almost do it, I almost put it right out of my head, but then a thought strikes me and it makes me catch my breath.

Sally Freemantle. That's what Merrily called her. Not Sally Carter. She used Sally's maiden name.

F R E E M. The writing in the mirror steam. It wasn't *Free me* at all. It was *Freemantle.* That's what the haunting was trying to spell on the bathroom mirror. The name of their killer.

51.

Emily

My head is in a whirl. Could Sally really have murdered her rival, right here in this house? Maybe that's what calmed her down. Maybe the trauma of what she'd done changed her? And what about Joe? Did he help her cover it up? Move the body?

The party has thinned right out, only Paul the vicar and our friends left, and we're all in the pool room. Paul's in close conversation with Freddie, who's now got a scarf around his neck. There's a fire blazing, so I don't know how he can be cold when Cat and Iso are both in thin tops and are fine. This house. This strange house.

'You all right, Emily?' Paul's broken away from Freddie and come to join me on the small sofa. 'You're lost in thought. Something serious by the looks of it.'

'Not that serious. Not really.' I play it down, but I'm also curious to see what the vicar knows about this missing woman. He's lived here long enough to remember it, surely. 'It was something Merrily was telling me about. A woman who went missing years ago. Last seen coming to this house, back when Joe and Sally lived here. Just was weird.'

'I don't remember anything about a missing woman. Are you thinking about your haunting?' He leans in closer. 'Who was the woman?'

ng artist called Georgina Usher.'

ee.' He looks down at his feet. 'And you think she's
.unting the Lodge?'

'Maybe she had an accident here. Maybe it's her vibrations I'm feeling.'

There's a long pause and then he talks, slowly and carefully. 'If there'd been an accident, then the police or an ambulance would have come.'

There's something in his tone, as if he's testing me. I sit up straighter and look at him. Maybe he's had his suspicions over the years. Maybe I'm the first person to say something out loud.

'Only if the people living here reported it.' I don't use the word *murder*. And I don't lay any accusations at anyone's door, even if it's all there in the subtext. The vicar looks at me for a long moment and I know he's picked up on exactly what I mean. I'm so sure of it, I almost don't hear what he says next.

'Emily.' He places a gentle hand on my arm. 'Georgina Usher isn't dead.'

I stare at him. 'What do you mean? Merrily said she vanished. Never seen again.'

'Never seen *back here* again.' He pulls his phone out and goes to Google. 'She's a famous artist now. She lives in America. I go into that school she used to work at when the kids are getting ready for confirmation. Even though she quit without notice they've named their art department after her. And they have prints of her work everywhere.'

He passes me his phone. 'Look.'

I stare at the dark-haired woman and the gallery wall of paintings behind her and then scan the text. I'm not really reading, my brain on fire and my face flushing. Everything he's saying is true. This is her. There can't be two Georgina Ushers with so much similarity in their past and of the right age. I've made such a fool of myself.

'Did Merrily say she'd died?' Paul asks gently. I know that tone of voice. Careful. Worried.

'No. I just—I just presumed.'

'Maybe you should let this idea of a ghost go.' He looks at me like I'm a child who's done something stupid. 'It's an old house, Emily. Old houses make noises. Their pipes and drains can smell. It's easy to get lost in your imagination about those things, and being out here on the moors probably doesn't help, but no one died in this house. There isn't a ghost.'

'I know that.' My voice is quiet. 'I'm so sorry. I just—I just got carried away for a moment. Please, please forget I said anything.'

I hurry out of the room, the heat stifling, and combined with my embarrassment, my chest is tight and I find it hard to breathe.

I go upstairs to the bathroom and lock the door, sitting on the side of the bath and taking deep breaths. He must think I'm crazy. God, what an idiot. How can I face any of them again?

When I come downstairs Paul is saying his goodbyes and he gives me a hug as if nothing has happened, but I feel a careful resistance there and I don't blame him.

As Cat pulls me away to put some music on, I want the house to swallow me whole.

52.

Emily

I smile and laugh and watch as Iso and Cat dance, Iso still necking wine, her dancing becoming dangerously close to falling, while feeling completely lost in a bubble of my own. Time drags on, and even though I want to go and hide under the duvet and block everything out, I force myself to stay up for another hour before sneaking upstairs, feeling awful. I'm hoping for some time to myself, but within minutes Freddie is dropping his clothes on the floor and stumbling into bed with me, the wreckage of the party waiting until morning.

'I'm so sorry about everything, Em,' he mumbles, pulling me close. I don't have the energy to push him away or remind him that he'd be in the spare room if we weren't hiding our problems from our friends. 'I really am,' he continues. 'I hate myself for it. I'm sorry I lied. I'll be better. I'll sort it out. I promise. I love you. I do. I really do.'

As he slides into a heavy sleep, his weight uncomfortably draped over me, I want to cry. Everything's crumbling around me. How has my life come to this? Surrounded by debt from my weak husband and losing my mind.

I lie there, listening as the others traipse to the bathroom, and then Mark's annoyed mutterings as he virtually carries Iso up to the second floor, and then finally the house falls quiet.

I stare into the dark as Freddie grunts and snores and moves about in his sleep, and by three a.m. I give up trying to get any rest of my own and quietly get my notebook from the side table drawer and creep out to the bathroom.

With the book balanced on my knee, my writing's a spidery scrawl as I splurge my anxiety and upset onto the page, under the light of my phone's torch. This is less a record of ghostly hauntings and more a reflection of my own mental instability.

There is nothing happening in the house. It's all in my mind. Hallucinations. Sally hasn't done anything. What is wrong with me? I'm fixated by a ghost that all evidence proves doesn't exist.

I've made myself look really stupid—and mentally unstable—in front of the vicar. I should call Dr Canning, I know I should. But I can't face going back into hospital. I just can't. I have to learn to ignore all this until it stops. I can't cope with it on top of everything going on in the 'real' world. *God*, I write, and underline it. *Maybe it would have been better if I'd just died?*

It's melodramatic and I don't mean it. I'm in no rush to die again. All that nothingness terrifies me. The nonexistence of it all.

The toilet seat lid is cold and uncomfortable and I'm calmer after getting my shame down on the page. Not happier but at least calmer. There's nothing I can do about it except try to talk to Paul next week. He'll understand, I'm sure of it. Everyone can be prone to flights of fancy, and given my extenuating circumstances and his Christian nature, we'll be laughing about it all by next weekend. It's not like I explicitly accused anyone of anything, and it's basically his *job* to forgive me.

I'm suddenly tired, hopefully now able to get to sleep, and turn off the phone torch. Before I reach for the bathroom handle to unlock it, it quietly clicks by itself and opens a few inches.

I freeze, staring at it, the cold draught around my ankles only part of the chill I'm suddenly feeling. I take a deep breath. I couldn't have locked it properly and the draught has pushed it open. That's all.

I reach forward to pull it open some more so I can leave, but the door, only a few inches wide, refuses to budge. I yank harder, but nothing gives, an invisible force holding it solidly, unmoving, from the other side. I stand back, confused. Is it me again? My stupid, mad post-sepsis brain? Am I imagining I can't open it?

I stare, not sure quite what to do, and then I hear something. Someone moving around. Very human footsteps coming down from the second floor. I pull at the door again but it still won't budge, so I press my eye into the gap. In the gloom I catch sight of Mark as he whispers urgently to someone out of sight and then there are more careful footsteps as they head down to the ground floor.

I stand back, confused, and then the door silently opens just wide enough for me to leave. I step out cautiously, feeling like I've walked into a secret. I peer over the banisters.

'She's totally out. What about him?'

'Snoring.'

A giggle and a *shh*. My breath catches. Is that Cat? What is she doing downstairs with Mark? I shiver in the chilly air—*maybe Freddie is right, maybe there is a draught*—and as they disappear along the boot room corridor, I give it a few seconds and then creep downstairs myself, rounding from the wooden floor onto the stone flagstones of the narrow corridor to the right of the front door.

The stones are like ice blocks underfoot, making my feet hurt, but I keep going, my racing heart warming me from the inside even as my extremities freeze. I grip my phone tight as I get nearer to the boot room door. It's closed, but maybe if

I press my ear against it I'll be able to hear them. Figure out what they're doing.

Deep inside, I know why they're up. There's only one reason two married adults would be creeping around together in the middle of the night, but I just can't bring myself to believe it without evidence. Cat and Mark? Cat of Cat and Russell and *marriage is teamwork?* And I can't grasp the idea of Mark cheating on perfect Iso, who is toned and slim and doesn't have the teeniest bit of cellulite and still acts like she's twenty-one. Everyone's in love with Iso.

I edge toward the door, remembering how much Iso drank tonight. Maybe there *is* trouble in paradise. Iso has always loved booze more than the rest of us, but there was definitely an edge to how she was at the party. But Cat? How could Cat do that to her? How could they do this to any of us?

My heart is pounding so hard when I reach the closed door that I'm not sure I'll be able to hear anything through it even if they were shouting at each other on the other side, but as I go to press my ear against the cold grain, the wood moves ever so slightly, opening.

I step back, my hand over my mouth, sure I've been caught, but the door stops at only two inches opened. It's a creaky old door with a stiff metal latch. It should have been louder when it opened, but there was nothing. A smooth silence as if it had just been soaked in oil.

A breathless moan escapes from inside. I can't help myself; I take a step forward. I have to *see.* I put my eye to the gap and it immediately widens. They're bathed in moonlight—Cat, perched on the shelf against the wall, her legs wrapped around Mark, who looks almost comical with his boxers down around his ankles as he frantically pumps himself into her. It's grotesque and revolting to see my friends, good-looking as they may be, like this, but without thinking, as an icy draught snakes up my legs, I lift up my phone and start to record.

Neither of them even glance toward the door as Mark groans, lowering his head to Cat's exposed breast. As his hands and mouth grasp at her breasts, she gasps and pulls her legs tighter around him. 'Fuck me harder,' she mutters, her eyes closed, and then wraps her hands around his neck. 'Fuck me till it hurts me.'

He stops then, pulling out, his dick hard and almost purple even in the darkness, and spins her around, bending her over the shelf, hand on her neck as he thrusts back into her, the cheeks of arse moonlight pale as he grips them.

'God, you're such a dirty bitch,' he mutters, gripping her by her hair, and they encourage each other with breathless words and commands and insults. I can hear his flesh slapping against hers, and yet, despite how uncomfortable it's making me feel, I keep on recording.

I have to, I tell myself. Iso would never believe this is real without evidence. Maybe of Mark but never of Cat. Neither would Russell. Neither would Freddie, and neither would I if I hadn't been seeing it with my own eyes. I feel sick. How long has it been going on?

I record them, lost in each other, for a few more seconds and then quietly step away and creep back upstairs to my own bed, climbing in beside my own disappointing husband. I lie there, wide awake and in shock, and maybe fifteen minutes later I hear two pairs of guilty feet carefully returning to their own rooms and their own unsuspecting partners.

53.

Freddie

The mood in the house the morning after the party is as grey and miserable as the sky outside. Iso has been throwing up since dawn, which put a damper on everyone's hangovers, and the cleanup is a long and reluctant process all round. Emily doesn't really help but she at least makes breakfast, although no one is really in the mood for it, especially her, and it becomes just more washing up to do.

She's quiet, not making much effort to pretend everything is all right, instead claiming a headache. It's actually a relief when the others clamber into their cars and head back to London with promises to visit again soon. Emily immediately goes for a lie down as if she can't stand to be in my company, which sours my already bleak mood. She's barely looked at me today, as if the energy we've had to put into pretending everything is fine to friends new and old is all my fault, but it's not as if the party was my idea.

I need some air, and figure now is as good a time as any to check the postbox for yesterday's mail as I'm not sure my mood can get any worse.

It's foggy again—god, I can't wait for spring—and I'm barely able to see more than a few feet in front of me as I stroll, but I'm happy to be out of the house. My phone buzzes and I'm surprised to see it's the vicar texting. I don't remember giving him my number.

Just to let you know that you can talk to me whenever you need to, totally confidentially, and that obviously goes for the concerns about Emily you shared last night too. Maybe you should talk to her doctor again?

I frown. I don't remember talking to him about Emily at the party. I scan through my memories and suddenly get vague flashes of being huddled with him in the pool room, talking earnestly, but nothing more than that. My head starts to throb, a nauseating stabbing sensation, as if the effort is too much. Seems I have got a hangover after all. If I had whole conversations last night I don't remember, I must have drunk more than I thought too.

I send back a quick reply. *I will and thank you.*

Three dots flash up as he types a reply. *I'm sure she won't harm herself. Although I do feel that's my responsibility for mentioning the suicide crossroads in the first place. I didn't realize she might get obsessed by it as you said.*

Emily's not obsessed by the crossroads. Why would I have told the vicar that? If anything, it's the opposite. Emily's terrified of getting injured again. She's in no hurry to die. Why would I have said she might be suicidal? Maybe the vicar got the wrong end of the stick from something I said.

I reach the mailbox and there's only one letter—no bills today, thank fuck—our life insurance policy renewal that needs signing and sending back, so I put the vicar out of my head, and as it starts to rain, I hurry back to the house.

The pipes are rumbling and I know Emily's settled in for a long soak in the bath before we cobble together an attempt at dinner, so I light the fire, which goes some way to keeping the endless draught at bay, and with a beer cracked open, I fill out the form. I canceled a lot of things when I started getting into this financial mess, but I never canceled the insurance. My parents died of carbon monoxide poisoning when working on a new house, and between that and what happened to Emily, I know how fragile life can be.

I sign at the bottom and scan the details and terms and conditions. I stare at the numbers mentioned. There's a lot of money for a payout in the event of the unthinkable. More than I realized. Definitely enough to get me out of all this financial trouble. I stare at the figure for a long time before licking the envelope and sealing it up.

As the fire crackles, outside the afternoon sky is sinking into night. There's a storm approaching and slowly the wind starts to whistle around the house. As gusts cough and wheeze against the bricks, my mind empties for a while with the sheer exhaustion of months of deception, and when the heavy splatters of rain come, I doze off.

I have half dreams of Emily tumbling from the ridge—*Did you push me, Freddie?*—her fingers reaching for mine, but this time she grabs me and pulls me down with her, and we fall in terror, staring at each other, the rocky ground hurtling closer.

I finally startle awake with the sound of Emily coming down the stairs, and only after I gather myself and shake away the cobwebs of my headache do I realize that, for the first time in what feels like forever, as thunder starts outside, I'm warm in this house.

54.

It's not the storm that keeps the raven awake.

He has weathered worse in this life on the endless reckless moor. He hides behind the warm chimney as the wind batters the front of the house and fluffs his feathers to protect the cold husk of his dead, accusing mate.

He turns his head away, preferring the cold wet air to her brittle feathers. Perhaps he should move backward and let the wind take her. Bright Wing is becoming impatient. She has gone back to the others tonight. She doesn't like the house either and doesn't understand why he has to stay. He can't explain to her why. He doesn't truly understand himself.

Unfinished business.

He wishes Broken Wing would crumble to nothing already. Is it only her lingering resentment of him—*You let me die. You murdered me.*—that keeps what remains of her corpse together? If she disappeared, then he would be free. She would be dust on the wind and he could fly far, far away from this place. To start again. With Bright Wing.

No more *before before before.* No more forevermore. He needs to do something. As the wind finally drops but the rain comes down harder, he raises his own strong wing to protect her remains.

This has to end. His mate is dead. He knows that.

55.

Emily

The morning refuses to lighten, the sky stubbornly clinging to a deathly grey mantle that none of the lights inside the house can dispel. It doesn't help that I'm so cold. For the first time since he's mentioned it, I think Freddie might be right about there being a draught in this house. Despite having had a long hot shower after he left for work, and lighting a fire as well as having the heating on, by the time I get back from a quick trip to the local shop for a pregnancy test, I haven't been able to get warm at all. Perhaps it's shock that's causing it. My head hasn't stopped spinning since finding Cat and Mark in the boot room.

I stare down at the test, unsure if there's a line there at all or if it's just shadows and liquid. It's not a brand I know. I should have gone into the center of town and gone to the chemist, but it's misty outside and I didn't want to drive more than I had to. Anyway, I've probably taken it too early. Maybe I've got my dates wrong. Maybe my cycle has changed since my accident.

And it's probably no wonder I still don't have a period. Maybe there is a slim chance that I'm pregnant again, but I expect it's more the shock of everything that's been happening. Not only has my husband been hiding things from me and gambled away our financial security, our best friends' marriages are a bullshit of lies and cheating too. We all started out so young and in love. What's happened to us?

On the sofa, I toss the test into the fire and then huddle close to the crackling flames and watch the video on my phone for what feels like the hundredth time. My stomach flips and twists and makes me feel queasy again. Yesterday the whole business upset me so much I spent the entire day quietly trying to decide whether to talk to Freddie about it to get his opinion on whether to tell Iso or Russell or to leave well enough alone and say nothing. It's hypocritical of me for sure. I mean, I cheated on Freddie. But only once and not with one of our friends. This is totally different. I could barely look Mark or Cat in the eye, and I've never been gladder for one of Iso's hangovers distracting her; it was a relief when they all left.

I felt so bad for Iso. Maybe the over-drinking was because she knew something was wrong. I was about to open up to Freddie when he went out for a walk, and then when he got back I was in the bath and he was in an odd mood. I decided to leave it.

Now I'm glad I did. I pull my cardigan tighter and glance around the room, trying to figure out where the draught is coming from as my brain ticks over. I realized earlier that the voices I heard on the landing when we had the late Christmas day must have been Cat and Mark meeting up when everyone was asleep. Had they wanted to come and see me at all, or was it just a good excuse to see each other without raising any suspicion? Using our home as a venue for a sneaky shag?

I throw more coal into the blazing fire. Sitting here in the relentless chill, my upset has turned very much to anger. The world is full of liars. There has been one slight upside. Cat—so much for her Christian values—and Mark's cheating has also put Freddie's gambling slightly into a different perspective. The gambling at least is an illness. And it was stress from *my* illness that made him do it. Yes, it was weak, but I do understand it. This sneaking around—and the way they were fucking was not first-time fucking, so they've been doing it a while—is something else. Iso would kill Mark and take him for everything he's got if she knew, and it would break Russell's heart.

Why would Mark do that to Iso? I am blaming Mark for it, I realize. He's charmed Cat. Made her feel special. That doesn't happen to her often; she's not a *shining* person like Iso. It's probably just a game to him. A game that could end up costing him a lot.

I sit up a little straighter and look down at my phone, a thought coming to me. It's like a jolt of electricity through my veins and almost makes me warm. It's not a pleasant thought. In fact, it's an entirely *un*pleasant thought, one that I never in a million years would have imagined I was capable of. It's the complete *opposite* of telling Iso or Russell or confronting Cat to tell her to stop it. But it would certainly solve all Freddie's and my problems. Or give me a get-out-of-my-marriage card if I decide I can't trust him anymore.

I stare at the fire for a long moment before reaching for my iPad on the coffee table. I'm going to need both my devices for this. Before I can talk myself out of it, I fire a text to Mark telling him to call me as soon as possible, and then I sit back and wait, my heart pounding. Mrs Tucker is due in to clean soon, and I want this done before then.

I only have to wait ten minutes before my phone rings and I nearly throw up on the spot. *Just do it, Emily,* I tell myself and take a deep breath before I put the call on speakerphone and press record on the iPad.

'So,' I start, 'how long have you been fucking Cat for?'

'What are you talking about?' he says, indignant. 'I'm not fucking Cat.'

'Yes, you are.'

'Is this a joke?' He tries to laugh, but I can hear his blustering panic. 'Why would you think that, Em? I know you've been having some weird moments since your accident, but that's just plain crazy.'

'I saw you,' I say, calmly. 'And before you protest some more, I took a video. In fact, I'll send it now.'

'Jesus Christ,' he mutters as it arrives. 'I told her we shouldn't do it in your house, but she's so fucking needy. She won't leave me alone.'

Bingo.

I watch the time ticking away on the voice note app as it records. *Gotcha.*

'Are you going to tell Iso?' Mark's voice is full of dread as he starts running through all the eventualities. 'I know she's your best friend, but this would devastate her. I'll end it. I've been trying to for a while but Cat won't let it go.'

'When did it start?' I keep my tone uncertain. *Give him hope to make him talk.* 'I need to understand it before I can decide what's best to do.'

'The holiday.' He lets out a long, shaky sigh. 'She's so different from Iso. You know what Russell was saying at the Christmas thing? About how people are illusions at first. Not Iso. Iso's still as high maintenance and full of life as she was on day one. It's exhausting. Cat's so calm, and she's had a little crush on me forever. It just happened one afternoon. I think you and Iso had gone shopping. It was a couple of days before your accident. Russell and Freddie were asleep on sun loungers and we were inside talking. Drinking. One thing led to another, as they say.' He pauses. 'Sex with Iso is all performance and all about Iso. Cat was so easy. And so grateful.'

I hate him on Cat's behalf for that, and the worst bit is I know it would be true. Mark's not worth half of Russell, but he has that blinding thing like Iso does and he has all that money. He would have made Cat feel special.

'It's only been a few times. Hotel meetups. Nothing serious. Not for me. Honestly, Emily, I feel shitty about it, I really do. Awful, in fact.' I can hear the panic in his voice. 'Please don't tell Iso. Please.'

'She'd destroy you if I did,' I say and sip my coffee. I'm amazed at how calm I am. 'How much do you earn, Mark? Two? Three million a year? I read that report in the *Times* on pay at Rolfman Bachus. And you're top of the tree there. If I tell Iso, she'll go nuclear. She'll shake out all the apples in the divorce settlement, and worse, she'll bad-mouth you everywhere she goes. All those charities you support for tax relief. All those foreign clients you're always entertaining. They won't want her noise. It won't be worth doing business with you to have to deal with her.' I pause and let that sink in. 'But the money aside, she'd never ever let you go. Every relationship you try to have she'd do her worst to scupper. Her ego would never forgive you for cheating. Her father cheated, remember? Broke her mother. Wrecked her childhood. You'd take the punishment for that.'

'What do you want, Emily? None of this sounds like you.'

He's defensive now, the pieces coming together in his clever head. I'm not shouting at him, calling him a bastard and saying I'm telling his wife. All I've done is point out the very compelling reasons he wouldn't want his wife to be enlightened.

'I want a hundred and fifty thousand pounds.'

He laughs momentarily but then stops when I don't say anything else and the silence between us becomes palpable. 'God, you're serious, aren't you?'

'It's a drop in the ocean compared to what Iso would take. I want you to set up some high-interest account for me and put it in there. Freddie's been gambling again.'

'I knew it,' Mark mutters. 'I asked him about it. He denied it.'

'Of course he denied it,' I snap. 'It's an addiction. You should have told *me*.' This new piece of information gets rid of any vestige of guilt about what I'm doing.

'Freddie's got me in a hole and you're going to get me out of it. You must have so many investments and accounts Iso knows nothing about. She's never been interested in managing finances.'

There's a long pause at the other end and I hear the puff of a vape. 'How do I know you won't come back for more?'

'You don't. Except I won't. You're just going to have to take my word for it.'

One hundred and fifty seems a big enough number to either leave and start out on my own or get me and Freddie clear of debts and get him into some rehab. I'll just need to figure out a way of explaining where the money came from if I stay with him.

'It will take me a while to do it safely,' he says eventually. 'A week or so at least.'

'That's fine. Oh, and by the way, I've recorded this conversation. So even if you think you can escape the video evidence, you've confessed all on here.'

When I hang up, a big fat grin on my face, I feel better than I have since falling, since those awful *I'm going to die, I don't want to die* feelings. Maybe everything is going to work out just fine.

56.

Emily

Mrs Tucker comes about half an hour after my call with Mark ends, by which time I'm a little vague on why I went for blackmail rather than telling Iso. My head thumps nauseatingly hard when I think about it. Blackmail. I go up to the bedroom and take a couple of pills, needing a lie down. I'm a *blackmailer.* The word makes me feel queasy and unpleasant. It's like the very worst of me came out for that call, but I can hardly ring Mark back and say I've changed my mind. I don't want to change my mind. I hate financial insecurity and this will save us. I don't want to be that person, but neither do I want to be drowning in debt and possibly a homeless single mother.

The sound of vacuuming downstairs soothes my head as I close my eyes and rest, and by the time the cleaner makes it up to the middle landing the sickening pain has thankfully eased. The bedroom door's open and I hear her cleaning the bathroom, humming to herself, before she runs a mop over the wooden floor and then checks the spare bedrooms, and I figure it's probably time I got up and made us both a cup of tea. In my socks I pad out to the hall to find her staring up at the second floor, eyes slightly glazed, as if she's looking at something that isn't there. My heart skips a beat. Is she feeling something odd up there too?

'Are you okay, Mrs Tucker?'

She startles slightly and then lets out a small laugh. 'Was lost in the past for a moment. That's all. A rush of almost forgotten memories. Funny how that happens. The smell of the wood did it.'

'The past?'

'Oh, you see, my father was the gardener here when I was small,' she says, taking another glance up to the second floor. 'When it was Fortuna Carmichael's place. I spent a lot of time playing here. I'd almost forgotten about it. The strangest thing happened to me here.'

'Oh really?' My heart flutters hard like raven wings against a chimney. 'I was going to make us both a cup of tea. I've got some carrot cake too. I'd love to hear about it. And upstairs doesn't need any work anyway.'

'Well, if you're sure.' She picks up her bag of cleaning prod-ucts and hurries toward me, smiling. Is she wary of going up to the second floor too?

She waits until we're at the kitchen table, mugs of tea in hand, before she starts to talk. 'Like I said, it was the strangest thing. Must have been a dream, but it was so vivid.'

'What happened?'

'When Fortuna had the place there was a cupboard up on that top floor. Might still be there, in fact. It looks like a radiator cover, but there's a storage space behind it. Carved holes in the wood, that kind of thing. They kept their luggage in there; it was my favourite hiding place when I was little. I'd make a den and pretend I was on a pirate ship or in a fairy castle. The usual thing. Anyway, Fortuna used that suite at the top as her creative space. It was where she'd drink and make her outrageous clothes and play music and, to be honest, do all the things that made me think she was utterly exquisite. I was in awe of her. And her husband, to be fair. Gerald, his name was. He was injured in the war so walked with a limp, but he was pure Clark Gable. We didn't have people like them living here. They were so different. And they had one of those passionate relationships you think you want until you're in one. All fire and ice. A lot of fights. A lot of making up. To a child, it was all so glamorous.'

I listen, rapt, drawn as much by the mention of the top-floor room as by Fortuna Carmichael's excesses.

'People would forget I was there, and from the cupboard I could listen to Fortuna's music and wonder what it must be like to be someone so unusual.'

'So what happened?' I ask.

'It was a very hot summer and it got stuffy in there. I dozed off and I must have had one hell of a dream because I was sure that when I woke up there was a racket going on—a fight—and then through the gaps in the wood I saw Gerald fall on the floor. I could see his face through the carved holes in the cupboard door, and I was sure he was dead. His eyes had *emptied*. Then I saw her drag him into her second-floor suite. I could hear her panting and everything.'

'Gerald died of cancer, though, didn't he?' I interrupt, confused. 'I saw his grave in the churchyard.'

'Exactly.' She shrugs. 'It must have been a dream. It felt so real though that I sneaked out of the cupboard and ran all the way home. When I went back the next day I was terrified to be inside the house with her, but then there was Gerald, right in front of me, coming down from upstairs, hale and hearty and off out for lunch with friends.' She lets out a laugh. 'No word of a lie, I was six years old and I almost wet myself right in front of him.'

'But what an odd dream.'

She picks up her slice of cake and bites into it and I make an attempt to do the same but my stomach is unsettled again.

What is it with this house and that upstairs room? Mrs Tucker had that strange experience, and I've heard all that oddness. It can't just be coincidence. She carries on chattering and I half pay attention but she's not talking about the house anymore and I'm still thinking about it. It must have been a dream or a child's imagination, but whichever, it's odd.

I see her off and then my phone pings with a text from Mark. *I've started the process. Will need some personal details for the account. I'm emailing you a form.*

When that money comes in, with or without Freddie, I'm getting out of this house. A fresh start. I try to imagine starting anew without Freddie. A part of me, maybe the same part that's capable of blackmail, is thinking, *Screw him. He deserves to be left in the shit.* But a larger part, the *me* of me, knows I can't leave him. I've been with Freddie for my whole adult life. I'm used to him. I love him. Most of him. I'm sure I do, and I've done some shitty stuff too.

Soon we'll be putting the house up for sale and moving on. It can be someone else's problem. I go upstairs and write what Mrs Tucker has told me into the notebook, just to get it out of my head, before putting it away, hidden from any prying eyes. I need to stop keeping the record if I'm really putting the top floor out of my head. I lie back on the bed, finally calmer, and doze and daydream about a life away from here as the rain comes down harder outside.

Thankfully, the house stays quiet.

57.

Freddie

My mood matches the foul weather as I pull up at the house. One of the credit card companies called me at work, chasing payment. They'd already rung the London office, which could have gone to shit if they'd said why they'd called. This time at least, they didn't. But next time they will. *Fuck fuck fuck.* That would be a one-way ticket to a polite redundancy. No one wants someone with a mountain of debts working in their accounts department. Also, there are the *other* people I owe the ten grand to. They'll come with more than a court order if I don't get their money back—plus interest—in a month. They'll bring a base-ball bat. The noose is slowly tightening around my neck.

'Dinner will be about half an hour,' Emily says as I come in. The house smells of roasting chicken, and it's such a change from her mood when I left that it backfoots me. What's she playing at?

'I would have cooked.'

'It's fine. I wanted to. I'm not working, so it's my job to take care of the house.' She leans against the kitchen side and looks at me, almost awkward. 'I do love you, Freddie. You know that, don't you? I really want us to get through all this.'

'You do?' I'm hoping my face looks grateful rather than just surprised and exhausted.

'Yes. I'm disappointed, but I understand why it happened. And marriage is teamwork, after all, right?' I give her a half smile for the attempt at humour.

'It's just going to take a little time.'

There it is. That superior and yet still-a-victim tone. She turns back to check a pan on the Aga. 'And maybe we should think about moving out of here.' Her words are so light that I know this is what she's been building to.

'Sure. Of course. If that's what you want.'

'Get a proper fresh start. You can go to meetings in a bigger town.' She smiles at me again, as if butter wouldn't melt. I give her a tight hug so she can't see my face. Doesn't she realize how much it costs to move house? And with my current credit record? Where will we go? A thought dawns on me. This is nothing to do with a fresh start. She probably wants to take whatever money we'd be lucky to get out of this place and run. Wants her share before the debt collectors come.

'I'm going to grab a quick shower. Is that okay?' My smile feels like a grimace, but she doesn't notice. Why am I so angry with her? I spent all these months not wanting her to find out in case she left me, and now she knows and is prepared to forgive me and I'm filled with some unquantifiable rage. What is wrong with me?

I head up the stairs, the temperature dropping as I climb, and start the shower running before going to the bedroom to get undressed. I sit heavily on her side of the bed and lean forward to pull off my socks. I'm so tired that every movement is weighed down with lead. I throw the socks in the direction of the laundry basket and then just stay there, slumped. What a mess. I'm about to drag myself to my feet to strip the rest of my clothes off when I notice that her side table drawer is open a few inches. I peer in, curious. There's a Moleskin notebook in there and a Montblanc pen, neither of which I recognize. Has Emily been writing a diary?

My heart thuds as I take it out. What's she said about me in here? With a glance toward the hallway to make sure she's not followed me up, I open the soft leather cover.

By the time I get into the shower ten minutes later, the bees are buzzing loud in my head and I let the hot water beat down on me, blissfully wonderful, as I try to take it all in. I knew Emily was having some weird post-sepsis moments, but the stuff she's written down is crazy. She really does think the house is haunted and that it's doing these things. Suddenly it all makes sense. The way she's been creeping around at night. So much paranoia. I don't need to quietly wish her to go mad; it seems like all the evidence is there that she has. *Evidence,* the bees buzz at me. *The evidence is there.* Despite enjoying the heat, I cut the shower short and hurry back to the bedroom to take pictures of the pages. *Why do you need evidence?* a small voice inside asks. *What for?*

I answer my own question by pinging a couple of the images over to the vicar, sharing my concerns. I almost email them to Dr Canning too, but hold off. It's enough that Paul has them.

'Dinner's ready!' she calls upstairs. I check the book is left exactly as I found it, close the drawer, and head down to join her. The bees abate slightly and we actually have a pretty pleasant evening, culminating in my return to the joint bedroom and some urgent if not adventurous sex. Once again, I forget to put on a condom and I should have pulled out, but I didn't. But anyway, after the miscarriage and everything she's been through, I doubt she'll get pregnant again so easily. A baby is the last thing I need right now, especially if she's planning to take what she can and leave.

That small voice keeps trying to speak up inside me—*Why would she do that? Why do you think the worst of her?*—but the bees buzz louder and drown it out. A part of me has always resented Emily. Her holier-than-thou nature. The way she judges me for gambling. I know she thinks I'm weak. And maybe I am. But at least I'm not smug. And there's an unpleasant part of Emily that is definitely smug. And she loves playing the victim.

As she lies on my chest, and we both drift into sleep, one underlined sentence from her notebook whispers into my dark oblivion. One I made sure I sent to the vicar.

Maybe it would have been better if I'd just died.

58.

Freddie

The smell hits me like a wave as soon as the alarm wakes me. A vague rotten stench hanging like mist in the room, so strong that it almost makes me gag. I go out to the bathroom, closing the bedroom door quietly on sleeping Emily. The smell is worse here, thicker, like food rotting in a bin in the height of summer. The landing window is closed, and I think this is one time she could have bloody opened it in the night and I wouldn't have minded. God, the stink is foul.

I should wake Emily up, but I don't want to face that *I told you so* expression that she does so well. And anyway, this smell might be something completely different to what she claimed to have experienced before. Iso was so drunk at the party she could have vomited somewhere upstairs, forgotten by morning, and not mopped it up.

My jaw's tight with irritation as I try to keep my breathing shallow and head barefoot up to the second floor. Iso has never been good at cleaning up after herself. I don't know how Mark puts up with her, banging body or not, because there's no way I could live with someone that high maintenance. After those few months living alone when Emily was in hospital, even she feels high maintenance. I find it hard to remember how much I missed her now. Did I really want her to come home?

Sometimes I'm so tired that I can't remember our lives before this house at all.

The stench of awful decaying wetness is even worse on the top landing, and I cover my face in the hope that will help. It can't just be vomit, surely? There's nothing up here that I can see, tiny droppings, no evidence that maybe rats or mice have died under the floorboards, although it would have to be a whole nest that had died to come close to this smell.

As I head toward the primary suite, which seems to be the source of the odour, I hate to admit it, but maybe Emily really did smell something up here. And if so, what's causing it? I push open the door to the bedroom and fight back a gag and cough as a wall of stink hits. Something is very wrong in here and it panics me. I avoided telling Emily but I bought this house without a survey. What if this is going to cost a fortune to repair before we can sell?

I stumble over to the window, holding my breath, and quickly tug at the lock and push the window wide, hooking the lever to hold it open. It's still dark outside even though it's gone six and icy air immediately tumbles into the room, embracing me, but I don't care. It's deliciously clean and sweet and I momentarily drink it in.

I wedge the bedroom door open and hurry back down the stairs, happy that the smell is already diminishing behind me even as the temperature drops. Still, I think, as I go back to the bedroom to get dressed, happy to see Emily is still fast asleep, she always goes on about the house being too hot. See how she likes it cold.

I don't bother with coffee and sneak quietly out to the car. Whatever's going on with the house is going to have to wait. We can't afford to fix anything anyway.

From somewhere on the roof of the house I hear a bird cawing into the dawn and another answering from somewhere on the moor. Emily will be up soon, I think as I head down the icy lane and pause at the postbox at the edge of the village to slide the signed life insurance renewal form in. A headache starts thumping behind my eyes as I watch the envelope disappear. *Why couldn't she just have died?* All my problems would have been solved. I'd have been free.

She could still die, a tiny voice inside whispers, and the headache blooms into a migraine. *The vicar thinks she's obsessed with the suicides on the crossroads and all the strange things in the house.*

There's a lot of medication in the house too. It would be easy for her to make a mistake. Take too many.

59.

The car sends clouds of steam and smoke up to the sky as it disappears down the lane. The raven watches it go, the man inside. The raven does not like the man, *no, not at all, not anymore, nevermore*, but doesn't know why. He used to like him, but now the man makes his feathers twitch and ruffle. The man has been in the house too long.

Bright Wing is waiting for him somewhere beyond the wall. It's the cusp of dawn, and as much as he wants to fly, he will wait until light. He does not like leaving his dead mate alone in the dark. It reminds him of how he left her to die in the darkness of the chimney, and then he finds he cannot move. Guilt turns his wings to heavy lead.

Bright Wing calls for him again, impatient. She is more impatient than Broken Wing was in the happy days when her wing was whole, before the shotgun blast brought out the worst in her. The pecking. The rage. The frustration. *Peck peck peck.* Sometimes he's sure he can still feel her pecking him in the night, her beak sharp and cold on his soft warm chest. He thinks she would still peck him if she could, for being whole and healthy and clean-winged.

He waits until the sky begins to wash away the blackness with blue hues, and then finally he prepares to leave for the day. To join Bright Wing and hunt and enjoy the skies with bloodied beaks and full bellies. It's only as he leaves the roof that he sees the window below is open. He hovers, staring at it, that slit into the house. The hungry house. He can't take his eyes from it.

Feed me, the open mouth whispers to him on the wind that his black spread wings surf across. *Give her back to me.*

Before he knows what he's doing, before he can change his mind, he darts to the roof and picks up her vanishing husk, now just a few feathers clinging stubbornly to brittle bones, and tosses her through the open maw of the house, into the upstairs bedroom.

She lands, facing away from him, a ghost of his love on the floorboards, and as soon as she does, a gust of sharp wind blows, and the window rattles free and slams shut. He stares through the glass, as inside, the bedroom door slowly closes too, trapping his dead mate's corpse inside.

At least she's in the warm, he tells himself as he turns and flies away, wishing that the heavy weight of guilt was so easily disposed of. *At least she's out of the cold.* He'll come back one last time tonight to say farewell. And then he'll be gone.

60.

Emily

I wake at seven-thirty just as a grey-blue washes through the darkness outside. Birds caw in the distance, already up and darting around the moor.

Warm under the covers, glad that Freddie left without waking me, I realise that for the first time in ages I've had a proper deep sleep. No bad dreams. No coma. No accident. And actually my leg doesn't hurt too badly this morning, rather than waking to the deep dull ache that makes me want to stay in bed rather than have to move it. Maybe I'm turning a corner.

And soon I'll have a hundred and fifty thousand pounds. It's a strange and alien thought, and for a minute it's almost as if it was a dream. I've blackmailed Mark. I really have. I don't know how I feel about that. Relieved, for sure. But also disturbed by how easily I did it.

My phone pings with a text from Merrily saying they'll drop some equipment over later in prep for starting the job next week. There's snow forecast and they want to get everything up the lane now in case it gets icy. I answer that it's okay, and if I'm out just do whatever they need to do as the gates are unlocked, but my stomach drops. At some point I'll have to find a reason to delay most of the work I've planned with them if we're going to sell the house. There's no way I'm spending that big a chunk of Mark's money on this place.

You wouldn't have a hundred and fifty thousand pounds if it wasn't for this place.

I pad into the bathroom. It's true, even if it goes in the *am I going mad or is this post-sepsis syndrome* list of crazy things in my head. If the bathroom door hadn't stuck at those couple of inches, then I'd have come out and bumped into Mark, who would then have panicked and made up a reason for being up and then gone back to bed. And then, if the boot room door hadn't opened, I'd never have been able to get the recording of him and Cat together. It's just a coincidence; it has to be. There's no such thing as ghosts, and if there is a draught then that could easily have opened the boot room door. It almost makes sense, but as I brush my teeth I push the bathroom door forward and back and it moves smoothly, no hint of stiffness. Maybe there was a door wedge I hadn't seen and the door had caught on it. I look around for one, but I can't see it. I look to the bathroom mirror, and no steamy writing appears to give me clues. *You will die here.* That gives me flutters of disquiet even if the library has since remained undisturbed. If it *was* me, it was probably my hospital fears coming out from my subconscious. But still. *You will die here.* No one wants to see that.

Stop it, I tell myself. *You'll be away from this house soon and it won't matter.*

Did I mean what I said to Freddie last night about wanting our marriage to work? I think so. He'd never do to me what Mark and Cat have done to Iso and Russell. I've started to think back on our old dreams of living in France and running a little hotel or Airbnb. Maybe if we're careful we could do that.

My period still hasn't come. I'll give it a few more days and then do another test. Who knows, maybe hormones have added to all the weirdness I've experienced. I let the hot water run over me and do my best not to think about Mrs Tucker's odd story. I won't feed my post-sepsis delusions. There is nothing strange about the second floor.

I'm still feeling chirpy when I'm dressed and check that Mark got the form I filled in. I need to find a way to explain the money to Freddie at some point. Maybe I'll tell him the truth when the cash is in? He'll be so relieved to be out of the hole I bet he won't even mind. If I'm okay with it, then that's his excuse to be okay with it too. I've kept one secret from him; I'm not sure I should keep another. Not if I want us to work.

I don't want to be around when Merrily and Pete come, so I decide to take myself out for the day, to Taunton. Buy myself something new to wear. Then do the supermarket in case snow does come. Maybe stop somewhere for lunch. Have a self-care day, as Iso would say.

I leave the heating on—maybe Freddie is right about the draught, but there's no way I'm going to admit that—and wrap up warm. It's going to be good to get out of Larkin Lodge for a few hours. A taste of the freedom to come.

61.

Emily

I get home just after eleven-thirty. The motorway was a night-mare and after twenty minutes driving the ache in my leg kicked in, so I turned back onto the country roads and ended up in a lovely café in a small market town having a toastie and getting lost in a book for an hour, a new twisty Harriet Tyce thriller, about a lawyer with problems that make mine feel like a walk in the park.

It's not been the full day out I planned, but I feel rested, and when I get back to the Lodge I'm glad to see that the Watkinses have already been. They've left a digger and various other bits of heavy machinery in the garden, and I feel a twinge of guilt that they probably won't get to use half of it. Maybe I'll make Freddie tell them we've changed our plans. It's his fault anyway.

In the I go upstairs I hang up two new tops I found in a little boutique, not wanting Freddie to see I've been out spending money, but when I get to the middle landing a thudding sound from the second floor nearly makes my heart stop. I drop the bag, forgotten, and stare up to the next landing. *What now? Is this my head playing tricks on me again?* There's another thud, and then a caw, and relief floods through me. A bird. Another bird is trapped in the house.

My hands tremble, but my fear of the upstairs bedroom has been slightly abated by the night of the party—*There are no ghosts at Larkin Lodge*—and I can't leave the bird stuck there until Freddie gets home. That's hours away, and it could have died of shock and panic by then. I take a deep breath and climb the stairs, grateful that while I still feel that chill sense of dread growing with every step, there's no awful rotting smell enveloping me. I reach the top, glad I came home while it was still daylight.

My heart pounds and, for a moment, while the bird thumps and caws against the bedroom door—*of course the bird is stuck in the bedroom*—I glance at the little stencilled cupboard on the landing. I can almost see Gerald Carmichael lying on the floor, eyes wide and dead. *Although he didn't die there*, I remind myself. *It didn't happen. He died of cancer.* It was just a child's imagination.

The frantic noise falls silent and my worry that the bird has knocked itself out overwhelms my fear of anything else, and without hesitation I open the door.

I stand in the doorway and stare for a long moment.

It can't be. It just can't be.

A raven is perched on the windowsill, and it hops around to look at me, expectant. It's calm now that it's got someone's attention, beady bright black eyes staring at me as if to say, *Come on then. Open the window. Let me out.*

I swallow hard. The raven is whole and healthy, glossy and firm. Even the space where its wing is badly scarred and feathers are missing looks strong. And the area of shocking white around the old wound is stark as fresh snow. I know this bird. I've seen this bird before. I took this bird's dead carcass out of the fireplace downstairs and threw it away when I set the other one free. It is the same bird. No other raven could have those markings. But how did it get in this room?

And more importantly, *how is it alive?*

It caws again, and I force myself inside, my mouth half-open still. It doesn't fly away in a panic as I approach but shuffles from foot to foot, eager to get out. Close up I can see the damage clearly. This *is* the same bird. I'd bet every penny of Mark's one hundred and fifty thousand pounds it is, even if it's impossible.

I open the window and the bird darts out, whirling into the fresh air in a dance of absolute joy, crying into the sky for all to hear that she's *alive alive alive* again.

It isn't possible. None of it is. And yet that bird that was dead, is alive.

I look back at the space on the landing where young Mrs Tucker was sure she saw Gerald Carmichael lying dead before Fortuna pulled him into this room.

It was just a dream though. Wasn't it?

62.

Freddie

'She's still convinced the house is haunted,' I say to Dr Canning, one eye on my office door. I've left it open just wide enough in case Alicia is listening. 'And it's made her paranoid. The vicar is worried too. He feels bad because he's the one who said about the suicides being buried under the house, which hasn't helped.'

A shadow falls across the carpet outside. I've been warned three times already that my assistant, Alicia, is a nosey parker. I'm not even sure why I want her to be listening in, but the bees are buzzing loudly, and it seemed like the right thing to do. *Just in case I need a witness to prove my concerns.*

'And she's veering between manic and depressed,' I continue, before hesitating and then adding, 'I don't think she's always taking the pills you prescribed, and I don't know how to make sure she does without her getting angry.'

'That doesn't sound good.' I can hear the doctor's pen scratching notes. 'I'll bring her next scheduled appointment forward, but it still will be a week or so. In the meantime, I'll email you some recommendations for some good psycho-therapists in your area. Not NHS, I'm afraid. But they should be able to see her quickly. And do what you can to persuade her to take her pills. The problem may be as simple as she's spending too much time on her own. Between the accident and the miscarriage, she's been through a lot. You both have.'

'You're right.' I infuse my tone with a hint of relief. 'That could be it.'

'Try to help her enjoy her new home. She's had a life-changing experience and it's quite natural that her mind is constantly in fight or flight. She's simply turned that toward the house, mistrusting it as a safe place. Self-preservation really.'

'Thank you again, Dr Canning. And sorry to have taken up so much of your time. Again. I just—I was so close to losing her.'

'It's perfectly understandable. And I'm glad you called. But try not to worry too much. She's a strong woman.'

'I know. Thank you.'

Outside, the sky hangs heavy, pregnant with the threat of snow, and staring through the glass, I get lost in the greyness of it. What am I doing? Why is the thought of the life insurance payout constantly needling my brain? Emily isn't going to kill herself. I'm not going to get that money. Why am I making her sound more unhinged than she is?

But what if she did? the bees buzz at me. *Or what if it looked like she did? No more smugness. No more holier-than-thou attitude. No more Mrs Always Right. Just a big fat cheque and no more debts.*

Do I really think those things of Emily? Sometimes she can be like that, sure, but not all the time. Not most of the time. Do I really want her gone? I want to be free of my own worries. I don't want someone coming to put *me* in hospital. But that doesn't mean I want Emily dead. Does it? My head is throbbing again. I'm so confused.

I need to get back to the house. Everything feels clearer back in the house.

63.

Emily

'Hello again, Fortuna.'

The old lady's in the same chair she was in before, a cup of tea beside her, but this time with a thick blanket over her knees. She looks like she's lost a little weight. More fragile than on my last visit. 'Do you remember me? I live up at Larkin Lodge.'

'I remember.' Her eyes dart my way, narrow and suspicious. 'The woman I don't know.'

'I brought you some chocolates.' I hold up a box I picked up at the local shop on my way. 'Thought you might like them.'

She doesn't thank me but nods, still suspicious but slightly appeased, and I peel off the cellophane and open them, putting them next to her tea.

'You know, I heard a funny story the other day about when you lived in Larkin Lodge. From a woman who played there when she was a little girl.' I smile, I hope in a kindly way. 'It was about your husband, Gerald. Something she thought she saw on the top floor. She was hiding in a cupboard there.'

Her eyes flash at me, sharp. 'Doesn't matter what she saw; he's dead now. He can't come back.' Her sudden staccato words are like tiny dry twigs snapping. A voice left too long unused. My heart beats faster.

'He died of cancer, didn't he? How awful.'

Her eyes drift out to the garden and she sighs. 'We were happy after I killed him. My beautiful Gerald.' I stare at her as she stares out into the past.

We were happy after I killed him.

My head spins with a sudden thought, crazier than the house being haunted. Is it possible that something in that room upstairs brings people—anything dead—that's put inside it back to life? That raven, so alive this morning, *was* the one I saw dead, I'm sure of it. But if the dead come back to life, then there can't be any ghosts. What's been trying to send me messages in the house if there are no ghosts?

Find it.

Fortuna takes a chocolate and chews it slowly, lost in her own thoughts of the past. I lean forward, closer to her, as if I'm about to whisper a secret.

'When I was last here,' I say gently, 'you said you found it but you put it back. You didn't use it. What did you find? Is it something in Larkin Lodge?'

'The book, of course.' She looks at me as if I'm stupid.

'Of course. The book.' I have no idea what she's talking about but I play along. 'You didn't use it.'

'I found it when we were moving.' She gives me a sly grin, little rivulets of chocolate-tinged saliva in the deep wrinkles around her mouth. 'I didn't use it. Too late now.'

The door opens and a nurse bustles in. 'I'm sorry to cut your visit short, but we've got doctor's rounds today.'

I almost ask for five more minutes, but Fortuna speaks first.

'She's leaving now.' Her expression hardens as if she realise I've gleaned precious information from her. 'She won't be coming back.'

I barely feel the cold when I get outside to the car.

Too late now.

My head is spinning. I need to get back to the house and think.

223

'Hope you weren't too cold. I forgot to say I'd opened the window.'

Freddie's home when I get to Larkin Lodge, and I'm so distracted by my visit with Fortuna that I'm momentarily confused and have no idea what he's talking about and then realise he means the second-floor bedroom window. He's coming down the stairs in jeans and a sweater, changed from work, and the house is baking again. How high has he got the thermostat?

At least now I know how the dead bird got back in. Through the open window. But how did it come through the window if it was dead? Had it somehow ended up on the roof and blew in with a wind? It was as if someone had thrown it back inside, but that's ridiculous.

'Where have you been?'

'Oh, just out for a coffee. Stroll around the village. Trying to get back into driving again.' I don't meet his eyes as I follow him into the kitchen. 'Thought I'd give it a go before the snow comes.'

'Be careful. Those turns can be dangerous in the mist.'

'How come you opened the window? I thought you were always cold here.'

'I could smell puke.' He pulls out a cheese slice from the fridge to snack on. 'You know, from Iso.'

'Of course.' My skin prickles. He's not being honest with me. The house didn't smell of sick. She didn't make a mess. She threw up, yes, but straight into the toilet. There *is* something going on in this house, and Freddie can't bring himself to admit he was wrong.

'I've volunteered to take on some extra stuff at work.' He changes the subject from the upstairs room, and I let him.

'Straight into it at the new branch then.' I don't have the energy to argue, and he's never going to tell me that maybe I *was* right. I was hoping he wouldn't be back for a while and I could have some quiet time to think and search again, but as that's not possible, I don't want to fill the evening with fighting.

'Yeah, covering some accounts while someone's on sabbatical leave. May have to work longer hours for a bit.'

'That's fine. Every little will help until we sell this place.' I reach into the cupboards to see what we can have for dinner. Pasta again, no doubt. And wine. Cheap and hopefully cheerful. Anything to help ease this awkwardness between us. I should tell him about the money that's on the way. I really should. We could play music and dance around the kitchen and feel the relief of all our money problems being solved. I *should* tell him, but his lie about why he opened the window has annoyed me. It makes me want to punish him a little longer.

Sometimes I wonder if this house is bringing out the worst in us.

64.

Emily

On the landing, I stare out at the night, pulling my thick cardigan around my pyjamas. The snow hasn't arrived and the darkness is crisply silent. A void. If I opened the window and tumbled out, I could be falling into that void forever. Maybe I'm still in the void of unconsciousness in the hospital. Maybe I never woke up at all. Another crazy idea to contemplate. I can't sleep, which given everything is hardly a surprise, but with Freddie beside me snoring I couldn't think either. And I need to think. At some point I have to start trusting myself instead of everyone else. I trusted Freddie and he was lying to me. Mark and Cat have been pulling the wool over everyone's eyes. Why not trust myself?

There *was* an awful smell coming from upstairs and even Freddie's experienced it, because why else would he air out the room when he's always cold? And why is he always cold when the thermostat shows it's baking in the house? He's feeling a little of what I have been. Not the writing on the mirror and the books flying and the Ouija board, but something more visceral. And there is *something* about this house. Something odd.

I know the bird that flew away this morning is the same dead bird I put outside on my first night in Larkin Lodge. There is no way there are two ravens with identically damaged wings. The bird was very dead when it fell from the chimney into the red room, but somehow, when it was in the *upstairs* bedroom, it came back to life.

This brings me to Mrs Tucker's tall tale of her daydream of seeing Fortuna Carmichael killing Gerald and dragging him into that room. I look up at the ceiling, imagining his dead body there. The next day he was fine, hale and hearty. Sure, that could be a child's imagination, except for that sentence that I keep hearing over and over in my head.

We were happy after I killed him.

But where does all this get me? Even if the upstairs room has some strange power to bring things back to life, that doesn't solve my problem of the haunting. The dead bodies get up, breathe, and walk—or fly—away. No ghosts.

In bed, I curl up behind Freddie, his back my pillow, and his body moves in a steady comforting rhythm. As much as I find it soothing, I cling tightly to him as I drift into sleep. I can't deny I'm afraid. Because if all the other odd stuff that's been happening in the house is real, then what about the message with the book. Was it a warning, a threat, or a prophecy?

You will die here.

Maybe if I solve the puzzle of the house, that threat will be gone. Just like we'll be gone soon. We'll have money and a fresh start. We'll leave the house behind and live our best lives. My period is still notably absent. Maybe two arrived at Larkin Lodge, but three will leave. But first of all, I have to know. I have to *find it.*

65.

Freddie

Three birds in the sky, slashes of black stabbing at the endless grey canvas overhead. Ravens, one with a shard of white in a damaged wing. It's flying beautifully though, perhaps even better than the others. After a moment, the damaged one and the larger bird, maybe the male, break away into a pair, pirouetting around each other, and there's such *joy* in their movement that I can't look away. The other bird is forgotten, the two cawing and darting and diving so fast and so close they should collide, but they don't, as if they've done this dance a million times before and can anticipate each other's moves, but there is nothing of dull routine about it, only complete and absolute joy.

Oh, for that joy. I'm exhausted.

I start the car, eager to get the heating working, and lean my head against the headrest. The bees buzz and my toes are still icy, and even Emily curled up close behind me last night couldn't warm me up. She was squeezing so hard at times I couldn't breathe.

I look back at the door where she's waving me off. I smile and half wave back and then pull away, the gravel crunching as I turn away from the house and down the lane.

Emily.

She's acting as if she's forgiving me, but how can that be? I've lost all our money. I've got debts. She's veering between completely distracted and overly nice. Why isn't she angrier? Is it post-sepsis, like this haunting business, or is it something else? The bees buzz louder.

She was out when I got home yesterday, and when she said she'd been for a coffee she couldn't even look at me. Emily's always been a terrible liar. So if she been for a coffee, where had she gone that would make her lie to me? What would she want to hide?

The answer rings loud as a church bell as the moors fly past me and the grey sky brightens.

A lawyer. Of course.

She's been taking advice. How best to divorce me, I imagine. She's got money in her bank account from her injury payout. She can afford someone good. She's going to take whatever is left and leave me with nothing. What if she presses charges too? She could do me for fraud, I'm pretty sure of it. One of those cards *is* in her name, but it's the one I've been paying the minimum payments on, so it won't affect her credit. Even if she doesn't press charges, if that comes up in the divorce case I'm totally screwed.

Who am I kidding? I'm totally screwed anyway. My phone pings with an email from Dr Canning, and I slow down to read it as I drive.

Please make sure she takes her medication, and I have attached some good local psychiatrists' details. My secretary is sending Emily some appointment times for the next fortnight. Reach out immediately if you feel she is a danger to herself or others.

I frown as I realise it's a response to an email I sent early this morning. I scroll up. It's saying I'd found her awake in the middle of the night on the landing staring out of the window and it was worrying me. I don't remember her getting up in the night. A jolt of memory comes to me—*the shower running, my fingers tapping out the email on the phone*. I must have been half-asleep. I'm so exhausted all the time; no wonder I'm forgetting things.

A horn blares and I look up to find I've wandered across the central line. I pull quickly back to my side of the road, and then as my pulse slows and I stare at the road ahead, I try to focus on what I need to do at work today. One line of Dr Canning's email plays over and over in my head as the road rolls under me.

Reach out immediately if you feel she is a danger to herself or others.
Even Dr Canning thinks she might kill herself.

66.

Emily

The air has that crystal quality that comes before snow and the frost is so thick on the moors that out there it looks like it's snowed already. Merrily arrived unannounced at nine to talk through some garden plans, and I listened and nodded and looked at the beautiful designs I wasn't going to spend money on and told her I'd show them to Freddie and we'd need a few days to mull it over. We agree to wait until this current cold snap is over before they fill in the septic tank and start on the paths. She's breezy and chatty and there's no mention of missing artists or Sally and Joe, so at least the vicar hasn't told her about my 'ghost' moment, but the time drags until she leaves because I want to get on with my own plan for the day: finding the book Fortuna was talking about.

After she finally goes, my phone pings with a message from Mark saying the money's in and paperwork is on its way, and while I do feel a small wave of relief—and a not so small twinge of guilt at what I've done—I put it aside in my head as I climb the stairs to the second floor, having remembered the only place in the house I didn't search already.

I'm sure the landing is suddenly darker than downstairs, but I ignore it along with the creeping dread that swirls around me in a cold breeze. I don't look at the bedroom door and focus instead on the latticed box that I'd automatically presumed was an old radiator cover, even though there's a radiator a few feet along the wall.

I get slowly to my knees, every hospital-stiff joint protesting, and after a moment find the small catch along the left side. The front cover swings open and, holding my phone torch out, I peer inside.

The empty space is about five feet deep and wide, and while I couldn't stand up in it, a small child could, and I can see why Mrs Tucker would have made a den here.

Even without the torch, enough sunlight comes through the lattice to keep the space bright enough to play. I can picture her in here, a suitcase as a table, maybe with a cloth on it, hosting teddy bears tea parties. But where would the book be hidden? Somewhere she wouldn't see it?

Fortuna found it when they were moving. So that would have been when she came in here to get the suitcases. And if there had only been suitcases near the opening, she'd just pull them out and not see any further in. But they must have had trunks too, wedged against the far wall, perhaps by Mrs Tucker as a child when she made her den? She'd have had to crawl in to crawl them out. Did Fortuna find it then?

A wave of the narrow torch beam gives me no clues, and after slipping one of my trainers off and putting it in the gap to stop the door from closing on me if the house has one of its draughts, I reluctantly, and on my hands knees, go inside.

The air is stale and dusty, undisturbed for god knows how long, and the walls are cool. I press and touch every inch along the side and back but nothing gives, no secret cupboard within a cupboard, and once I'm done, sitting back on my heels, my back aches from hunching over. Maybe I got it wrong. Maybe the book isn't in here at all.

I'm reversing toward the door when I see it. A small line in the skirting board in the corner. I look closer and see another line, maybe eight inches along. My heart beating faster, I reach out and touch it. There's no click or secret door, but as I push, the skirting is loose and comes away. My cheek presses against the floorboards, while I look at where the wall has been dug away. My heart patters faster as I hold the phone out to see better. There *is* something in there, filling a slot that has been dug out to fit only that item. It's a book. I can see the yellow of the pages. One finger each side, I wiggle it from the tight space, ignoring the disturbed brick dust making my nose itch, and slowly it comes free. A bound ledger, heavy in my hands despite its slimness, the cover grimy and faded and the leather spine worn in places, but I can make out the carefully printed writing on the front: *Christopher Hopper, Surgeon.*

It's the book. I've found it.

67

Emily

I don't linger on the second floor but bring the book downstairs into the sitting room, light a fire, and then get a cup of tea. My whole body is tingling with the treasure of a mystery about to be solved. If I can just understand what it is that's so strange about this house, then I can put it all behind me and move on with Freddie. Get away from here. But I need to know. And the answers are going to be in here. I can feel it. I settle into the sofa, pulling the blanket over me, and carefully start turning the yellowed pages.

I can only consider what led me to this house to be fate. The weather was fierce when the burned man was brought in to the hospital, and several of the staff had not managed to get to work that evening. So it was I, and not a nurse, who sat with him through his final hours. I was alone with the dying man as he muttered to me through the night, no others there to hear his strange story that could be mistaken for the babble of the insane.

Perhaps I too should have thought of his story as madness. He was, after all, very badly burned, but after my years of marriage with Hannah, I know how mania can sound, and this man, broken and dying, did not sound like that. I sat at his bedside and listened rapt as he whispered to me the secrets of the house that had forever stood on the crossroads in the middle of nowhere and that had brought him to his fate.

Three years have passed since he died, and some might say I am now as mad as he was. I left my position in the hospital and sold our house. I bought the burned-out shell and have painstakingly restored it to be exactly as the dying man described. With every brick laid, I've felt the strange lure of Larkin Lodge. The hunger of it. The joy it has to be alive again. It called me to it through his words, I'm sure. It knows I need its help.

Hannah has remained mainly in our apartment in Bath, which has suited us both. She enjoyed being a leading surgeon's wife—that part of her I never really liked cares far too much about impressing others—and has not forgiven me for leaving my position at the hospital.

When we first met, when I found her refreshingly challenging and intelligent and so charming and witty, a true equal, I did not realise she hid a lack of ability to forgive. That while she loved me, she loved my growing position in society as much as my person. Perhaps now she loves it more. She'd told me back then that, like me, she wanted a more equal society, but she cherishes her standing in the present one too much for that to be entirely true. When we first met she had been excited about the prospect of travelling and setting up a missionary hospital in Africa or India, but perhaps again she feigned more excitement than she felt. She was very quick to find reasons that we could not go, even though we have not been blessed with children.

Perhaps soon, all that will change. The house is rebuilt. The room on the top floor is ready.

The next entry is two weeks later. I keep reading, rapt.

Hannah finally came to visit, and she was in such surprisingly fine spirits after realizing how large and beautiful our new home was, and how she would be a leading lady in local society, that, prepared as I had thought myself, I couldn't bring myself to kill her.

It was only afterward, as I waved her off in her carriage back to Bath to spend the month closing up the apartment, that I realised what a godsend that choice had been. I had not thought through all the consequences of my endeavour. What if the dying man's tale had been naught but fantasy and I had poisoned Hannah as planned? I would have had no alibi for her death, and it is no secret among her friends in Bath that we have not been on the best of terms recently. Before long the truth of her death would be discovered and I would be hanged for murder.

I have decided what I will do. I'm a scientist and have been a fool not to think of it before now. I need to test what the dying man told me before I kill my wife.

The writing is less fastidious in the next entry, and I take a sip of the tea that is growing cold beside me.

I can hardly credit it, and perhaps it is I who is mad, but what-ever is in the bones of this house the dying man did not lie about the strange peculiarity of its skill. I chose my test subject carefully. It had to be someone I knew well enough. Someone perhaps I cared for. After much deliberation I chose a fellow I had known in the army, who I had been for a while great friends with, a chap called James Masterton, who I knew to have fallen on some-what hard times in Bristol. His situation did not surprise me. For while James had a warm wit and could be very kind, he loved and discarded too easily, his vanity requiring constant validation, and his temper was too quick to flare, especially when he had been drinking. These situations always made him remorseful, but not enough to stop his bouts of vileness. It was one such unpleasant altercation that had led me to back away from our friendship despite his pleas for forgiveness. I found it terribly upsetting, having felt such a kinship with him when we first met, but there was no alternative, especially once I had begun courting Hannah.

In the intervening years, I'd heard that he was living separately from his wife in small rented rooms by the Bristol docks, that his drinking had got worse, and that the business he had inherited from his father was failing. He had been a good army medic, but those days were behind him. His life was a misery, and for all his charm his failings caused misery in others. As I arrived in Bristol to track him down and bring him home with me, I told myself that should my experiment fail, then his death would be no great loss to our society.

He was happy to see me, of course he was, and it was easy to persuade him to come and visit in a week or so.

The weather was on my side. He arrived on horseback—having no funds for a carriage—in a terrible storm that raged for days, and he had paused to talk to no one nor had he been seen by a soul as he'd neared the house, and he was in such a state of shivering cold that I thought for a while I might not have to do the deed at all.

He dried out by the fire, merrily commenting on its warmth, although I seem to be forever cold in the house, and we ate a supper of bread, cold mutton, and cheese and he bitterly bemoaned his current predicament but also toasted his joy to be reunited with me as we shared some wine. And then, when I knew he was in his cups, with my heart in my mouth, I laced his large brandy with more than a dash of laudanum, and before it could fully take hold I suggested we retire for the night.

I pause and stare into the flames of my own fire. *Forever cold in the house.* Just like Freddie. My head is a swirl of past and present. Us, Fortuna and Gerald, and Christopher and Hannah Hopper, all linked by this strange house.

He stumbled up the stairs and complained at my insistence that he sleep on the second floor—I made some excuse about the middle floor not being ready yet and that perhaps he could help me with the work needed there. His legs began to crumple beneath him as we reached the second bedroom, and I held him up until he could flop onto the bed. He was muttering something and laughing and then within moments he was unconscious. I would like to say that I had some misgivings about what I was about to do, but I was cold and wanted to be by the fire, and all my friend's failings had begun to irritate me once more.

As the storm raged outside, I saw only the worst of him and loathed him for it. I had worked so hard for everything I had achieved in my life and he had been gifted so much and thrown it all away. I did not even have his charm, but a solid stoicism I have overheard Hannah describe once as dullness.

I had hoped that the laudanum would be enough to slip him into that endless void but, damn me to hell, while his breathing was shallower he was still very much alive. Perhaps he'd developed a taste for it over the years and had some tolerance to its effects. I had prepared for this eventuality and took the sections of rope I'd hidden under the bed and tied his wrists to the bedposts. He was a few years younger than me, and even despite his debauched life-style, more powerfully built, and I couldn't risk that as he fought for his life he would overpower me.

I was right to do so for as I straddled his body, the pillow gripped in my hands, his eyes flew open, and the realization of what I was doing—along with not a small amount of confusion—was clear in them.

'I'm sorry,' I muttered. 'But I have to know.' I pressed the pillow over his face as his body bucked and convulsed underneath me, desperate to stay in this world of the living. It was probably over in minutes, but it felt unfeasibly long before he fell still and I slowly stepped away. The pillow slipped to the floor and the sight of his face, frozen in a death mask of fear and rage, made my chest burn suddenly and I vomited violently all over the floor. A lifetime in the service of saving lives and now, in such a short space of time, I had become a murderer.

I sat in the corner of the room for hours as the storm raged outside, my head throbbing and my throat sore from vomiting. I was desperate for water, but I did not leave. By morning his body had cooled and rigor mortis was setting in, and there was no room for doubt that my erstwhile friend was anything other than dead. When dawn came I untied his hands, and despite having no energy I managed to haul his body from the bed and across the landing, his boots dragging heavily across the polished wood. Finally, out of breath and my whole body aching, I pulled him into the room that would decide both our fates, the room I built the house for, the master bedroom on the second floor. Outside, the storm was easing, and the first streak of dawn light broke through the clouds and streamed in through the large window, casting a spotlight on his grotesque corpse as I laid him in the centre of the empty bedroom.

Exhausted, and sure my mind was on the verge of cracking, I closed the door behind me and went downstairs to my own room, where without even getting undressed, I fell soundly asleep.

I woke to silence and the conviction that I'd damned my soul to hell and that I had a body to dispose of. But, as I crawled out of my bed, the fool who had believed a raving madman, I heard whistling from downstairs. My robe about me, I flew down the stairs, and there he was, in the kitchen, James Masterton, a picture of health, making eggs on the stove.

'I fear I owe you a breakfast of apology, my friend. I must have drunk far too much last night and vomited in the bedroom. I cleaned it up with some rags and have scrubbed the floor, but perhaps only one or two glasses of wine with dinner tonight.'

He was alive and had no memory of his own murder.

The entry stops there, and my own breath is shaky. This is what Mrs Tucker said happened to Gerald. He came down the stairs as if nothing had happened. There's one more entry left, from two weeks after that, and I turn the page. Will there be an answer to my ghost here?

It was exactly as the burned and dying man had told me. I watched James for a week and he was truly a reformed character. Everything I liked about him was still there, but his drinking was moderate and his humour good. He was all I had thought him to be in the heyday of our friendship. He did not question this change in himself but was determined to get back to Bristol and start work on repairing his business and his marriage.

But I had to test the second part of the story I had heard so long ago in the hospital.

James had gone to Exeter overnight to visit with an estranged brother, and I took one of his unwashed shirts, socks he had ridden his horse in, a handkerchief, and cleaned his brush of loose hair, and then put the strange collection in a bed warming pan and carried it to the top floor bedroom. I waited until I heard him return, and then set light to the contents, ensuring the flames stayed within the pan. I would not set fire to the house like the dying man had. They shot up unnaturally strong, and I was glad there were no furnishings for them to reach, and I knew in that instant something had changed. I could feel it in the air of the house and hear it in the rage of the boots that ran up the stairs and the angry bellow of my name.

'Christopher? Christopher?'

I got to my feet, the other item I'd brought upstairs hidden behind my back, and braced myself for his entry.

'You murderous bastard,' he said in the doorway. 'Part of me was stuck in this awful room, in the darkness of it, trapped in this house for a week. I will kill you for that, I swear, you

odious nothing of a man.' He rushed at me, his temper of old fully returned, but I stood my ground, and as he threw himself at me and we fell to the ground I pulled the carving knife from behind my back and he impaled himself on it.

Once again, I had murdered my friend. This time I would not let the dark part of him out.

James has left. He has gone back to Bristol full of cheer. He did not see the blood in the upstairs room that I will now go and scrub clean. I cannot keep this journal because they will put me in the madhouse if anyone finds it, but neither can I bring myself to dispose of it. Before I leave this house and country for good, I will find a place to hide it. It belongs in this house. A secret within a secret.

And now I must go and clean the room again. Because Hannah arrives tonight.

I cannot wait to kill her.

I close the cover, the journal creaking with age, spine threatening to give way, my head reeling. If I've gone mad, I've not gone mad alone. Suddenly, the 'ghost' is starting to make a crazy kind of sense. I summarize what I've learned from these old pages.

First: If you put a dead body in the room upstairs, the person comes out alive and well and with no memory of their own murder.

Second: Not all of the person comes out. Only the best version of them. Part of them—the *worst* parts, the parts the murderer doesn't like—get trapped inside the room.

Third: If you burn some items of their clothing or hair, items with their DNA on them, the two parts become whole again. Then they remember.

That's why Fortuna had that odd collection of Gerald's possessions in a box. In case she felt guilty and decided to make him whole again. Too late now. That's what she'd said.

It was too late because Gerald died of cancer. So the part of him trapped in the room would have died with him.

It's not a ghost in the house. It's part of a person.

My skin prickles as I remember my accusations at the party I was so embarrassed of. Maybe I wasn't wrong. Could Georgina Usher have been murdered by Sally Freemantle after all? Has part of her soul or essence or whatever been trapped here for two decades? I stare down at the book, my mouth drying and hands sweating. I'm not mad. Mrs Tucker wasn't either.

I google Georgina again, rummaging through her artwork and her biographies, clicking into various articles and interviews, scanning them for any great changes in her life or the way she was mentioned. There's nothing. Then I read one that stops me dead. It's an interview from two years ago, and in it she's chronicling a lifelong battle with drink and drugs, an addiction she says she'd been struggling with since her late teens.

I carefully open the journal again and look back at the last entry, where Christopher Hopper talks about the changes in James after he'd come out of the room.

Everything I liked about him was still there, but his drinking was moderate and his humour good. He was all I had thought him to be in the heyday of our friendship.

His drinking was moderate. The element of his personality that drank too much, that veered toward addiction, that part was left in the room. Wouldn't the same have happened with Georgina?

I lean back against the wall, my head and heart both racing. If not Georgina, then who else could be stuck in the house? Who else could have been murdered here and come out changed?

The obvious answer strikes me so suddenly that for a moment I don't even breathe. There's only one person it can be. One person whose radical shift in personality has been commented on while I've been living here. I think back to those letters appearing on the bathroom mirror that morning.

Yes, the entity was trying to spell FREEMANTLE.

But not to spell the murderer's name. The person trapped in the house was writing her own name. Her maiden name, as she wasn't married when she was killed.

Half of Sally Freemantle is trapped in this house.

From outside comes the surprising sound of tyres on gravel—it's only midafternoon—and I hurry as best I can up the stairs and replace the book before Freddie sees it.

68.

Freddie

'Are you sure you're going to be okay?'

She's in the kitchen when I come downstairs with the small overnight bag. I wasn't entirely honest with her when I said that I had to stay in Taunton tonight. Yes, we do have a client dinner meeting, and yes, the boss has booked our team into the Travelodge in case the snow dump happens as expected, *but* he did say I could duck out and stay at home, given Emily's situation. I said no. A night away from Larkin Lodge is just what I need. Maybe this headache will clear. It always feels better when I'm somewhere else. I should really get someone to check for a minor gas leak. That would explain my headache and odd times of confusion and maybe some of Emily's strangeness too.

'Yeah, fine. I'll go to the book group in the pub.'

She turns away and faffs around wiping a side down, avoiding looking at me.

'I got an email from Dr Canning's secretary earlier,' she says, and my eyes dart involuntarily to her pills on the side. 'He's going on holiday and needs to bring my next appointment forward. Pain in the ass really, but we'll have to go to London.'

'Better to be early than late.' Everyone's lying, even the good doctor. He must think she's getting paranoid or he's protecting my involvement in the discussion, or both. I have a flutter of something akin to excitement that I don't understand—I don't *want* to understand.

'And after you called him, I guess he was always going to bring it forward.'

I look back at her pills again as her passive-aggressiveness rankles. There are a lot of them. *There are enough of them.* 'I was worried about you. You know that.'

'I know. I get it.'

If she gets it, why does she need to mention it at all? Trying to put me in the doghouse again. The useless weak husband who's always going behind her back. Will that come up in the divorce too?

'I'm leaving in half an hour or so. I can drop you at the pub on my way and maybe someone can give you a lift back. Then you don't have to drive in snow if it comes.'

I'm glad she wants to go. The vicar already thinks she's losing her marbles, so it's a win-win situation for me. If she behaves normally, he'll think she's faking it, and if she mentions any more strangeness in the house, that's more fuel to my fire.

I go back into the lounge while she busies herself doing nothing in the kitchen, still pondering her pills. Anti-anxiety pills. Pills to help her sleep. There are plenty that she could use to kill herself with. I didn't increase the life insurance this time; it's the same policy we've had forever. Nothing suspicious there. I stare in the flames and under the crackling wood I hear the hum of a beehive.

If Emily overdosed, my debts would immediately come to light and would make people suspicious, for sure, but they would never be able to *prove it.* On top of all her paranoias about the house, maybe finding out about my problems would be seen as sending her over the edge. Has she consulted a divorce lawyer though? That could go against me. The flames lick the back of the grate, hungry, the heart of the fire almost white with heat. Everything could go against me. But they would have to *prove* that I did something. And I have plenty of evidence that she's mentally unstable.

I take a deep breath and then have a moment of joy as my body thaws out, as fast as an ice cube dropped in boiling water. The house is warm, and so am I.

Maybe I'm going to kill my wife.

It's a strange and surreal thought, but it doesn't fill me with horror.

69.

Emily

'I'm not sure we should stay out too long,' Paul says to our small gathering at a corner table in the quiet pub. 'No one wants to be driving the lanes in a blizzard.' It's quiet in the pub, and outside, while the snow isn't falling heavily yet, the flakes are getting thicker, sticking to the windows, creating an oppressive claustrophobia. There's a claustrophobic atmosphere around this table too. The only people who've showed up are the vicar and Sally and Joe, and I couldn't feel more uncomfortable if I tried.

I take a large sip of my red wine and watch Sally and Joe over the top of my glass. One of the girls he was painting at the studio is behind the bar, and she glances over at him occasionally with such longing I'm sure he must have slept with her. If Sally notices she doesn't mind. They're sitting side by side, his hand on her thigh. His is a guest appearance, not a normal book group member, but he decided to stay when he saw I was here. Despite what he said at the party, is he thinking I'll be his next conquest?

'I didn't really enjoy the story.' I break the silence. 'It was a bit grim.' I'd quickly finished 'The Murders in the Rue Morgue' while Freddie had got his overnight bag together earlier. I wanted to see Sally and the book club was the perfect excuse.

She's funny and charming and beautiful and has no idea that the man she loves murdered her. No wonder she was getting headaches in the house. She's been separated from herself for a long time now and perhaps her body could feel it.

'And a bloody monkey,' Paul adds. 'All very clever, but really? Not exactly satisfying.'

He hasn't said a word about what happened at the party, and I'm glad. I'm trying my best to appear perfectly normal, and he seems to be believing it.

'It's a classic though,' Sally adds. 'First of its kind and all that. Although I'm not sure those 'best twist you'll read all year' book blurbs on Amazon could get away with the killer being an escaped gorilla.'

'We should try something lighter next. Perhaps a romcom. Cleanse the palate.' Paul glances sideways at me, clearly worrying that all the talk of murder might send me back to my paranoid suggestions. I was premature thinking he'd forgotten what I'd said. Still. We'll be moving soon and I'll never see these people again.

'Good idea,' Sally says. 'Murder stories stop me sleeping.'

'Are you okay, Emily?' Joe's studying me, concerned. 'You're a bit pale.'

'Sorry, I do have a bit of a headache.' It's surreal sitting opposite them. Perhaps he's even persuaded himself that killing his wife was all a dream. They're happy, anyone can see that. Happier than they were when she was constantly jealous back in the days Merrily Watkins described. *That* part of Sally Freemantle is stuck in my second floor bedroom.

'Maybe it's something in the house,' Sally says, quietly, her brow furrowed. 'I got a terrible headache there.' Joe leans across and kisses her, soft and sweet, and she looks so joyful and so does he. A quiet perfect love, if unconventional. And all it took was a little murder. It's hard to believe when I'm out of the house and she's clearly alive and well. Maybe the book is the rambling of a madman, and maybe Mrs Tucker found it and read it and then dreamed Gerald's death. Maybe Fortuna never killed him at all.

Too many maybes. Joe's still looking at me thoughtfully as I pull my coat on and say my goodbyes, and I have a moment of panic that he can see right into my head.

You will die here. A warning.

Would he kill me too if he knew I knew? No. Because no one would believe me. There isn't even a victim.

'I'll drop you back now.' Paul cuts in just as I think Joe was about to suggest he do the same thing. 'The weather's getting worse.'

'I'm sorry about what I said at the party.' It's freezing in Paul's car, the heater blasting out air that's barely above the temperature outside, and the snow is turning to ice on the windscreen. We've made small talk about the weather and Poe, but there's been the elephant of my talk of Georgina's murder between us. 'Obviously I'd got carried away with my imagination. It was stupid and I'd had some wine and . . . well.' I shrug as if that's enough of an explanation.

'Oh good.' The gears grunt as he speeds up along the road. 'Freddie's been very worried about you.'

'Freddie?' I look across at the old man, surprised. 'What's he said to you?'

'Nothing very much. He was talking to me at the party. Said you'd still been having some unusual experiences in the house.'

'He shouldn't have done that.'

'I'm a vicar, Emily, people talk to me. That's the main part of my job, hearing the problems of others and trying to help them.'

'We don't need your help. I'm fine.' I'm quietly seething, part anger and part embarrassment that they've been whispering in corners about me. 'And it's not like he's perfect himself. Not by a long shot.'

'In the words of Billy Wilder, nobody's perfect, Emily.' He looks across at me. 'But he loves you. And I think you're a lovely person who's been through a lot, and we are both concerned for you, that's all. He's worried you may have some anxiety and depression after your accident.'

'What is it you're so worried I'm going to do?' I stare at him as he pulls into the drive. 'Kill myself maybe?' He looks sheepish in the gloomy light as the car comes to a halt and I realise that's exactly what he was worrying about.

'Jesus Christ,' I mutter and get out of the car, slamming the door behind me, ignoring his pleas to listen. What does he know about me and Freddie? Nothing. Maybe I should tell him how Freddie hasn't exactly helped any of my anxieties by getting back into gambling. But I won't do that because I do my best to be loyal. Because I'm the better person. I hobble toward the house and don't look back.

70.

Emily

Sally and Joe are not my business, that's what I told myself when I got home, climbing into bed still angry at both Freddie and the vicar. They're happy, and I've got enough problems with Freddie's debts. Whatever part of Sally that's trapped here might also be dangerous. She threatened to slit Georgina Usher's throat all those years ago. What might she do if I set her free? I went to bed decided that I'd leave it well alone, get the money, get out of this place, go to France. Work on my own marriage, if I decide to stay in it. My period still isn't here, and surely if I do another test soon I'll get a clear answer.

A rattle from the hallway startles me out of my near sleep. It's only ten but feels like the dead of night as I push myself up to half-sitting to listen. There's no wind buffeting the outside of the house, and the rattling from the landing is an island of noise in the silence. The rattling stops and there is the scraping and grunt of wood, followed by immediate icy air. It smells fresh, not rotten. It's air from *outside*.

I get up, the floorboards already cold underfoot, and wrap my dressing gown tight, my heart starting to race. I pull the bedroom door open slowly, peering cautiously out as I reach for the light switch. I can see it, even before the sudden brightness of the bulbs makes me squint. The hallway sash window is open upward, the bottom panel *lifted*, not the top panel fallen. Thick flakes of snow drift in, appearing as from nowhere, spat out by the endless, unforgiving darkness beyond.

My skin prickles with more than just cold, and something glints at my feet, demanding my attention. I stare at that tiny space in the floorboards.

The nail. The nail is back. Of course it is. I skirt around it, and when I reach the window I can't bring myself to shut it immediately, a sudden fear of closing myself up in here and the house becoming my grave. I grip the windowsill, letting the cold air encircle me, ignoring the heavy flakes of snow that land on my face and hair. I take in a deep breath. *Sell the place. Get out of here,* I think. *Larkin Lodge isn't your problem. Sally Freemantle isn't your problem.*

The window slams shut so fast that I barely have time to pull my hands away, and as the wood comes screeching down hard, it traps my little finger, white pain exploding through me. Splinters tear and cut at my skin as I stumble backward, pulling my hand free, the window snapping that final inch shut. As I cradle my hand, the lights suddenly flicker overhead. For an awful moment I think I'm about to be plunged into the pitch-black, but the yellow bulb sputters back into life and, moaning, I go into the bathroom. My finger's throbbing hard and already swelling, and worst of all, it's bleeding around the nail. *Sepsis sepsis sepsis,* is all I can think.

At the sink, almost sobbing in my fear and panic, I stick my finger under the tap and open the bathroom cupboard to find the TCP and plasters.

I shriek as the water turns from freezing to boiling in an instant, the hot water coming out in a jet, splashing up my arm, and once again I'm forced to yank my hand away and stumble backward. In the hallway the window creaks open and slams shut, over and over, so fast and angry I think the glass might break.

'Stop it, stop it, stop it!' I slide down to the floor, gripping the small bottle of TCP in one hand as my cut finger pumps blood over my dressing gown. 'Please! I'm sorry! I'm sorry!'

My knees under my chin, I hide my face, curling up like a child, just wanting it all to go away. This madness of the house. I want to be back in hospital. I'd rather be in a coma than dealing with this. I want it to stop.

The noise goes on, a cacophony of bangs and slams and rattles and creaks, taps around the house coming on and off, the shower starting up, doors slamming, and I keep my head down, curled in on myself as if I can make myself disappear. Finally, when I can't take it anymore, I look up and scream, 'Okay, okay, I'll do it!'

Everything stops, an instant silence.

'I'll do it,' I repeat, more softly. 'I'll set you free.'

71.

Emily

I sleep like the dead; it's only the sound of ploughs clearing snow from the lane outside that finally wakes me. The house is warm and calm, and if it wasn't for the throbbing pain in my little finger I could half convince myself that it had all been a dream. It's swollen but not red and hot, and I'm still going to drown it in more TCP and tape it up, but I don't have a panic of sepsis today. There are too many distractions. In the hallway the nail has once again vanished, and the window is shut. I check the fastenings and see it's locked too.

'Sally Freemantle,' I whisper, looking up to the second floor. 'Are you here?' There's no answer, as if the madness of last night has drained her energy too.

In the bathroom I bathe and tape up my little finger and then get in the shower—tentative at first and ready to leap out if the temperature changes suddenly—and let the warm water run over me. I flinch slightly as I soap. My breasts are so tender and heavy maybe my period is coming after all. I add that to the list of things to think about later; while I'm in town I can pick up a better test. Before that, I have one job to do. Empty this house of unwelcome residents.

It's bright outside, the fresh snow sparkling, but the ploughs have worked hard so the road to the village is clear. With my sturdy boots on and my stick in hand, I make it to the car without incident. I'm going to the studio to talk to Sally, and my plan is to suggest we go next door to their cottage for a coffee to discuss how it works if Joe paints me. While I'm there, I'll go to the loo and steal whatever I can of Sally's to hide in my bag and bring home to burn. Surely I can grab a few things. A hairbrush maybe. Underwear from a laundry basket. I guess anything with DNA on it will do. I'm so lost in thought that when my car loudspeaker starts ringing, I realise I'm halfway to Wiveliscoombe already. It's Iso calling and my nerves—already rattled—ratchet up another notch. What if Mark's decided to come clean and told her that I've blackmailed him? I let it ring for a moment longer and then take a breath and answer.

'Hey.' I'm pleased to hear that I sound normal. 'I'm driving so can't talk for long. The weather's a mare.'

'But you're driving, that's great!' Her voice crackles through the speaker. 'I haven't said it recently, but I'm so proud of how well you're doing.'

'Getting better every day.'

'Good on you, best bitch. You're my superhero.'

She used to say that when we were at uni, even though she was the beautiful shining one, and it made me feel special. I realize it still does. It has always felt great to be important to Iso.

'I wanted to apologize for drinking so much at the party. And throwing up. I'm so embarrassed, and Mark's been even more moody so I know he's ashamed of me. There were strangers there, and you know what he's like with new people. I don't know why I did it. I've not been feeling that great, and he was . . . Anyway, it'll all be nothing, but it wasn't fair on you.'

'We didn't care, Iso. I didn't really notice you were pissed until you threw up. You held it together with panache.'

She laughs at the other end, relieved. 'I try, I try.'

'But are you and Mark okay?'

'Yeah. I think so.' She doesn't sound certain. 'It's just hard sometimes. He's so successful and I try to be the perfect trophy wife but sometimes I feel like it's not enough, you know? And none of us are getting any younger. Sometimes I think if he's not one hundred percent happy we should maybe part ways as friends and try our luck on someone new. You ever feel like that with Freddie? Or am I having some kind of early midlife crisis?'

It's rare to hear Iso sounding insecure. I'm her best friend. I should tell her to have it out with Mark if she's got some niggling doubts. I should tell her that I know *exactly* why Mark's been so moody recently. I should tell her about Cat, even if I spare her the video.

'You're perfect, Iso, and he loves you,' is what I say instead. 'And every couple has those moments. He's probably stressed about something at work.'

'Yeah, you're right. And sorry, I didn't mean to dump my shit on you. I just have that kind of paranoid feeling that something's going on.'

'Well, don't. You have nothing to worry about, okay?'

'Okay. I love you, Em. I was lost when you were in the hospital. So drive carefully, yes?'

'I will. And I love you too, and I'll call you later.'

Guilt twists in my gut like maggots eating at me. Iso's my oldest friend. I should tell her what I saw Mark and Cat doing and let them all figure it out from there, not stay silent while leeching money from—*blackmailing*—her husband. Sometimes that feels like a dream too. Did I really do that? How awful. This need to protect myself above others has always been a part of me, but maybe this is taking it too far. Maybe I should call Mark and give the money back.

But still, I think, as I pull into a parking space next to the chemist. He's sent the money now. And it's not like I'm using it just for me. It will get us out of trouble and get Freddie some help with gambling rehab and for all I know we have a baby coming. And anyway, Mark won't even miss it.

'Emily!'

As I get out of the car, I turn to see Joe there, wrapped up in a jacket and scarf, and I'm suddenly afraid that he *knows* that I know, but he smiles warmly.

'How's the headache? All gone?'

'Yes, yes, just needed a good night's sleep. Actually, I was on my way to see you and Sally.' My heart thrums hard in my chest. 'I was wondering if you were serious about painting me.'

'I'm always serious about painting. So yes, I was. I would love you to sit for me. I'm picking up Sally from the hairdresser's, then we're going to Carmello's for lunch.' He smiles. 'Why don't you join us? We can talk about it there.'

'That would be great,' I say. I take the arm he's holding out and feel his biceps under his blazer. Despite everything I suspect of him, he's still magnetic. I can understand how that girl in the pub looked at him. The idea of being naked as he paints. There's a sexual thrill I can't deny, even though I'm never going to do it.

We get to the salon just as the stylist is showing Sally the back of her head and giving her a waft of hairspray, and she grins and waves in the mirror.

'Emily's joining us for lunch.' Joe leans in and kisses her full and lingering on the mouth. 'You look gorgeous.'

'That really suits you,' I add.

She's had a fair amount cut off, three or four inches, maybe more from the amount hair littered around the chair, and a bunch of choppy layers cut in. It's a super-cool style. Let's hope *whole* Sally likes it. It feels surreal thinking that some of this woman's essence is stuck in my house. Maybe I am mad—maybe more than maybe—but I still believe it.

'Thanks.' She saunters over to the counter and Joe follows her, reaching for his credit card as a junior takes the robe from his wife and fetches her coat.

'Get that floor swept please, Sasha,' a stylist calls across to the junior, who nods, and my stomach does an excited flip as I look down. *Hair. Sally's. A lot of it.*

I lift my keys from my pocket and accidentally drop them at my feet, and as I lean down to pick them up, my back to the others at the counter, I also quickly grab a few cut locks and wrap them in a tissue, stuffing them away, hopefully before anyone sees. When I turn, head thumping with a rush of blood, Joe is still at the counter chatting and Sally has joined him. One item down.

'Lunch then, ladies?' Joe says as we come outside. I take one arm and Sally takes the other as he leads us to the restaurant, where we take a corner booth, Joe between us.

I study their dynamic as they talk me through the process of the artwork and the percentage they'd pay to me as a model. It's not a small amount. Joe really *is* a sought-after artist if they're making that much. Sally's constantly looking at him, adoration in her eyes. Maybe that's what he needs from women. Adulation. Maybe that's why he fell in love with her in the first place. She had her wit and charm and she adored him. But the downside was that she couldn't ever share him.

As the plates are cleared, I surreptitiously take the wet towel that Sally wiped her hands and mouth on after her garlic butter prawns and pocket it. Two items down. Then when we leave and Sally pops to the loo and Joe pays despite my protests, I sneak her napkin too. I don't need or want to go back to the cottage really, but I don't have a good excuse not to, so I impatiently drink my tea, have an obligatory toke on a joint as Joe rummages in their record collection for something to play, and then make my excuses, saying I need to get back before Freddie's home from work.

'I can walk you to your car, if you like?' Joe says.

'I'll be fine. It's barely fifty feet from here. But thank you. I'll talk to Freddie about the painting. See what he thinks.'

I leave them to it, Sally already swaying to the music, mildly stoned, and I know that as soon as I'm out the door they'll be dancing together and probably very quickly fucking. I let myself out, taking the silk scarf she was wearing at lunch, now draped on a coat hook, and get back out into the icy air.

Fuck it. By the time they notice anything is missing, it will be too late. The strains of music drift out to me as I walk away. Some seventies folky-sounding band I don't know. *Enjoy it while it lasts, Joe,* I think. *Your chickens are about to come home to roost.*

The drive home is uneventful. When I get there, without giving myself any time to think, I go to the kitchen and grab a roasting pan, matches, and firelighters before heading straight upstairs. It's getting dark already, and who knows when Freddie will get back. Even with the lights on, the upper landing is edged in suffocating shadows. As I push open the door to the primary bedroom, there's an awful chill hanging in the air, and the floorboards creak heavily under me as I walk to the center of the empty space. I don't stop though. I know what I have to do.

Seated on the floor, I empty my Sally collection into the roasting tin and add the firelighters. It takes two goes for my trembling hands to light a match, and I throw it straight onto the firelighters before any draught can extinguish it. The flames appear immediately and shoot up unnaturally high toward the ceiling, and I sit back, heart racing, and watch it start to burn.

I know straightaway that something strange is happening. It's as if all the air in the room is being sucked into the roasting tin like a whirlpool and expelling the flames, bright white with a swirling black smoke. The smoke expands and expands, filling the room fast, dark, sulphuric and ashy, and I scuttle backward, my eyes already burning and watering. I try not to breathe in, but I have no choice, and the hot smoke goes into my lungs and suddenly—

72.

I'm not in the upstairs bedroom. I'm not anywhere and yet I'm everywhere, watching the action. I'm the house perhaps. The power that was built into the house sensing what's about to happen.

They're fighting in the bedroom. They look so different, so young, but it's them. A small suitcase is open on the bed, and while Sally, red-faced from hysterical crying and rage, still launches accusations at him—I know there was something happening! I could see it in the way you looked at her. How was I supposed to sit by and watch that and not say anything? How could you do that to me!—*he's yanking her clothes out of a chest of drawers and putting them in it. He looks wild, his pupils so dilated his eyes are nearly entirely black.*

'I can't do this anymore,' he finally says when her tirade of anger and jealousy and insecurity pauses for breath. 'You're exhausting me. I need to breathe.'

'I thought you loved me.' She tries to tug a sweater out of his hands, but he pulls it free and folds it into the case.

'I did love you. I do love you. But I can't deal with this *you. All these questions. I barely knew Georgina and you've run her out of town. Do you realize how crazy that is? I can't go the rest of my life without talking to another woman, Sally. I can't go through the rest of my life without sleeping with another woman. I won't. I'm an artist. I need that freedom. You said you needed it too!'*

He storms out, slightly unsteady on his feet, and I'm pulled with him, tugged through the air like a balloon on a string as he goes to the bathroom and clumsily gathers up her toiletries.

'You can't do this! I'll change.' She's followed him, and the rage has turned to fear and upset as she realizes he means business. Her heavy eye makeup—a look that I somehow know, maybe because Joe does, isn't her usual but is Georgina's that she's made a pathetic attempt to replicate—has streaked down her face, a tragic rejected clown.

'You say that every time.' He pushes past her and back out onto the landing, dragging me with him.

'I mean it this time!' She rushes out of the bathroom and clings to his arm. 'Please, Joe. Please. I'll kill myself if you leave me. You know I will. Please . . .'

It's too much for him though, this ritual that they've been through so many times in their relationship. His love is never enough for her, and it never will be. That black hole of jealousy and need just gets bigger and bigger. This time, this final time, her fingers clinging onto him, and her tears, do nothing but disgust him. The weed is strong and he's still tripping a little from the acid he did in the studio last night, the light and colour and emotions glitteringly surreal. Her fingers turn into dirty talons digging into him and momentarily her face contorts. She's a vulture that won't let go. Why can't she just be the Sally that he loves? The Sally who was so cool with everything that he is in a way that made him love her so much more. He's at breaking point. Even the drugs can't calm him down. It's all snapping inside him, and as she tries to pull him toward her, he pushes her hard away. 'Enough!'

He pushes her too hard.

Surprised, she stumbles backward, trips over her own feet, and falls flat on her back.

'Oh.'

It's the only sound she makes, and then nothing. She just lies there, silent and still.

Joe hesitates, confused. Maybe she's been drinking or she's so overwrought that she just can't bring herself to move, because he's sure he didn't push her that hard, did he?

'Sally?' Colours glitter brightly, trailing at the corners of his vision.

She doesn't answer. Her hand twitches and then so does her leg. Her eyes, wide open, look left and right as her mouth tries to move.

'This isn't funny. You know I've been tripping. Don't freak me out. Get up. We can talk about things.' He's afraid now. He doesn't know quite what's happened, but he knows, deep down inside, that with that push something went very, very wrong.

It's when he kneels beside her that he sees the blood starting to pool behind her head. 'Oh god.' It's his turn to sound distraught now. Her throat gurgles. She's desperately trying to say something, her eyes darting this way and that, confused, not understanding what's happening to her.

He *suddenly understands though*.

The nail.

The one that he was supposed to take out from the loose floor-board after she nearly trod on it a week or so ago. He doesn't even know how it got there. An inch of nail sticking up the wrong way, a floorer's revenge perhaps for a snotty homeowner not happy with their work. He almost trod on it himself once and has skirted around it since then, too busy creating art to find pliers and a new floorboard and make the repair himself.

Now it's too late.

He lifts Sally's head and shoulders carefully away from the floor and hears the awful squelch as the base of her skull comes free from the bloody metal spike underneath. He wonders how something so small can have done so much damage and that maybe in a minute when the shock wears off she'll get up and start shouting at him again. As his adrenaline fires up, whatever's left of the LSD momentarily makes her blood a beautiful bright red, but it's sticky on his fingers and he's worried he'll never get it off. Her eyes are terrified, and he knows, deep down, that something irreparable has happened and that she's not going to be getting up ever again.

'I'm sorry. I'm sorry,' he whispers, sitting back on his heels, eyes wide in horror, not knowing what to do. That's not strictly true. He might be high, but he does know what to do. He should go downstairs, pick up the phone, and call for an ambulance. That's what he should do, but he can't bring himself to move. What would be the outcome of that call? A wheelchair maybe. A life spent feeding her with a teaspoon. Cleaning up her shit. Maybe he could do all that if she was the Sally he loved. But the jealousy and insecurities will still be there. They will turn to hate. He'll be chained to her in something awful. He can see the years stretching endless ahead, a prison of a life.

A prison of a life for her too.

He moves forward a little. 'Sally?' he whispers. The air vibrates with his word, but he ignores the shimmer of acid trails in his vision. They're not real. Sally is real. What he's done to Sally is real. Isn't it?

Her eyes dart toward him, no movement at all in her limbs now, and they stare at each other, and for a moment all he feels is a rush of love and warmth for her because she's so afraid and helpless. And then he sees it. The tiny kernel of rage, a splinter of it clear in her expression.

'I'm sorry, Sally,' he says again, as if there's any way she can forgive him for what he's about to do. 'I'm sorry.'

He closes his eyes so he doesn't have to see his bloody hands as they press against her mouth and nose. Her face feels like cold dough, and he wonders if his hands will sink right through it. He doesn't have to hold tight because she can't struggle, but he twists his head away even as he sobs, wondering how he got into this nightmare. After a minute or so he takes his hands away and slowly, so slowly, turns back to look at her.

Her eyes are still wide and staring upward but there's no life in them, no life or love or jealousy or light or darkness. She's empty. She's dead.

Time passes. Hours. Day turns to night. He sits on the floor beside her and tries to think. It's done now. It can't be undone. Can he say he found her like this? He was in the garden collecting flowers and came in and she was dead? He smokes skunk until his throat and eyes burn from the weed and exhaustion.

When he finally straightens out a little, he looks at her splayed body. She fell backward. In the middle of a hallway. There's no way that could happen without a push. Even the local yokel police would have suspicions about that. So what else is there he can say? Tell half the truth? They argued and he shoved her away and she landed unluckily. Could he get away with saying she died fast? Would they be able to tell? It's been hours already since she landed on the nail and he still hasn't called anyone. He's not local. Will they turn on him? He can see the headlines now.

Drugged artist murders local girl after fight over another woman. Crime of passion. Life imprisonment. His life is over. He doesn't know what to do.

So he does nothing.

For three days he does nothing.

I watch him through the endless hours, the sleepless nights and days of it. Sometimes he laughs. Sometimes he cries. He drinks. He smokes weed. Takes pills. Not acid, he won't trust himself on acid, but the time passes in a haze. He plays music. He sits in the garden and howls at the moon. It's a fever dream I live through with him. He thinks very hard about killing himself too, but doesn't know how to do it and very much wants to live. He thinks about running but he has nowhere to go. No passport even.

It's a hot summer and this week is the hottest, dampest of the year. Thunder bugs hang in the air, nature holding its breath, waiting for the weather to break. On day two, Sally, forever on the middle landing floor, starts to stink. She smells bad, rotten and sweet, and if he gets too close, he thinks he can hear little popping sounds coming from inside her.

He opens the landing window to let the stench of her out, but the upstairs is becoming unbearable. Still, he can't stay away. He goes and looks at her and sometimes he can't remember a time when she wasn't just a body on the floor. He wonders if the world outside has died. Or maybe he has died, and this is his hell. He wishes he could sleep. If he could sleep, then there is half a chance that this might be a dream when he wakes up.

But he's not asleep, he's high and drunk, and Sally's rotting and time is moving on.

On day three her mother calls. He doesn't answer at first, the noise so alien and not part of this new universe of him and rotting Sally and the stench and his madness, but finally he does. He hears himself saying she's in Taunton for the day. He's going to pick her up later. He says yes of course they'll visit this week. Yes, she is feeling better. When he hangs up, he has no recollection of calling in to her work sick on her behalf, but he must have done. His self-preservation instincts working for him even if the rest of him is failing woefully.

In the middle of the third day he decides enough is enough. He'll hide her for now and then find some way to dispose of her. The septic tank perhaps, if he cuts her up into small enough pieces that will rot down. Buy some sulphuric acid and throw it in. Put her in a drum. Something. But he needs her gone. He needs to sleep and he can't do that with her on the landing.

He stares at her fizzing body, watching the fly crossing her eyeball. He's opened and closed the window so many times, afraid that the stink may waft down and carry his guilt straight to the local constable, that now he thinks it would be odd without the smell. He looks up the stairs. He'll put her on the top for now and think on it all. The small part of his rational mind that remains knows that by tomorrow, one way or another, the game is up. They can't stay here, just the two of them, how jealous Sally always wanted it, forever. He must either confess or get rid of her.

266

He has washing-up gloves on when he wraps her in a sheet and ties the end off with thick garden wire. He's never thought of himself as physically strong, but all that time spent outside digging the plant beds and laying fresh lawn has given him some summer muscles, and combined with his sheer desperation, he manages to haul her up a few steps and then leverage her over his shoulder. He's rubbed Vicks under his nose, and taken a couple of uppers, but it's no match for the new Eau de Sally enveloping him.

He starts to cry when he reaches the top landing and wobbles slightly, his legs shaking and tired, and momentarily thinks he may fall backward himself. But he grips the banister hard and yanks himself forward. He won't be found at the bottom of the stairs suffocating and broken under the rotting body of his girlfriend. The door creaks open, and as he drags her in, the heel of her shoe, poking out from the sheet, scrapes on the wood like fingernails before the door creaks and clicks shut again.

He drops the body in the center of the room and staggers out, closing the door behind him. He opens the windows on the landing again. He changes the bedsheets so they're fresh. He unpacks Sally's case of things she kept in his house, putting them all back where they were, sobbing some more, remembering how lovely she could be when she wasn't so jealous. How perfect they were in those heady first days.

He scrubs the landing floor and burns his bloody clothes in the fire. Finally, he has a long bath, and eventually, after three long days and nights, he crawls between the clean sheets and falls asleep.

He has somehow, just by moving her, resigned himself to his fate. He can't cut her up. He's not that person. One last sleep in his bed, and then tomorrow he'll face the music. There's nothing left to do.

He is fast asleep when the upstairs door opens. He doesn't hear Sally come down the stairs and then go down to the kitchen and boil the kettle.

He only wakes up when she's beside him on the bed, a cup of tea on the table for him, sitting cross-legged in her leggings, hair Bardot-sexy around her perfect face.

'I had the strangest dream,' she says. 'But I can't remember it. Everything is a blur.' The confused look only lasts a moment before she shakes her head and smiles at him. 'Anyway, I'm cooking eggs. You coming down?' She gets up, then looks back from the doorway, frowning. 'By the way, did I have a fight with Georgina about something?' She's puzzled, a memory not fitting quite right. 'I should call and apologize. So silly. Maybe we should have her over for a drink. Maybe you should paint her.'

He stares after her as she goes.

The sheet is gone from the upstairs room, back in the laundry cupboard. It smells fresh and clean. It's as if it never happened. Maybe it didn't. Maybe it was all a crazy, long acid trip. That has to be it. There's no other explanation. Only weed from now on. No more nightmares like that. Still, he locks the upstairs bedroom door and decides he won't use it anymore. Maybe it's time to move out of this house—

73.

Emily

And then I'm back in the room, gasping for breath. There's no black smoke, just the pale light of the bulb and the remnants of ash cooling in the baking tray. I look around me. I *feel* for something in the house. Nothing. Just me and the bricks and mortar. No bad smell or oppressive atmosphere. It's a lovely spacious primary suite ready to be moved into.

I sit back on my heels, and while the world has righted itself, my head still spins with what I've seen of the past, what I've just *lived*, and it takes a few moments before I feel like me again. Now that I've experienced it, I understand everything that's been going on.

The nail in the hallway that kept appearing and disappearing. That was where Sally died. The window opening and slamming. The sound of the bedroom door opening and creaking shut. Bits of the past being visited on me. Clues as to what Joe did to Sally.

Thinking of her body lying rotting for days on the landing outside our current bedroom makes me shiver. It's so horrifying, and it's left me shaken, but I know it's all true. As my breath slows down, I know with absolute certainty that Sally Freemantle was murdered and her soul torn in two. One part free and one part trapped in this room until I freed her.

I stay there in a daze until pins and needles force me to my feet. I pick up the pan and hobble out into the hallway. Still nothing. No smell. No awful sensation. Just a house with only me in it. Will Larkin Lodge get hungry again? Want a new occupant in the room? Does it attract couples with secrets? Couples like Freddie and me?

You will die here.

No, I won't. I know the secret of the house now. I'm prepared. And despite his debts, I'm not killing Freddie. We are not like those other couples. Hannah and Christopher Hopper. Fortuna and Gerald. Joe and Sally.

Sally. Has she *joined* back up already? Would that be instant? What was she doing when it happened? Would Joe know? Has he noticed a change in her yet? Is she angry with him? Will she even know what happened? More than that, will Joe? My head is a whirl of questions and I'm afraid of most of the answers. But I did what Sally wanted. She can't come after me for it, and their marriage isn't my business.

We need to sell this house and get out. Start again some-where else.

It's a relief when Freddie comes home. We order Chinese, curl up together on the sofa, and watch a movie. Despite my sore breasts my period still hasn't come, and as I lie there in his arms, I realize that I really am hoping that I'm pregnant. Freddie wants to put his mistakes right. I need to do the same. A baby that is truly ours. No guilt attached. A fresh life for a fresh start. We're not like the rest of them. We're really not.

74.

Bright Wing is gone.

She's flown back to the roosts where the others gather, nevermore to return. He barely remembers that she was here, as if she too was part of the strange dream of his life these past few seasons.

Broken Wing is back!

Her chest is plump, feathers glossy, and her black eyes shine with the fierce bravery and intelligence and humour that made him want to nest with her so long ago. Before the white came into her feathers and brought with it the mean streak that had hidden inside her.

The white patches are still there amid the damage, but the mean streak has gone, and she flies as well as she ever did. They soar together above the frozen moors, cawing to each other, dancing together. And while he knows that this is *not right*, this is not the way of beasts and birds and man, and dead is dead whichever you are, he finds he does not care. His mate is not dead. That is all he knows.

His mate is not dead and she no longer pecks at him.

They turn their backs on the strange house on the moor and fly away toward the warm roofs and nests of the villages and towns. They fly away from farmers' guns and strange houses that sit and wait to lure them in. They fly away from other birds. They don't need them. His head bends in toward hers, warm and inviting.

They have each other again.

Forevermore.

They fly away and they don't look back.

75.

Freddie

'Another beer?' Emily nods at Paul's empty bottle.

'I'll go.' I start getting to my feet, the dutiful husband, but she waves me back down and smiles.

'I've got to keep moving. Been a lazy day and my leg is aching.'

'How's she doing?' Paul watches her thoughtfully as she heads out to the kitchen. 'She called me to say sorry for snapping in the car.'

'She was pretty dark this morning but seems better this afternoon. She's got an appointment with her specialist next week, so once that's done I'll feel happier.'

As it happens, Emily hasn't mentioned any strange events in the house for the past couple of days, and in fact she laughed it off the last time I mentioned it, saying how embarrassed she was that she got so worked up in her imagination. It's been an odd few days. I tapped at one of the pipes that leads from the kitchen upstairs when she was in the bath last night, but she had no reaction. Maybe she didn't even hear it.

'I still worry that she's emotionally unstable,' I add. I don't know why. Emily's not suicidal, and I'm not going to kill my wife. Even if I really wanted to, she's making it difficult. She's been ridiculously nice over the past few days. Almost like the old Emily. She's been affectionate. Joyful almost. 'Not that I think she's going to—'

I'm cut off by three loud toots of a car horn coming from the front of the house, and the moment is gone. 'More visitors it seems,' I finish as we get to our feet.

Emily is already on the drive, and we join her in time to see Joe and Sally getting out of an overloaded estate car.

'What's happening?' I ask.

'We're going on a road trip!' Sally smiles. 'Rented a place in Scotland with a studio. Getting back to nature for a month. We've always wanted to go, and now the weather's turned milder we figured why not. Joe's going to paint me again.'

'Exciting.' Paul peers into where the back seat is covered in cases. 'Are you sure you're only gone for a month?'

'The plants from the studio are in the boot,' Joe says to Paul. 'We wondered if you could look after them? You weren't in so we thought we'd try here.'

'I can do my best. Hopefully I won't let you down.'

'Brilliant. Jump in and we can go down to yours and unload them. Some of the pots are pretty heavy.'

'Sure.'

'I'll give you a hand,' I say. It won't take long to get the pots out between me and Paul, and then when Joe leaves to pick up Sally I can labour my worries about Emily more with Paul.

'Great,' Sally says. 'I'll stay here for a chat with Emily while you men do the manual labour.'

I look at Emily still hanging back on the house steps. 'Is that okay?'

'Of course. Make sure you carry the heavy ones.'

I don't know if it's the sudden shadow of clouds across the winter sun, but she looks tense. I dash inside and grab my keys from the hook, then jump into my own car. 'Okay, let's go.'

As I wave goodbye out of the window, Emily half raises a hand back then folds her arms protectively at her chest again. What is wrong with her? Her good mood has evaporated. I wonder if Paul noticed it too.

76.

Emily

'So,' Sally says as the cars round the corner onto the lane, disappearing out of sight. 'Here we are.'

Her whole demeanour changes now that the men have gone. She slouches slightly, one hand on her hip, a wry smile on her face, but all her *ease* has vanished. There's a sudden hardness in her expression. Something brittle.

'Joe hasn't noticed a thing. Since you released me.' I must look stupefied, because she laughs. 'Hard to get your head around it, isn't it?' She glances up at the house. 'I won't come inside again if it's all the same to you. I've spent far too long in there for one lifetime.'

She takes a few steps forward and then leans against the small wall by the steps where I'm standing, watching her, this *new* Sally.

'But now I'm free. Thanks to you.' She looks down at her hands. 'So strange to be in such an old body. Enjoy your youthful skin while you have it. Getting out of the shower in front of the bathroom mirror has been a horror story that's taking some getting used to. But I shouldn't complain. I thought I was stuck in there forever.'

It's so strange, listening to her. She's still Sally, but with added ingredients. An edge. An anger. Is this because of what happened to her, or was it always there? Is it part of why Joe killed her?

'And maybe I nearly was.' She shakes her head. 'In that godawful room upstairs you eventually start to mesh with the house. It sucks you in and it gets harder to be *you*. It eats you up. Devours your being. Fortuna Carmichael's husband, Gerald, eventually died out here so that killed him in there, but there are echoes of others trapped in the brickwork. People who lived too long out here to ever truly release the bits inside when they died. They feed the house. It likes it.'

She shivers and I realize that however bad the feeling I got from her presence in the room was, it was nowhere near as awful as the room felt for her.

'The books,' I say eventually. 'Was that you?'

'You will die here.' She lights a cigarette and exhales. 'I needed to get your attention. And it was a warning. This place. It brings out the worst in people. It's been doing it with you two. I saw everything.' Her eyes are flint sharp. 'Your husband's hidden gambling.' She nods down the lane. 'You should leave him. He's a weak piece of shit. What's going to happen the next time you have a crisis? All your money down the drain again?'

'He needs help,' I say. 'I've got some money coming—'

'Ah yes, the blackmail.' She laughs. 'You surprised me there. But like I said, there's something in this house that brings the worst parts of you to the surface. I was always jealous, yes, and there's no way I could have done the open marriage thing long term, but being in this house made me worse. It made Joe more selfish too. The bastard murdered me, after all.'

'Do you think, after you came back, he realized there was part of you trapped in Larkin Lodge?'

'I don't think he gave it a moment's thought. Joe is all about Joe, and I was compliant and adoring. I honestly think he's persuaded himself it was just a bad trip. That he never killed me.' She takes another fierce inhale. 'But he did. And he has to pay for that.'

'What are you going to do?' I can hear the rumble of an engine heading back up the lane, Joe come to collect his loving wife. *All* of her. I watch her posture and expression change as the car comes into view, straighter and more serene.

'I'll think of something,' she says before coming forward and kissing me on the cheek, enveloping me in her perfume. 'Take care, Emily.' She squeezes my arm. 'I owe you one. And I mean that.'

As she jumps in and they drive away, I wave as if everything is perfectly normal.

'Safe travels!' I call after them, and then Sally twists around and smiles a vicious good-bye at me, and I know in that instant that I'm very unlikely to see Joe ever again.

77

Freddie

The drive up the lane with a slight beer buzz doesn't take the edge off the frustration of not having the time to reinforce my worries with Paul. As soon as Joe was on his way back to Sally, I'd begun to tell the Vicar that this calmer and happier Emily was only a show for visitors and that behind closed doors her moods were entirely different, but his phone rang and it was a sick parishioner who needed a visit.

Still, I think as I drive. *There's no rush.* The bees buzz behind my eyes, impatiently contradicting me. Of course there's a rush. Every day the noose of debt gets tighter and I get closer to losing my kneecaps. The road is full of grey slush, the snow melting into dirt. I wish Emily wasn't being so nice. So much like her old self. Maybe she isn't thinking of divorcing me after all. I can't decide if that's a disappointment or not. How far down the road of setting up her suicide am I?

Setting up her suicide. I'm so weak. I have to laugh at how I sugarcoat things even to myself. Plotting her murder, that's what I really mean. If I gave her enough sleeping pills, it wouldn't even hurt. She just wouldn't wake up. I wouldn't want to hurt her. God, I'm so tired.

I pull up at the postbox to empty it of any final demands and credit letters that I'm not even going to open before I throw them on the fire. The dread makes me stare at my phone for a moment, the temptation to have *just one go* on the PokerPlayUK app that I've deleted and added back so many times. I shove my phone into my pocket and get out. If I'm really considering doing the unthinkable to get myself out of this mess, I need to stop now.

There are three bills waiting for me in the box, and I screw them up and stuff them into my pockets, but there's something else.

A white A4 envelope neatly addressed to Emily.

A business envelope, and it feels like there's a fair amount of paperwork inside. She *has* filed for divorce.

I look more closely and see that it's come from the company Mark works at. What the hell is Mark doing sending paperwork to Emily? It's not like they've even ever been close. Is he somehow advising her on how to get the best out of this awful financial mess? Moving her pension somewhere out of reach maybe?

I open it as carefully as possible although the paper still tears, but nothing I can't tape up and pretend it came that way. I pull out the documents, immediately recognizing them as paperwork for a Jersey account—*Why the hell does Emily have a Jersey account?*—and then look at the short note written in Mark's busy scrawl paperclipped to the front.

The 150k is all there. We're done. Destroy the film of me and Cat. Get out of your friendship with Iso.

I stare for a very long time, totally confused. What film of Cat and Mark would Emily have? One hundred and fifty thousand pounds. Why would Mark give her so much money for it? The obvious truth slowly sinks in as a chill wind cuts through me. Mark is fucking Cat. Emily knows and has blackmailed him. Now she has a hundred and fifty thousand pounds hidden away. She's got a get-out plan for herself and is going to leave me in all the shit.

That fucking bitch.

78

Emily

I've done a lot of thinking in the couple of days since Sally and Joe left and the house fell still.

We are not like those other couples. We are going to be okay. Mark's paperwork didn't arrive, so I've chased him and he's emailed me copies as proof while he gets a second lot of papers prepared. I've told him to send the replacements recorded delivery. That way the postman will have to bring them to the house, but it doesn't matter if Freddie sees them. I've finally made my decision. I'm going to tell him about the money and we'll work through his problems together. We're both flawed. We can both be selfish. He's gambled away all our money because I nearly died, and I've coldheartedly black-mailed one of our friends to save us. Neither of us is perfect. But at least we're whole.

We've been together a long time and I won't give up on us now. I don't want us to become like all those other couples, staying together out of habit, love having curdled into mild contempt. We're better than that. And I've got the money and a plan. Yes, Freddie can be weak under his sweetness, but I need to accept that, and anyway it leaves space for me to take charge. I've found four potential places in France that could work as a home with space for a little bed-and-breakfast or

Airbnb. We could leave everything behind and start again. Live our best lives.

I've gone into Wiveliscoombe for the day, and while the librarian prints out Mark's documents, I've found a comfy chair and am browsing a book on living in France. I'm not keen on spending too much time in the house alone, especially after what Sally said about it bringing out the worst in its residents. I'd thought about that all night after they left, and she's right. I would never have blackmailed Mark before we lived in Larkin Lodge. And the way Freddie and I fought about the nail. That wasn't like us. There were plenty of things happening in the house that weren't Sally too. The cold draught. The way the bathroom door opened just enough for me to follow Mark and Cat but not enough for me to get caught. Who knows why the house is the way it is—there was no explanation in the ledger—but maybe it came from the energy of the miserable souls buried so awfully at the crossroads for hundreds of years. So much misunderstood unhappiness. Maybe that's why the house draws couples with problems to it. I was angry with Freddie when I was looking at the house, and he said that the house was there on my iPad when I was in hospital, but I'm pretty sure I'd closed the window down. I always do.

The house wanted us. But I'm wise to it now.

After an hour or so a group of nursery children come into the library for story time, so I get some lunch at a cute café, grab some beef from the butcher for dinner, and then, after going to the chemist, on my drive home I pull in at the vicarage.

'Hey.' As Paul opens the front door I hold out a cake box. 'I was in the village for lunch and they had such a great cake selection I bought you a couple.' I'm on a charm offensive after seeing the cautious side glances he kept giving me when he came over last Sunday. It may take us a couple of months before we sell the house, and I want to get our friendship back on an even keel.

'That's so very sweet of you. Thank you.'

'I can't stop but I wanted to thank you for being so supportive since we've moved in. You've made us very welcome in the village.' Behind him the narrow hallway is filled with the plants from Sally and Joe's studio and my stomach flutters wondering how they're getting on. 'And I'm sorry again for getting snappy in the car. The pain can really affect my mood sometimes, but I've been taking stronger painkillers and they're really helping.'

'I'm so pleased to hear it.' He steps a little back into the house. 'Are you sure you won't come in?'

'I can't today. But don't be a stranger. Maybe we can keep one another company while Sally and Joe are away.'

'I would like that. And it's good to see you looking so well. You're positively glowing.'

'Honestly, I feel great, I really do.' *Glowing*. Am I glowing or is he being polite? I guess the pack of three pregnancy tests in my bag will answer that question soon enough. 'I've turned a corner and my head is much clearer. I think I'd underestimated the effect of my accident on my senses. Looking forward to seeing my specialist and getting the all clear.' I nod at the plants before he can comment. 'Are you managing with those okay? Any news from Sally and Joe?'

'I'm doing my best. And I had a text to say they'd arrived but that was it. I expect they're too busy having fun.'

'I expect so.' I can only imagine. 'Anyway, I should get back. I'm attempting a beef Wellington for Freddie today. Wish me luck. And feel free to pop up any time.'

I breeze off to the car, and his smile as he waves me off is much more relaxed. I feel good and my leg is hardly aching today. I want to get home. And then there is the pregnancy test. I can't fight the excitement. Time to expunge my guilt.

It'll be like I never cheated. I can pretend all that was just a dream. I'm going to be a good mother. I know I am.

79

Freddie

She cooked beef Wellington for dinner tonight and had got dressed up and was all smiles and affection. It took every ounce of energy to play along while in my head the wheels kept turning to the rhythm of *fucking bitch fucking bitch fucking bitch*. Two long days since I found the envelope from Mark and she's been sweetness and light and not said a word. I chewed the meat and pastry—at least one of us can afford to buy a huge lump of organic finest beef—until it was a pulp, not trusting my dry throat to be able to swallow.

I can't figure her out. What game is she playing? She's got this one hundred and fifty thousand pounds from Mark hidden away, but she's still here playing the forgiving wife. I did the washing up, insisting she go and relax, and she kissed me, telling me to hurry so we could watch a film together. She had lipstick on her teeth and it suddenly revolted me. My wife felt like my enemy. I made a work excuse, ignoring her disappointment, and hid in the red room with my laptop and pretended to work. Eventually she went to bed, and I promised to join her as soon as I could.

I haven't joined her. I've been staring at the crimson walls, lost in the heavy flock wallpaper, thinking of her cold dead body. The insurance claim. The money that would be all mine.

Even Mark's one hundred and fifty thousand would come to me. What's good for the gander is good for the goose.

The house cools as the night thickens outside. She said she'd been out all day today, in the local town, and once again I'd noticed her eyes slip away as if she was hiding a secret. I can't stop thinking about her seeing a divorce lawyer. Maybe they've told her she has to keep up the charade of pleasantries. Don't give me time to launch a counterattack. Devious little Emily. My stomach gurgles, the heavy dinner too rich for my nerves, and I get to my feet. I should go to bed. Sleep on it. Be fresh in the morning. The bees are buzzing so loud in my head I think it's going to burst.

A lamp is on in the sitting room, and as I reach to turn it off, I see Emily's iPad on the coffee table still has its screen lit even though she's been upstairs a while. It's weirdly not locked but open on her emails. I pick it up, sitting on the sofa, and am about to go into search to see if she's been chatting with a divorce lawyer when I realize the email thread that's open is from her old work account. And the date is from a few weeks before the holiday. I didn't even know she could still get into that account. I presumed it was deleted when she left, but maybe she archived them for reasons I can't fathom. What other explanation could there be?

It's not a group thread, just Emily and her old boss, Neil, who she always raved about but who I thought was a bit of a smug prick. Handsome in an older man way, I guess, but even if Em couldn't see it I knew he looked down on women a little, like they always needed looking after or rescuing. One of *those*.

I pause before hitting the search button, my eyes catching on a phrase. *I have no regrets and we're both adults but I perfectly understand. And this is premature, but please know that you're getting the promotion tomorrow. Not because of this, obviously, but because you deserve it. It had already been decided before the conference, in case you had concerns.*

Not because of what? And why was he talking about no regrets? Them both being adults?

I open up the whole thread and feel steadily more sick as I read the whole thing through. I remember the conference she went to. It was over a weekend. A bunch of them from work were going and she said it would be good for her promotion chances.

The written phrases make my vision swim. *Shouldn't have done it. We were drunk. It was great but it can't happen again.*

Emily fucked her boss.

I toss the iPad down, not wanting to touch it. She drunk-fucked her boss for a promotion. My Emily. Holier-than-thou Emily. She cheated on me. No wonder she was so shitty during the holiday. Was it because she was struggling with the guilt?

A second, more awful thought dawns on me. The drinking on holiday when she was pregnant and hadn't told me. In the long weeks she was in the coma, I'd fought those niggling questions in my head about why she'd been drinking if she thought she might be pregnant. Why she was so moody. Now the answers are coming to me with crystal clarity.

The miscarriage she had in the hospital. The pregnancy I grieved for.

Was that baby even mine?

80.

Freddie

Fucking bitch fucking bitch fucking bitch.

Have I ever known her at all? Emily the blackmailer. Emily the liar. Emily the cheat. I drank more whiskey and went to bed at about two but only managed maybe forty minutes of restless sleep, then got up early and came back downstairs again. I can't be near her. The walls of the house are more comforting, like a protective womb around me.

I pour myself a third cup of coffee, my nerves jangling as the rumbling pipes overhead come to a stop. She's out of her shower, and that's my cue to start her breakfast. I need to stay calm. I need to figure out my plan with a cool head. I have to be kind to her just in case she talks to anyone. She needs to think I still love her. I still care. I *do* care. I care about that one hundred and fifty thousand pounds. On top of the life insurance, that will leave me very comfortable. Maybe I could move to France for a while. Spend time with my mum's French family. They've always wanted to see me more since her death. I could start a little bed-and-breakfast there. A life with no stress.

There's a friendly knock on the door as I'm about to start chopping the peppers, onions, and mushrooms Emily says she wants in her omelette, and it's Merrily Watkins there, a big smile on her ruddy face. Another wave of irritation passes through me. No wonder she's smiling. Emily happily gave her a twenty-five-grand job. Why would she do that? Is she thinking she can kick me out with nothing? Pay the mortgage herself?

'Sorry to bother you.' Merrily cuts through my thoughts. 'But our Portaloo hasn't turned up yet. Not going to be here until the day after tomorrow. Will it be all right for us to pop in the house when the need takes us? I'll tell the boys to take their boots off.'

'Of course, no problem. I'll leave the door unlocked. Help yourself.'

'Excellent. We'll get on. Hopefully we won't be too noisy for you.'

'Great.' I smile but don't encourage any more conversation or offer any drinks, and she treks back toward the wreck of our garden.

I grip the waxy green pepper tight, but still the small paring knife slips as I try to cut into it so I swap it out for one of the larger, sharper knives and start to slice. I have no appetite myself. It was bad enough finding out about the money, but the thought of Emily cheating has destroyed me. How could she do that? What happened to the Emily I fell in love with? How much did she want that promotion?

There have been times over the months when I've wondered if maybe I nudged her over the edge when we were on that ridge, but I know I didn't. Deep down I know I didn't push her and I did my best to grab her hand. God, if I had that time again.

The words keep going round in my head, *Fucking bitch fucking bitch fucking bitch*, and they mix with the buzzing of the bees and I chop harder and harder.

Marriage is teamwork, Emily, I think. *It's time you played your part.*

'Freddie.' She breezes into the kitchen in a pretty dress and with makeup on. What's all that for? She looks happy, *smug*, as she comes up close to me and touches my arm. 'We need to talk.'

This is it. The woman who cheated on me is now going to say she's divorcing me. *Fucking bitch.* All thoughts of keeping her sweet vanish from my mind.

'I know about the money, Emily,' I growl as a red mist comes over me. 'And I know you fucked that wanker behind my back.' A red mist, the same colour as the red room walls, fills my vision, as if it's crept inside me overnight and wants to escape. 'You're a fucking bitch.'

Her eyes widen as I step closer, at first confused, and then horribly surprised.

'What?' I say. And then I look down.

81.

Emily

'Freddie.' I virtually bounce into the kitchen, almost without a limp, and get right up close so he can see I've made an effort. I wanted to do this last night but he was tired after work and clearly not in a great mood, but this morning is different. He's cooking me breakfast even though I'm too excited to eat. I thought I wouldn't sleep last night, but I was out like a light so I'm fully refreshed. I'm *glowing*.

I'm wearing a dress, one that I last wore on a date night before I did that awful thing—a different life ago. I smile at him, unable to contain my happiness. I was thinking of hiding one of the three tests I've taken in a row—I had to be certain this time—somewhere he'd find it, but I want to look him in the eyes and share the news. Maybe I'll even be honest about the other thing. I need to go into this with a clean slate, and maybe if I tell him how much I instantly regretted it, he'll forgive me. Secrets are the death of trust. I've kept the tests though—they're tucked away in the back of my underwear drawer for now. Mementos already. I'm so excited. He's going to be so happy. I go up close to him and touch his arm. 'We need to talk.'

It's only now that I'm inches from his face that I can see that something's wrong. His arm is so tense under my fingertips that his muscles might snap. His eyes are dark and angry. More than angry. He looks *mad*.

'I know about the money, Emily.' He growls at me like an uncaged wolf. 'And I know you fucked that wanker behind my back. You're a fucking bitch.'

He steps in close as I try to protest—this isn't how this is supposed to go, not at all—and then something feels horribly wrong. I'm confused, my eyes widening as I gasp.

'What?' he asks, and then looks down.

'You hit me.' I find it hard to get the words out, he's knocked the breath right out of me. He actually hit me.

'Oh god,' he says, and then the madness drains out of his eyes and all I can see is fear and my own shocked face in his pupils. Suddenly I'm very afraid, but I have to look down too. *Oh god.*

All I can see is the knife handle. *Where is the knife?* I grunt slightly, not able to catch my breath. The knife is inside me. I can feel it, cold in the middle of me.

'Oh god. Freddie.' My words are barely air. *It was only a little knife though, a paring knife. It can't do that much harm, surely. Can it?* I grip at the kitchen counter, my whole left side losing strength, and then I see it. The paring knife is on the side.

'Oh god,' I try to say again, and then I clutch at his chest, trying to keep upright, trying to keep alive, there is a knife inside me, and then I'm crumpling to the kitchen floor, and there must be something, there must be, and then it all goes black.

82.

Freddie

Oh fuck oh fuck oh fuck.

I slide down the kitchen side to the floor, unable to take my eyes off her. She's dead. Her eyes are empty and her hands have stopped moving. How did she die so fast? I didn't even realize I'd stabbed her. I was so angry and I gripped the knife tighter and then . . . I can't finish the thought. I think I'm going to puke. *Oh fuck oh fuck oh fuck.*

This is not a suicide. There is no way I can make this look like a suicide. There's blood all over the kitchen floor. Oh god, I'm going to prison. I've murdered my fucking wife.

From outside I hear feet on the gravel, men smoking and laughing, and my sudden white-cold panic forces me into action. I quickly lock the front door and then stare at Emily's body. She can't stay there on the kitchen floor. Until I know what I'm going to do, I need to get her out of the way. Put her upstairs. The spare bedroom maybe? I scrub blood from my hands and then take a few deep breaths, trying to calm my shaking body. I need all my strength to pick up her dead weight, and she slips and slops around as I try to get purchase. I take a breath and put into practice how I helped lift her in the hospital before she could walk.

Oh fuck oh fuck oh fuck.

The spare bedroom will still be too risky. What if more than one worker needs the loo?

The room at the top of the house. That's where I'll put her. She can stay in there for now.

83.

Emily

'God, that's awful.' It's only the start of March but it feels almost like a spring day in the little suntrap courtyard the Watkinses built by the orchard where I'm sitting with the vicar sipping tea.

'Yes, it really is. Terribly hard to get my head around. He was always so alive.' Paul's so distraught he's aged a decade. I want to hug him. But then, despite this awful news, I'm in such a good mood I want to hug everyone.

Instead, I stroke my currently flat tummy. I can't wait for Freddie to get home to share our brilliant, brilliant news. I thought my queasiness might have been down to my medication, but then I found some used pregnancy tests in my underwear drawer and had a hazy memory of taking them a couple of weeks back. It must have been just before I banged my head. Freddie says concussion can do that to you. Mess with some of your memories. A few things are a little off, but I'm fine in myself. I need to remember that. I'm right as rain now. Even righter than rain. I went down to the pharmacy and got a fresh test and yes, we are very much pregnant.

'What happened?' I ask, bringing my focus back to the present.

'Sally said she'd gone out for a hill walk while Joe was going to stay in the rental and paint. He was doing an enormous canvas of her, but she'd started spending the first couple of hours of the day out on the hills and moors and then bringing back breakfast from the bakery in the village before settling in to lie still for the rest of the day while he worked. She said he'd said he had a bit of a headache and was feeling off, but to go just the same. So she went on her walk and picked up breakfast and some medicine in the village, and when she got home he'd either slipped or maybe felt unwell or fainted in the shower and cracked his skull.'

'Oh god, the poor man.' It makes me shiver.

'And poor Sally,' he adds. 'He didn't die instantly, apparently. Bled out in the bath. It was quite a mess when she got back. She called an ambulance straight away, obviously.'

'It's such a nightmare for her. She must be in a terrible state. If only she hadn't gone for that walk.'

'That's what she kept saying to me. I told her that accidents happen all the time and you can't live that way. And he knew she loved him.'

'They did love each other so very much.' It's strange, but I always get a weird heavy headache when I think about Sally, as if there's something about her I can't quite remember. Maybe I should take a painkiller, even though I'm trying to avoid medicines at the moment to protect the baby. 'And having you visit for the weekend must have helped.' I touch Paul's hand, a gesture of comfort. 'When is she coming back here?'

'She's not.' Paul gets to his feet. 'She says she wants to live abroad. Maybe go to her niece in New Zealand. She says there are too many memories here. Anyway, the reason I called by was that she gave me something for you before I left.' He takes out a lilac envelope and hands it over. 'She says it's only for you.'

'Oh, that's nice.' I'm surprised though. I can't imagine why Sally would have anything to say to me. We weren't that close, I don't think. Were we?

After Paul's gone, I make a cup of tea and curl up on the sofa to read the letter. It's beautiful, neat cursive written carefully in ink pen.

> *Dear Emily,*
>
> *So, Paul has spent all weekend telling me how happy you and Freddie have been recently, and what a positive change there's been in you, and it alarmed me to the point that I figured I'd better write. If you remember everything that happened with us, then nothing in this letter will come as a surprise. But if you find you're a little muddy and confused in your recent memories when you think about them too hard, which I suspect you are, then read on. The last time I saw you I told you I owed you one. Well, this is it. Me paying my debt.*
>
> *This may seem like a wild story, but it's one you found out about, and you set me free. I think perhaps, by luck or design, maybe your husband found out about your blackmail cash and put you in the second floor room too . . .*

My head starts throbbing and the words blur, but I force myself to read on. What is she talking about?

> *. . . but I'm getting ahead of myself. I need to explain this to you one step at a time so you can understand what your darling or not so darling husband has done to you.*

I read and read as she tells me everything that I suddenly feel like I already knew, and then I go back and reread it all again, my head spinning. I look at the last line again.

> *And when you've read this, burn it. For both of us.*

I do as she requests and lean forward, lighting the paper with the fire matches. The sun is sinking by the time it's ash, and I sit back and stare out of the window for an hour or more. It can't be true, can it? Can it? It's crazy, but at the same time I feel the very truth of it. I remember a vague feeling of guilt.

Mark and Cat. I was blackmailing Mark, that's what Sally said. The inside of my skull itches as if there's a scab over an empty space.

I don't have any extra money anywhere. The whole thing is insane, but I humor it. If I had an account with money in, and Freddie knew about it, then where would he hide that from me? I'm sure I did. But when I try to remember it, there's nothing. Just a fuzzy haze that makes me want to think about other, nicer things.

I go to the red room that Freddie uses as a home office and rummage through all the drawers, fighting my every instinct that this is lovely sweet Freddie who would do nothing to hurt anyone, especially me. I'm about to give up when I pull a drawer free and check underneath like they do in old spy films.

There's an envelope taped to the underside of it. An envelope addressed to me. My heart in my mouth, I take the papers out and read.

A hundred and fifty thousand pounds sitting there in my name and an awful note from Mark. God, why would I have done something so grotesque? Does this mean that everything in Sally's letter is true?

Oh, Freddie. Tears sting my eyes, anger and upset and hurt, and I touch my stomach where our little baby is growing. *What did you do?*

84.

Freddie

'I'm up here!'

Her voice drifts down from the second floor and my stomach tightens. Oh god, she's up in that room. My foot hesitates on the bottom step. I've only just started relaxing around her, this new vibrant joyous Emily, but I can't entirely trust the situation.

Some days I manage to persuade myself that none of it really happened, but the strained muscles in my shoulders that still hurt in the mornings are testament to the fact that I did indeed haul my dead wife's body up three flights of stairs, shut her in the second-floor bedroom, and then scrub the house clean, crying and drinking myself to sleep while trying to get up the guts to call the police before, lo and behold, the next morning she came down them all by herself. I almost had a heart attack. I thought I was going mad.

Sometimes I still think I've gone mad. I know I killed her. And yet she's alive. And she's her, but different. She's so much more lovable again; that's the only way I can describe it. She's happier and I'm happier. It's like the old days when we first met.

In the main though, I've persuaded myself that I hadn't stabbed her as deeply as I thought, or maybe hadn't even stabbed her at all. I did nick myself with the blade, and maybe the blood was all mine from that. Small cuts can bleed a lot. Maybe she simply passed out and I *thought* she was dead. Maybe I had a small psychotic episode and hallucinated it. Anything to convince myself that she didn't actually die.

Still, we need to sell this house and move on as soon as possible. I can't live here much longer. It's all just too odd. While Emily cheating death is in many ways a blessing, I don't trust this place.

I need to figure out a way to get Mark's money out of her Jersey account, or at least find a way to make it sound plausible. She doesn't even remember it's there. Her memory is hazy around the events surrounding whatever happened in the kitchen, like a cloth has been pulled across it, wiping out anything that links to it. She doesn't question anything. I told her she'd had a fall in the kitchen and she looked confused for a moment and then accepted it.

Turns out she's not the only one capable of blackmail. I got more money out of Mark too once I'd found the video on Emily's phone and transferred it to mine. I didn't go too greedy. Just enough to pay my debts. To buy us some breathing time.

'Come up!' Emily calls down, head peering over the top banister, hair falling free around her grinning face. She is beautiful when she wants to be. When she's happy. 'I want to show you something! And I've got beer!'

'On my way,' I say. I feel a little uncomfortable seeing where she is, but I shake it away. There's no way she could know what I did. She's just got a plan for the top floor, that's all. Maybe a way to make the house more sellable, or maybe she's gone back to her idea of renting the second floor out as a private apartment to bring in extra money.

She's standing in the bright sunshine in cute pink dungarees and hands me a strong Belgian beer, one of my favourites, before wrapping her arms around my neck and kissing me.

'Drink that before I show you.'

She smells a glorious combination of apple and peach. I'd forgotten how good it feels to be properly loved by her. When she first *came back*, I was so relieved to be out of trouble—no prison for murder—that I was giddy with love. I thought that would fade. I thought within a week I'd want to feed her all her sleeping pills and go back to my original fake-suicide plan, but I didn't.

She's not judgmental of me like she'd been before. She's not got that irritating 'always right' and 'slightly martyr passive-aggressive thing' about her anymore. She's supportive. She believes in me. She forgives me for my problems. I don't think she even remembers cheating on me, and everything I did to her feels like a dream now. We're actually happy. She's a proper wife again. If she thinks I'm weak now, she doesn't show it, and that in turn makes me stronger.

I drain half the beer and it tastes good, bitter and strong, and the buzz goes straight to my head. 'You're an angel,' I say. 'This is just what I needed.'

'Finish it.' She's bouncing up and down on her toes, like an overexcited child. 'Don't worry, I've got another.'

'Okay.' I do as I'm told, laughing along with her. 'Go on then. What's the big surprise?'

As soon as I put the bottle down, she pulls something out from her back pocket. At first, I think it's a Covid test, but then I realize it's not. It's a pregnancy test. Two thick red lines in each box. I look up at her, my mouth falling open, surprised but not unhappy. Definitely not unhappy. In fact, my heart leaps. A child that is definitely mine.

'Are you . . . .?' I stare at her, not able to finish the question. She nods and squeals and leaps into my arms. 'Are you having a baby?'

'Yes, yes, yes,' she says. 'We're pregnant. Eight weeks. I saw the doctor this morning.'

'Oh my god, Emily. Oh my god! That's amazing!' We squeal together and hug and my head spins with the news. *A baby. She's got a new baby growing inside her. We're having a baby.* We really are going to have a fresh start. This Emily would never cheat. And I wouldn't kill this Emily. None of that happened. Once we're away from here it will be easy enough to forget. After all, she'll be alive and well and happy beside me.

She turns round to look at the bedroom suite while I reach for the second full beer, my heart racing and elated.

'I thought we could move up here. The baby's nursery could go where the dressing room is. A family suite?' She looks back at me for my thoughts.

'Up here?' My smile falters. I can think of nothing worse than moving up into this bedroom. I'd rather forget all about this room. I feel so guilty up here. When I think of it I reach for the betting apps again.

'Maybe,' I say. 'Or maybe we should just use the middle floor. More child friendly?' Suddenly, the world feels off-kilter, and with a sudden wave of seasick dizziness, I clutch at the wall.

'Are you okay?'

She's swimming a little in my view line, her face distorted, and heat rushes up through me, a cold sweat forming. 'Sorry,' I mutter, trying to smile. My face feels strangely lopsided. 'The surprise of the pregnancy must have gone to my head.'

'Oh, that's not surprise at my news, Freddie,' she says softly, kissing my cheek. 'That'll be all those pills. In the beer.'

'What?' The wall's moving under my touch and I groan as my legs buckle slightly. She's not making any sense. I look down at the bottle in my hand, or at least I try to look down at it, but I can't focus. *What the fuck did she just say?* I look at her, confused, trying to speak, and stagger toward the door.

'I know what you did, Freddie,' she says, harder now, following me as I lose my balance and fall to my knees on the floor. *I can crawl downstairs. Call an ambulance. There will be time.*

'You killed me. For money. For money I was going to share with you to get you out of trouble. I was going to tell you what I'd done that I felt so bad about. But you're weak, Freddie, and you stabbed me. And that broke my heart,' she continues. 'My first instinct was to bring myself back, obviously. There's a way, you know. I found the book. I did it for Sally. But that's a story for another time. But then I changed my mind. I realized, you see, that I don't want to be that Emily anymore. I don't want those negative parts of myself. Why would I? I want to be my best self. But this got me to thinking.'

'Emily, please . . .'

Ignoring my plea, she follows me as I haul myself out into the landing, which sways and lurches under me.

'I realized that our baby needs two good parents. People it can be proud of. Who won't fuck it up. I didn't want to let those parts of me out. But I don't want all the weak and negative parts of you either. So there was really only one solution left to protect our family.'

'Don't do this,' I mumble, dragging myself toward the stairs.

'It's already done.' She stays in the doorway, watching me, impassive, as I try to focus. My mobile phone is on the downstairs hallway table with my keys. If I can get there, I can call for help. I feel sick, the world swimming around me, but still I drag myself onward.

'Are you thinking you can somehow make it downstairs?' she asks, coming up behind me.

'You can try if you want to.' She steps over me and goes down two stairs before crouching in front of me, our faces level. 'But you need to understand something before you make that choice. It won't stop you dying. Even if you do manage to call for an ambulance, no one will get here in time, and it's a redundant scenario anyway, because despite my bad leg, I will definitely get to your phone first.

'But. And this, for you especially, is the really important part.' She pauses for effect and to make sure I'm really listening. 'I am too physically weak to carry you all the way back up here when you do die. You need to understand that. If you die downstairs, you're gone for good. I can tell them it was suicide. All your debts weighing you down. It's an awful thing, but I'll have to live with it. For the good of our baby.' She strokes my hair. 'But you don't have to die, Freddie. You can crawl back into that room and our child can have the best of both of us as parents. You've always wanted a family to come first. This is your time to prove it. I can help you if you want. But you need to choose, Freddie. And you need to choose fast.'

I look at the stairs ahead of me, and then I turn my heavy head to the open doorway behind me. The edges ripple and I think I'm going to throw up. I feel awful.

I'm dying. I'm actually dying. I don't want to die.

I can't believe this is happening. I can't believe she's drugged me like this. I'm going to be a father but I'm never going to see my child.

I moan and tears slip from the corners of my eyes. *I don't want to die. I want to see my child. I want to have a family. I want so many things.*

My vision is getting black at the corners. I'm running out of time to make my choice. She's right in everything she's said. I won't get to the phone before her. And she definitely wouldn't be able to carry me. I have to make a choice while I still can. She hasn't really left me with one, I realize, as I stop crawling forward. Life or death. What would anyone choose?

How bad can it be? I'll come back out alive. Some of me will. I'll still be alive.

Sobbing, I try to turn myself around, to face the door before

I pass out completely. 'The room,' I mumble, even though the words are a mess. 'I choose the room.'

'I love you, Freddie. You know that, don't you? I want the best for you. I want the best *of* you. You'll just fall asleep,' she says softly as she crouches beside me and rests my head in her lap. 'It won't hurt. I promise.'

And she's right. It doesn't.

Them

85.

Emily

*The raven with the dull damaged wing pecks at the window relent-
lessly. The sharp* tap tap *is almost constant. I am so fucking tired of
the cold and the dark and the fucking awful stench and Freddie's
relentless weak whining about the fucking unfairness of it all. The
bird caws, then taps some more. If I could kill it, I'd gladly throttle
with my bare hands.*

'Just look at them.'

*Freddie's over by the window and I join him and the raven even
though the daylight is so unnaturally bright against the constant
gloom of the room, and the sight of the other us—*them—*makes me
want to scream with rage. Freddie said I screamed for three whole
days solid once he'd joined me, but I don't remember. I remember
that our other selves—the best of us—carried on downstairs all
sugar and spice and everything nice as if we weren't even here.*

*'They're finally moving out,' I say, and it's like a punch in my
hollow gut seeing my body down there with full pregnancy bump,
Freddie's arm around me, tanned and happy.*

*Laughter drifts up as Freddie hands the house keys over to
Russell and Cat and the other Emily chatters some more and
smiles as if she has no cares in the fucking world. Russell and
Cat look so happy. Russell can't believe his luck. This house, a
new life in the country.*

Cat looks like she's making the best of it now that it's over with Mark. I know what she'll be thinking. At least Russell didn't find out. Not yet, anyway, Cat dearest.

I understand the house now. The kind of couples it attracts. The type it's hungry for. Couples in trouble. Couples with secrets. Couples it can play with. Russell was snared by Larkin Lodge the moment he saw it, just the same as Freddie was.

If I hadn't been so susceptible to picking up Sally's energy, maybe it would have been me the house targeted. Freddie was the one with the secret—maybe I would have killed him and he'd never have known. It could be me free down there with the wonderful version of my husband. Even with the way things turned out, it still could have ended that way. But no. Instead I betrayed myself. I could have made myself whole and killed Freddie, but no, holier-than-thou, butter-wouldn't-melt idiot Emily decided she liked being the good little woman. Nevermind the raven, If I could throttle myself, I would.

'Which room do you think they'll choose to sleep in?' Freddie asks me. 'Want to bet on it not being this one?'

I don't answer. He's always trying to bet on something. God, why didn't I kill him first?

I can't look away from my own happy pregnant body. One about to disappear into the sunset.

'I can't believe they're going to France. With my hundred and fifty thousand pounds,' I mutter.

'And the money I got from him. We could have got more if we'd worked together. We could have got out of here laughing.'

'We could, we could, we could,' I mimic. 'If you hadn't fucked up in the first place, this would never have happened.'

'If you hadn't fucked your boss and got knocked up, maybe you wouldn't have been so distracted and moody you fell off the cliff.'

There's a moment of silence where we both bite our nonexistent tongues because otherwise we'll go round and round in circles of recriminations, like we have so many times in however long we've been trapped in this hell. Months, judging by my stomach below.

I touch the damp windowsill—everything's always so wet in here—and feel the liquid suck at my fingers, wanting to pull me in. I tug my hand away. I haven't been into the house yet. I'm going to have to start trying though, if I ever want to get out of here.

We stand at the window, shadows in shadow, and watch them, the other Freddie and Emily, get into their car, suitcases and passports packed, and head off to their new lives full of love for each other. Neither of them looks up.

'Don't worry.' Freddie puts his arm around me. It's a surprise, but I let him. He's the only thing I can touch in here, other than the pecking bird, that isn't trying to absorb me, and vice versa. 'There's plenty of our things up in the attic in storage.'

'How will that help us?' I ask, shivering into his cold chest, my leg and my stab wound both throbbing. But I'm already seeing what he means. We have stuff here.

Things to burn.

If somehow we can get them to feel our presence, maybe they'll be curious enough to dig around into the house's history too. I wish I hadn't burned the letter from Sally, but there's still the ledger hidden in the suitcase cupboard.

I glance sideways at all the weaknesses of my husband, then smile up at him. 'Ah, I see what you mean.'

As the raven caws angrily—nothing to burn for her, no hope for release—my thoughts race ahead. I look back down at the mouldy damp windowsill. I'm going to have to get braver at going into the house. Trying to make noises. Get some attention.

'We just have to make sure they know we're still here,' Freddie says, his eyes burning bright as he looks down at our erstwhile friends.

'We do.' I nod and let him kiss my head as I realize that if

311

anyone's getting out of here first, it has to be me. I have to make contact with one of them before he does.

Get them to FINDITFINDITFINDIT.

Freddie will never set me free if he gets out first. Just as the same is true the other way around if I get out before him.

He smiles down at me, and I know exactly what he's going to say. We end up saying it together.

'Marriage is teamwork, after all.'

Acknowledgments

First off, a big thank you to Sam Eades at Orion and high five on the start of our publishing journey together. Publishing, like marriage, is teamwork, and I'm glad to be part of this new team and I extend my thanks and eternal gratitude to all the people who have worked on this book to make it so much better. Thanks as always go to Veronique Baxter at David Higham, agent and friend and confidante. One more book in the bag!

This book was a hard one to write for plenty of reasons – injury being a big one and over-busyiness (is that even a word?!) writing a TV show being another and I could not finish this book without a massive shout out to author Harriet Tyce for the constant text contact and keeping me going. We got this!!

And also thanks to Teddy, my idiot dog, for forcing me to get out in the fresh air every day.

Credits

Sarah Pinborough and Orion Fiction would like to thank everyone at Orion who worked on the publication of *We Live Here Now* in the UK.

Editorial
Sam Eades
Snigdha Koirala

Proofreader
Sally Partington

Audio
Paul Stark
Louise Richardson

Contracts
Dan Herron
Ellie Bowker

Design
Charlotte Abrams-Simpson

Editorial Management
Charlie Panayiotou
Jane Hughes
Bartley Shaw

Finance
Jasdip Nandra
Nick Gibson
Sue Baker

Production
Paul Hussey

Marketing
Lucy Cameron

Publicity
Jenna Petts

Sales
David Murphy
Esther Waters
Victoria Laws
Rachael Hum
Ellie Kyrke-Smith
Frances Doyle
Georgina Cutler

Rights
Rebecca Folland
Tara Hiatt
Ben Fowler
Ruth Blakemore
Marie Henckel

Operations
Group Sales Operations team